HARDER

BY

SHA

THE FIRST LADY OF GHETTOHEAT®

Copyright © 2006

A

PRODUCTION

Published by GHETTOHEAT®, LLC
P.O. BOX 2746, NEW YORK, NY 10027, USA

Library of Congress Control Number: 2006930850

ISBN: 09742982-4-7

Printed in the USA. First Edition, September 2006

ACKNOWLEDGMENTS

First and foremost: All Praises due to the ever living, ever faithful, ever loving Lord and Savior. God gave me this talent. Without HIM, I am nothing.

Thank you to my family who has supported me with all of my endeavors. Daddy, I'm exactly like you. Thank you for giving me your strength. You're the best father in the whole wide world.

Gaby, girlfriends come and go, but sisters are forever. Yes, that means you're stuck with me! Thank you for helping me edit my book, and your stern discipline throughout the years. Thanks for being so smart and talented. I couldn't ask for anything more than that in a perfect role model. Without your encouragement, this novel would've still been sitting next to the computer, unfinished.

Junior, if I never had you, I would never enjoy reading or school. Thanks for giving me healthy competition and keeping me in check when I got out-of-order.

David, Ana and Mat, my little lovely angels, I love you dearly.

A special thanks to Mr. and Mrs. Guitteau.

Thanks HICKSON for giving me this once in a lifetime opportunity. Understand that we will make HISTORY! Peace and blessings to my entire GHETTOHEAT® family.

Thank you to Mrs. Young (RIP), Ms. B. Kaplan, Professor Slaymaker, Professor Villegas, Professor Swoboda, Dr. Mormon (RIP), and Professor Colbert. You all believed in me when I needed it the most. Wendy Williams, thank you for your motivation and inspiration.

Sunshine, your input and support with this novel was very much appreciated. To Joseph Porter and the ladies of Triple Threat Talent, for your support, even though you didn't know what I was up to.

Lastly, thank you to every single last person that tried their best to make my life a living hell. You only made me stronger, and I still love you. *Run tell dat!*

Dedicated to King David, Queen Anabella and King Matthew

You inspire me everyday. When you grow up, I know this will inspire you to follow your dreams. My Kings and Queen, anything is possible. The world is yours.

HARDER

prologue

Gasp…
Breathe.

My eyes open slowly as the piercing pain at the back of my head overwhelms me.
Where am I?
My head feels light.
Have I been slipping in and out of consciousness?
Strange.
Somewhere nearby, there's water dripping. Every drop makes the pain in my head worst.
Wherever this is, it's hot and I'm wet.
I can smell *Wrays and Nephew* rum, Calli weed and *Guinness Stout* in the air.
No, stout is on me.
The over-proof rum and weed?
…Rippa's infamous signature.
Shit.
Things are becoming clear.
Damn you Rippa! Damn you to Hell!
I can hear *Luciano* playing in the background so I know that you're around here somewhere. What I don't know is where I am or why I can't seem to move. I just wish it wasn't so dark in here. Maybe if I call for him: "RIPPA!"

My vocal chords move, but my lips don't.
Shit!
My lips are taped!
What the fuck is going on?
Ok. Think. Think, baby girl. The last thing I can remember…is…getting ready to leave New Jersey for a little getaway before my son was born. I've been hiding out for the past several months, and Nicky thought it would be good for AJ and I to go on a little vacation in Puerto Rico.

Arturo, sweet loving Arturo Jesus. I put that man through Hell and back. I know that. But, I've cleaned up my act and were going to be one big happy—

Fuck!

Where's AJ?

My mouth is taped and I'm bound to a hard-ass mattress.

Holy shit—noooooo!

Rippa must be holding me hostage, but how?

He did promise this.

Fuck! Fuck! Fuck!

spring of '97

Things couldn't have gotten any better. I'd just turned 18, and everybody with a dick was hooked on my ass. Even those dyke-broads tried to holla, but whatever!

Wherever I went, my name rang bells. A hood-legend, as they call it, I was the most wanted female out here without a care in the world.

I was the shit!

* * * * *

"I'm just *so* damn fly with my long, light-brown hair that falls right above my butt, to my sexy-ass shape! Not to forget, my pretty-colored shifting eyes and caramel complexion.

HUMPH!

There *ain't* a chick in New York, let alone Queens, that's hotter than me! The only one to even come close is my ace-boom, Shelly; Shelly Wakes.

"We're the same sign, got the same body type, and everything. Only differences are she's quiet, humble and like dark-skinned cats. I'm all about the limelight, confident and only stay with the light-skinned, *Al B. Sure*-looking brothers! But Shelly's pretty much down for whatever."

Whatever!

"Kai! Kai...um, are you done with ya little monologue? I can almost see the words written on your forehead while you're over there making goo-goo eyes at yaself in the mirror. You're so damn narcissistic and vain."

"Oh please, Shelly, quit bugging! I ain't making 'goo-goo' eyes at myself."

Damn!

I always had to wonder about Shelly always trying to break up my vibe. "Come on, Shells. Hillcrest is about to get out and I'm trying to check for dude that was at that party."

"What dude? Jordan Richardson? Gurrrl! Quit bugging! For starters, you know damn well every chick across the county wants a piece of him. Second, you're only digging him because he's sitting on old money. What you *really* need to do is figure out if you're going to *Baruch College* in the fall or not and *stop* chasing dollars. School is what you *really* need to be worried about."

I contemplated punching Shelly in her eye for trying to play me. Jordan Richardson was official!

"Aye, dog, for real-for real, there's more to it than that, yo. Dude is crazy-fly, just like me. Let's be honest, everybody knows that I'm the *only* chick around these parts that makes his perfect match.

"He and I are cut from the same cloth. You watch and see me become Mrs. Richardson one day!" After all, I was the flyest thing walking! "Besides, I'm *through* with school. What is there left to learn except how to make money. I don't need school for that."

Shelly never understood the thing I had for Jordan. She said, "So what are you going to say to Jordan if you see him today?" Shelly always countered with some good questions. "We might as well talk about him since attending college is a dead issue for you."

What was college really good for? They charged you outrageous amounts of money for textbooks and tuition, and for what?

Nothing!

As for Jordan, I didn't know what to say to "Mr. So Damn Fly." I never did, but Shelly wouldn't know that.

"Ma, I won't have to say a *damn* thing! He'll take one look at me and know *exactly* what's up! YA HEARD?"

Jordan Richardson was like a rainbow that broke in the middle of a summertime thunderstorm, bringing sunshine and singing birds. Yeah, yeah, I know that sounds like somebody's poetry, but if you saw him, he would make you feel the same exact way.

He stood about 6'2", 210 pounds, solid muscle with a dulce de leche (caramel) complexion. He drove a '95 *Acura Legend* that was black-on-black and had shiny chrome wheels.

Most other seniors in high school were driving 'hoopties' if they were even driving at all. I swore every time he passed by me, I heard Sade's *Sweetest Taboo* playing in the background while his *Nautica* cologne intoxicated me. He was too good of a catch for me to pass up.

"You know what, Shells, forget him." For years I tried to. I tried not to give him the satisfaction of having me go out of my mind like the other females.

Whatever!

That day, I was eager to explore my options. The options on a warm Friday afternoon would either be on Jamaica Avenue or at Green Acres Mall.

"Yo, Shelly, let's just go up to Jamaica Avenue. I need to pick up some '54-11s', and if I see him, I see him. But if I don't, his loss and some next dude's gain."

Shelly replied, "Baby girl, you are wild! You know *damn* well that you're too scared to say anything to him. Besides I ain't got no dough for The Ave."

Come on, who did Shelly think she was talking to? Money was never a cause for worry, especially back then. I had been working at *McDonald's* for about three months and got monetary gifts from my little admirers on a regular basis. You couldn't put 'Kai', 'money', and 'problem' in the same sentence.

That was unheard of!

"Shelly, you need some '54-11s', too, because them *Jordan's* you have on are looking tired as hell. Think of it as a belated birthday present. I got enough to cover several pairs of sneakers; so what's really good?" Her broke-ass had to go at that point. Who passed up free kicks? Not big foot Shelly.

When we got to Jamaica Avenue, it was nothing but a whole bunch of high school kids out there. It was the first warm day of the year so everybody was out. Damn. Maybe I should've waited for another day when all those *wack-ass* females wouldn't have been in attendance.

We'd just gotten off the Q5 bus and I could already feel the hate raining down hard on me and Shelly. Well, mostly me. I was used to it. Fuck it—we were already there. I figured that we might as well deal with it.

Not five minutes went by before drama introduced itself.

"Bitch thinks she's just so fly...but let me see her try to act cute with a bubble." It was this girl from Springfield named, Rhazza. She had a bad temper and looked like a man. Rhazza hated my ass ever since I moved to Rosedale. For what reason? I don't know.

She was a *sad* story.

To think Rhazza was about five years older than me (still in high school), but would still try to punk me on a regular basis. I made that day the final day she would ever try to disrespect me, or anybody else for that matter.

"Fuck is you talking to, you Magilla Guerilla-looking-type-bitch? You better go 'head with that bullshit!" I came back at her with fury in my voice and confidence in my swagger.

Rhazza got in my face.

"Oh word? You's a hard rock now? You forget who the *fuck* I am? I'ma take that switch out ya walk fa good, ya lil' bitch!"

As she said that, I quickly ducked her approaching right jab. "Rhazza, go home to ya baby, I'm really not tryna' fuck wit' you today." I was never one to pass up on a good fight. However, I wasn't about to let Jordan see me acting less than lady-like.

Rhazza persisted.

"Fuck you, Kai. I'm about tired of ya bullshit!" The next thing I knew, she pulled out a metal baseball bat and started swinging it at me. A crowd started to form around us. They were clearly in favor of her beating me down mercilessly.

Being outnumbered, I pulled out my mace: "Yo, dumb-dumb…take this!"

I sprayed it dead in her eyes and she started screaming, "Bitch, I'ma kill you! I'm blind, I'm blind." Mace should just be called 'bitch spray'. It turned the hardest individuals into suckers on impact.

Rhazza lost her balance and stumbled onto Archer Avenue with both of her hands covering her eyes. Too bad for her, a N4 bus was quickly approaching. It hit her dead on. She never saw it coming; she never had a chance.

Problem solved.

* * * * *

"Why you *always* got to walk like that? Maybe if you toned it down you *wouldn't* have so much beef." Shelly was supposed to have my back, not reprimand me like an authoritative figure.

"Dammit, man, like *what*, Shells? What are you *talking* about?"

15

Shelly gave me a once over, "Like you're the female version of Scar face! That's why we *stay* in some shit. You got a serious attitude problem. You and your 'I'm so damn untouchable and too damn fly' attitude. Are you even gonna go back and see if she's alright."

There was no need to. I already knew that Rhazza was either dead or was about to be. Shelly was absolutely right, it was back in high school when I adopted the "greater than thou, almighty ruler personae" that I couldn't shake.

That's when all the bullshit really started.

I never openly admitted to it. Instead, I started yelling at her: "Yo, for real, I got an *attitude* because I have a *fucking* personality! Personalities clash and whosoever don't like that can kiss...my...ass! Listen, we're fly-as-hell, so pigeons stay hating!

"It isn't about the walk, it's about us! It's always going to be this way so get used to it! And no, I'm not going back to see if she's alright! The bitch could *die* for all I care!"

Two months later, just before graduating, we found out that Rhazza did die as a result of her injuries.

Oh well.

After being saluted by the Grand Marshals of the 'hate parade' that day, we finally made it to our destination: the *Coliseum Mall.* Shelly and I were clowning these boys who were trying to holla at us, as we approached the glass doors.

Just my luck, I bump into him, himself—Jordan! Oh my God, it's him. Dammit! I was geeked like he was *L.L. Cool J* or somebody. I was cool and composed on the outside, but inside, I was star-struck!

I could've sworn the time stopped, as he opened his mouth to speak: "Sorry, my bad, ladies." Then he was gone. I kept it moving, but not before making a mental note that he was with Day-Day and Morris. They both went to Springfield with me and the conversation was bound to go in Mr. Richardson's direction one day.

"Kai!" *For real, why did Shelly have to scream my name like that?* Shelly gave me the look of death and continued, "um, wasn't that just Jordan? You straight bump into dude like you're 'bout it-'bout it, but don't say a thing? Don't tell me old boy got you shook? Not you, Kai, it ain't a good look."

Shelly was right. Me losing my composure over some boy was not a good look.

"Shelly, listen. In case you ain't notice the flock of birds hovering around him as my reason for not saying anything, then I don't know what to tell you. That's just *not* my style. Please, I ain't having no bird-bitch all in my face over someone that I *don't* know two shits about."

Who let the pigeons out the coup? They sure were out there flocking that day.

After buying a couple of pairs of *Reebok* sneakers, Shelly and I rolled up the block to the pattie spot, *Jamaican Flavors,* and that's where I first met him.

Rippa.

Just as we were about to leave the patti spot I heard him say, "Wh'appen, pretty?"

Shelly and I were so used to that every time we went up there. That time really wasn't any different. At least that's what I thought before I turned around.

When I did turn to that raspy voice, *"vic, vic, vic",* went running through my head at full speed. I was used to gaming the fellas for whatever they had to offer and this one looked like the usual suspects.

The boy, yeah, the boy stood about 5'5" (a whole two inches shorter than myself) and looked like he weighed 125 pounds, wet. Rippa had short nappy hair, and his chestnut complexion was blotchy. The kid couldn't have been any older than fifteen. That was fine by me, just as long as Rippa had access to some type of money.

My conscious tried to kick in with the statutory law thing, but all I could see through his mismatched clothes was a victim that was mine for the taking. After all, a-vic-is-a-vic, and something was telling me that Rippa would be a *sweet* vic. So I let him run his mouth.

I listened to Rippa ramble about my eyes (he said they reminded him of the ocean back in Jamaica) and my *Coca-Cola* bottle shape. I stood there and smiled politely. Shelly had no choice but to stand around while I listened to what Rippa had to say. When I heard my fill, I told him to have a nice afternoon and walked away.

Rippa must've been the shit back in Jamaica because he had this dumbfounded look on his face like I was supposed to fall in love with him right then and there.

Please!

He was definitely no Jordan Richardson! They were like the prince and the pauper. If this pauper didn't wise up, I planned to take Rippa for everything he had, and then some.

"Kai, you were just on 165th talking to a dude that was young and definitely not your type. What if Jordan peeped you?" Shelly asked.

Jordan was cool and all, but that situation right there—was about running game. I ran game, it was my thing. If a dude fell too quickly for me, best believe the plans were to tap him dry and bounce! It was always my plan to be retired by twenty-five and *McDonald's* wasn't going to do that!

* * * * *

Less than a week later, I bumped into Day-Day in the cafeteria at school. We started talking about nothing in particular when Jordan's name came up. Day-Day thought he was so slick, saying, "I know you're feeling Jordan something serious, just step to the boy. You know he lives a couple of blocks away from you."

I had to take a deep breath to still my racing heart. Just the mention of Jordan's name alone had me drifting into a daze. I nonchalantly replied, "It's *not* that serious. Jordan's cute and all…but so am I. Tell your boy to come and talk to me because it's *obvious* that I've been a topic of ya'll discussions!"

Day-Day just smiled at me like he was the *Cheshire* cat. That meant I was right; my name had come up. I just didn't know in what context. Morris came around, so being that I was outnumbered, I left the cafeteria before it became a "100 reasons to call Jordan event".

for the love of money

A couple of weeks later, Jordan retired to the furthest recesses of my mind. I met a guy named Ricardo Jones, and with that came my initial introduction to chic clothing and the 'real' value of money.

Ricardo was a wealthy real estate investor from Jamaica. I met him at my new job in the mall. I started working there right after graduation. I had only been there for about a month when I realized that every Sunday, around 4 PM, Ricardo would stop by to say, *"Hello."*

He was much taller than Jordan and had pretty, jet-black hair, which Ricardo kept pulled to the back in a neat, curly pony tail. The day I finally gave him my number, Ricardo was in the regular t-shirt and jeans giddy-up. I just gave it to him to shut Ricardo up. I had no idea what I was in for, until he came over to my house.

It was a regular day to me. I didn't feel the need to put my best foot forward because Ricardo didn't seem worth it.

Surprise, surprise.

I nearly fainted when he hopped out of his crisp 1998, navy-blue *Acura TL*. 1997 still had a few months left to the year.

If that wasn't enough to make me pass out, the brother had the nerve to wear a nice fitting *Brooks Brothers,* pin-stripped, navy-blue suit, with a matching fedora hat. I was almost too discombobulated to open the door. Ricardo came over straight from his office. I momentarily thought about pretending I wasn't home.

Knock-Knock-Knock.

"Hello," I tried to sound sexy and seductive, but ended up sounding like a hyena in heat.

"Hey baby, it's me, Ricardo."

Oh, Jesus, his voice was like melting caramel; sweet and hot—making my mouth water. Funny, Ricardo didn't have that effect on me when he wore his t-shirt and jeans the day before...

When I opened the door, I was totally mesmerized. Ricardo was absolutely gorgeous from head-to-toe. From that moment, I knew that I had to make him my boyfriend. I forgot all about gaming Ricardo because I knew he would spend on me; naturally.

That night, he stayed over for about three hours. We chatted about this and that. Come to find out, the fine vanilla brother was married, and a full ten years older than me!

A week later, we went out on our first date. At that time, I'd gotten used to *Red Lobster's* and *Sizzler's* scene. I so hoped that Ricardo would take me somewhere nicer, and he did. He took me to an Italian restaurant named, *Mateo's* in Long Island.

It was on a Saturday afternoon in July. It was hot as hell outside, and I really wasn't feeling going out. I just wanted to be with Ricardo. He pulled up to my house in a chauffeured, white Rolls Royce. Everything on my block came to a stand still when Ricardo stepped out, wearing a white linen suit—a designer brand that I couldn't name.

I was still trying to get dressed when I peeked at him through the blinds of my living room window. I noticed that Ricardo was carrying a large white box.

Knock-Knock-Knock.

"Hey, you're early," I replied as I answered the door, feeling embarrassed in my 'mall special' sundress.

"I came a little early so you could slip into this before we went out," he said coolly, as Ricardo handed the large box to me.

I reached for the box and smiled at him: "Awww, sweetie, you shouldn't have." I raced back to my bedroom and realized that yeah, he shouldn't have. What laid neatly in the box was an expensive white *Christian Dior* strapless dress.

* * * * *

For weeks I tried to shake Ricardo, but the fleet of fine cars, classy suits and promises to leave his wife had me stuck-on-stupid.

Along the way, Ricardo urged me to attend college in the fall and said that he would pay for all of the expenses. He even promised to give me one of his cars as a gift.

Things were really sweet between Ricardo and I. His main office was at the Cross Island Plaza, which made things more convenient for me; it wasn't too far from my house. We even went out every weekend to *Club Liguenea*, and I had the time of my life. Ricardo made sure that *everyday* was like Christmas day, and I quickly fell in love.

I thought shit was really sweet until early, one Sunday morning. I awoke to my phone ringing off the hook, and my cell's voicemail box was full. I usually didn't answer calls with unlisted numbers but I took the chance.

"Hello!" I made a point to sound extra bitchy.

"Hello, is this Kai?"

"Yeah, and?"

"Can I speak to you woman-to-woman?"

My first thought was to hang up on her stupid ass. I watched enough *Jerry Springer* episodes to know that 'woman-to-woman' only meant one thing.

Ricardo's wife was on my phone and very upset. She had to be much older than him. She sounded like someone's grandmother. Being that it was God's day, I chilled and attempted to hear Ricardo's wife out.

She started screaming at the top of her lungs, "WHAT'S GOING ON WITH YOU AND RICARDO? I SAW YOUR PICTURES IN HIS CAR!"

I remained cool: "Sweetie, Ricardo is my boyfriend. If you *really* must know, he's at my house a lot, and we've been going out every weekend since the summer started. Ya might wanna keep ya eye in the mail for the divorce papers instead of wasting your time calling me."

"WHO DO YOU THINK YOU'RE TALKING TO? I'M HIS WIFE, YOU LITTLE BITCH!"

Who the *fuck* was she calling a 'bitch'?

I took a deep breath and gazed over some of the things Ricardo had gotten me: a diamond tennis bracelet, the *Bose* stereo system, and my party outfits from *Neimann Marcus* and *Bloomingdale's*.

"Well, I don't think Ricardo knows that *you're* his wife…bitch!" I hung up and turned off my phone after saying that.

Later that day, Ricardo came up to my house upset. He told me I was being childish and stormed off before I could calm him down. I tried to call Ricardo to apologize, but he wouldn't answer his cell phone that day.

1st year at college

Ricardo did pay for my first semester like he promised. However, after the summer ended, he was no longer physically around. We never got the chance to get sexual, but Ricardo kept me at arms length, for whatever reason. I'd only really see him whenever he needed me for a special social function. Later, I would find out that I was Ricardo's 'trophy side-chick'.

I should've known.

Every time that I would complain about him not being around, Ricardo would shut me up by throwing money at me or buying me expensive things. For a while, that was alright but, I really thought I could settle down and start a family with that man.

* * * * *

By mid-November of 1997, Shelly and I were having the time of our lives at *York College*. The only bad thing was that I'd seemed to bump into Rippa at least once a week. I found out that he went to *Hillcrest High School* and was only sixteen years old. Rippa also had two jobs at two different Jamaican restaurants.

My better judgment was telling me not to lead this boy on, but Rippa was so stuck on me, I had to indulge. Besides, Ricardo only came around every once and awhile to drop a couple of hundreds. Ricardo wasn't there like I needed him to be, and I was lonely.

"Shelly, after class we're going up to Hillcrest!" I announced.

Shelly responded, "For what? I *know* you're not about to go chasing after some young boy! Don't let Ricardo find out before he cuts off your allowance. Come on, we'll be nineteen-years-old soon, and Rippa is how old?"

There was a three year age difference between Rippa and me.

Shelly never seemed to understand my policy of 'a-vic-is-a-vic'. True, I already had a sugar-daddy, but the money, in itself, wasn't enough. I needed more, so I became determined to find out what was really up with Rippa.

* * * * *

After class, Shelly and I walked into Hillcrest like we attended the school. The security guards didn't even bother to ask us for I.D. I finally found Rippa on the third floor in his Spanish class. When Rippa saw me, he could not stop smiling.

Enter game.

"Hey Rippa," I whispered, "come here for a minute." Rippa did as he was told, and was front and center with the quickness. Yeah, Rippa was hooked and to think he barely knew my name. I snatched the bulky *Nextel* phone off of Rippa's waist and put my info in.

"Rippa, sweetie, call me when you get home."

He was star-struck: "Uh-huh, will definitely do, Empress." I started walking away when Rippa called out my name: "Kai, you know mi *love* you? Mi a go marry you one day an' give you all di babies you want."

I didn't know what to say to that, so I smiled and continued walking away.

* * * * *

Rippa called as promised that same night. We talked for what seemed like hours. He had only been in Queens about six months and was from Waricka Hills in Jamaica, West Indies— Rippa lived up here in New York with his Dad in Springfield Gardens. I wasn't too keen on him living ten minutes from me, but I thought it was going to be oh so worth it.

I must admit, at that time, Rippa was doing pretty alright for himself. He got good grades in school and was even about to graduate soon. Baby boy even had a little car. Something I needed, but didn't have the ends for as yet. Ricardo said he would give me one of his, but never did.

Rippa's car was a 1991 modded-out Teggie. It was a well-known fact that I lived for car racing.

I'm still an enthusiast.

I lived for speed. In retrospect, perhaps that was a warning sign of my impending reckless behavior.

23

Rippa was equally excited when he found out that car racing was my thing. I asked him, "So what kind of things have you done to the *Integra*?"

I could hear Rippa taking a long pull of his spliff before answering, "Well, ma, mi and my friend dem take out the catback and change up di exhaust system and ting, so di car deya loud as fuck!"

Then I went to ask him about the wheels and this-that-and-the-third, and Rippa was honestly thrilled that his hobby interested me so.

I must say, he was really mature for his age. The conversation went well that night.

Too well.

I had to make a mental note: *Don't catch feelings for Rippa.*

And of course, I did.

* * * * *

Days turned into weeks, weeks turned into months and I started catching feelings hard for Rippa. I didn't want him to catch on, so I pretty much steered cleared away from Rippa and talked to him every now and then. Shelly had been M. I. A. since she started talking to this guy named, Ty that went to our school, so I was on a chill-out session.

spring of '98

By the time spring rolled back around, I was still debating on a course of action with Rippa when Ricardo found out that he'd gotten two different women pregnant at the same time. There were no more allowance from Ricardo, and his visits altogether stopped.

No matter how much I ignored Rippa, he was still stuck on me. His father even called me a couple of times, begging me to give his son a chance, so I did.

I alerted Rippa on his *Nextel* and within seconds, he was on the radio: "What's up, ma-ma?"

What was up was springtime was here and I needed some clothes—I got straight to the point: "Rippa, can you take me shopping for some spring clothes?"

"How ya mean, take you shoppin', eh?"

Um, yeah, fool, the mall closed at 9:30!

"Rippa, darling, I wouldn't ask you if I didn't need some. I've put on weight, and I can't fit my spring clothes from last year."

"So wha' ya do wit' your money? Don't ya have a card you cyan put it pon?"

Unless he was paying the bill, I wasn't about to charge it. Ricardo told me that I *never* should have to spend my own money. If I work, *all* that I made should go in the bank. Rippa would just have to understand.

"You know what, Rippa, forget it!"

He got back on the radio two minutes later: "I goin' come look fi you likkle lata and we can go shoppin' when I get off of work."

Yeaaah!

For the next two hours, I congratulated myself on my ability to mess with Rippa's head. I couldn't wait for him to come get me. I started to make a list of the stuff that I wanted as I waited for Rippa. It totaled up to around a thousand dollars in my head.

Unfortunately, my first love, Robbie left me with a serious *Ralph Lauren 'Polo'* addiction that broke my pockets to finance. That would be Rippa's job; or so I thought.

I was stunned to see Rippa getting off of the dollar van in front of my house. It's fucked up that he didn't have enough money to take the bus.

"Where's the teggie?" I asked, as I stepped out of the house.

Rippa dug his hands into his pockets and bowed his head.

"Ma, I wasn't even gonna tell you dis, but mi have speeding tickets mi haffi pay today, but you come now and say you need clothes, so I mus' park up the teggie for awhile."

Shit!

I felt kind of bad for a second, and then it passed.

"Fuck was you racing for?" I asked. Rippa just sucked his teeth.

When we got to the mall, I was about to make a mad-dash to *Mony's* clothing store until Rippa stopped me; pulling me close to him.

"Ma, don't even so think to go crazy up in here. Dis is all I have." I looked down at Rippa's hand and wanted to smack fire out of him! He only had two-hundred dollars! Mony's would have to wait for another day.

That day, I hit the '*Polo*' clearance rack in the women's section in Macy's.

south side jamaica, queens

Rippa was *definitely* no Ricardo! About a week after our "big shopping spree", I started dodging his calls again. I gave my life a really hard look, and decided I had to be doing *something* wrong. There were other inferior-type chicks getting broke off properly, while I starved.

I wasn't really starving.

I went through more than a couple of hundred dollars every week or so. That shit had to change, and it had to change quickly!

No later did I think that a change would come. It came in the form of an ex-con named, Tony Cartagena. I met him at work one day in March.

Tony was tall, lanky, and light-skinned. His almond-shaped eyes were what hypnotized me. I never would've guessed that Tony just had come home from a ten-year bid that same day. Then again, I didn't know anything about jail or the life that preceded it, except for what I read in books and saw on television.

Tony was anxious in the beginning. He tried to make our relationship move too quickly. We started talking on a Sunday and on that following Monday, Tony took me out. I could tell from that gesture alone that I could wrap him around my little finger—if I played my cards right.

Tony was straight to the point, while being sweet and sincere. All I saw in him, at first, was another opportunity to trick-off. Our first date ended up back at Tony's house; I don't even know how. One minute we were at *USA* diner chatting it up, the next, Tony and I were in South Side Jamaica, Queens.

I've always heard about the horrors that went down at that side of town, and nearly passed out when I realized that he was driving in that direction. As tough as I was, I knew that I couldn't mess with the broads out there.

We pulled up to a decrepit-looking house a few blocks away from *Baisley Projects;* I was so scared that day. I feared Tony was going to do something horrible, and leave me for dead up on "Pebble Beach". Many chicks had been found dead on project rooftops, and I *wasn't* about to be one of them!

Tony must've seen the fear in my eyes because just before he opened the door to his house, Tony gently grabbed my face and pulled it close to his. Locking his eyes with mine, Tony said softly, "Don't worry, kiddo, you're with me." I just nodded as I tried to remember my daddy's speed dial number on my cell phone.

Damn these men and their surprises!

When I walked into Tony's house I had to do a double take. The inside of his house looked like it was just featured on *MTV Cribs*. It was definitely *Lifestyles of the Rich and Famous* status. Since it became obvious that Tony had a lot of money, I straightened my back and prepped myself to cash in.

Instantly, the fear was gone and I went back into game mode. Tony would definitely have to come up out his pockets.

Enter game.

"So, Tony, why did you bring me here?" I said with a sexy smile.

"Kai, if it really makes you that nervous we can leave."

"Nah, I ain't nervous, just curious as to why I'm here. I will tell you though, you *ain't* getting no ass." I always laid down the rules in the beginning so there wouldn't be any confusion further down the line.

Tony broke out in laughter and just shook his head.

"Baby girl, listen. I brought you out here so you could get to see what I'm all about before you fall in love with me."

Tony was bold.

Yeah, he was cute and all, but *me* fall in love?

Please!

That wasn't *even* on the agenda.

"So what are you all about?"

Tony slowly pulled off his knit *Polo* sweater to reveal two holsters carrying twin, black nine millimeter handguns.

My heart stopped…

I had to bite my bottom lip to end its nervous quiver.

"I'm about a lot of things, Kai. First and foremost, I'm about my money! I've been gone a long time and money was the only friend I could count on. Money was the only thing that kept me sane on 'The Island'. So now that I'm out, it's *all* about money!"

I didn't know what to think at that point. I looked dead in his eyes and realized that Tony was being serious. We stood there looking at each other for what seemed like an eternity. He grabbed my hand: "Come on, let's go upstairs."

Oh shit, I'm about to be fucked. Or so I thought.

Tony instructed me to sit down on his king-sized bed as he took off the holsters. At that point, I was shaking like a fiend in need of a fix.

I was *so* nervous!

Tony then kicked off his new black *Timberland* boots and continued to undress, revealing yet another holster, holding a .22.

He came right up on me and whispered in my ear, "You really need to stop being so scared of me; I ain't gonna hurt you. You're fresh and smart—I need that. Trust that if you roll with me, you'll be rolling with royalty. You'll be the Queen-of-the-city."

I nodded as Tony broke away from me. He then reached underneath the bed and pulled out a huge photo album. I was like: "Ooh, pictures." Finally, something to break the tension in the air.

The pictures didn't have that calming effect that I needed. They were of Tony and his cronies with all types of machine guns, semi-automatics and coke. Raw cocaine, cooked cocaine, crack-cocaine.

I'd never seen so much cocaine in my life!

The photo album was a like a photo essay of Tony's life. I was still scared, but became intrigued, as he talked about the pictures.

I didn't know it at the time, but, Tony had fallen in love with me at first sight—hard! That day he told me everything about his operations from soup-to-nuts. Tony even showed me where his workers cooked up the coke. Tony broke sacred codes of the drug game—left, right, front and center.

Over some pussy that he ain't even *smelled* yet!

* * * * *

In the beginning, I only rolled with Tony when instinct told me it was okay to. It quickly became obvious that he was a dangerous man with dirty tricks. Before Tony's incarceration, he had a heavy hand in the crack game that infected New York City like the plague. Now, Tony's hands were in any and everything that would bring him a dollar.

As Tony took me around his neighborhood, I kept mental notes of who was who and what was what. He introduced me to every hustler, pimp and drug dealer in New York City. Tony just kept spoon-feeding me the game like I was his successor. I just kept soaking it all up like a sponge.

I couldn't wait to tell Shelly about Tony, I knew it would make her jealous as fuck. I went to Shelly's house one day sporting a brand-new, pink *Avirex* motorcycle jacket.

"Where did you get the ends for that?" was the first thing that came out of her mouth when Shelly saw me.

"Oh, this?" I smoothly replied as I dusted off the sleeves. "This ain't nothing. Its compliments of my boo, Tony."

"Who's Tony? Dammit, Kai, every time I turn around, you got a new dude hooked on your *trifling* ass. First it was Ricardo, now it's Tony? That's fucked up! That's *really* fucked up, Kai! I do all the shit Ty wants me to do, and this *nigga* still manages to cheat on me!"

Shelly just had to rain down on my parade; as usual. This visit was supposed to be about Tony and I. How did it turn to her?

"Shelly, what are you *talking* about? You are always with Ty, when did he have time to cheat on you?"

"Whenever I was at work or in class. I got Ty's password to his voicemail, and there's this chick named, Maritza talking about how much she loves him. I called the bitch back, and she was like how Ty is *her* man. Kai, what am I going to do?"

Truth be told, Shelly really did love Ty. I knew he wasn't any good for her though—Ty was grimey. Every time he'd see us together on campus, Ty would call Shelly on her cell phone, telling Shelly that he wanted to speak to her; even though Ty was standing less then a foot away from us. He could never look me in my eye.

Game recognized game.

"Does Maritza go to our school?" I asked coolly.

"Yeah."

Enough said.

"Alright, so come Monday, we'll find that bitch and see what's *really* up with her and Ty."

"But I don't want any trouble."

"Shells, the girl is calling *your* man, *her* man! There already is trouble."

Shelly went on to tell me that she thinks Maritza worked at the Financial Aid office at *York College,* because Maritza's been hooking up Ty with fraudulent financial aid.

Monday afternoon, I strutted right into the Financial Aid office pretending to look through some brochures. After about five minutes, someone finally called Maritza's name. She was a short, little Spanish chick that physically couldn't compare with Shelly.

I didn't get it...

I left the office on that note and found Shelly. She was upstairs in the library.

"Shells, ya girl should be called 'Lil' Magic' cause she's funny-looking as hell! Little short piece of shit!"

Shelly looked like she wanted to cry.

"Where that *bitch* at?"

"Downstairs in the Financial Aid office, just like you said."

We ran from the third floor to the first. I started snatching off my jewelry along the way. I had another two hours before my night class started, and was good and ready to beat Maritza a.k.a "Lil' Magic" senseless.

As Shelly and I hopped off the escalators, we saw Ty and "Lil' Magic" walking out of the Financial Aid office together. The two were hand-in-hand, smiling like they had just gotten married. Shelly had rage in her eyes and screamed out Ty's whole name, as loud as she could.

"TYRRET! MOTHERFUCKER, YOU HEAR ME!"

"Lil' Magic" turned around and flipped her hair like she's a Nuyorican Queen. "Lil' Magic's" audacity alone made my blood boil.

Ty turned around and had the nerve to say: "Shelly, what's the problem?" before leaving the building with "Lil' Magic".

I quickly turned to Shelly: "Yo, son, you gonna let the limpy motherfucker play you?"

"Nah, Kai, let it go. Fuck him!"

"No, you did fuck him, Shelly! Damn near twenty-eight days out of every month, and for what? Simon says that little flaky diamond on her finger is from Ty. What's up with that? You ain't got no fucking diamonds!"

"You're *fucking* lying, Kai!"

"Fuck that! Ty gotta answer to *me* now!"

I stormed out the building in search of Ty. Shelly followed behind me. Ty had the nerve to start walking down Archer Avenue

31

towards Merrick Boulevard. Shelly and I went and followed him on foot.

I tried asking Ty to tell me what was going on, but him and "Lil' Magic" just kept walking down the street like they didn't hear me. By the time we got to 109th Street, I gave up.

There would be another day.

Shelly and I retreated and ended up at a nearby *Taco Bell*. We went downstairs to watch their TV while we ate. Shelly and I got a good laugh off of how much Ty resembled 'Mojo Jojo' from the *Power Puff Girls*.

The next day, I received a frantic phone call from Shelly, begging me to pick her up from Ty's house as soon as I could. Apparently, Shelly went over there to get her stuff and Ty beat her up.

I got to his house and almost cried when I noticed that there was a fresh bald spot on the side of Shelly's head. She just got her braids done over the weekend, and Ty had literally snatched Shelly bald.

"SHELLS, WHAT HAPPENED TO YOUR HAIR?"

"Ty flipped out, yo! We started arguing and one thing led to another. The motherfucker grabbed me by my hair and tried to throw me out of the window."

Ty knew he was in the wrong. Why did he have to put his hands on Shelly?

A week later, Shelly and Ty were back together, and I was too through with her dumb ass. "Lil' Magic" would try to stare me down in the cafeteria when she was with her friends, and Shells was never around.

* * * * *

One day while waiting for Tony to pick me up in front of the school, a little, black, dingy *Dodge Neon* pulls in front of me.

"Yo, bitch, you stepped to my friend?"

Was the girl for real?

Oh shit!

"Lil' Magic" and some chick had just rolled up on me.

"Best believe, if you're talking to me, you better come up out of the car where I can see you!"

"Lil' Magic" was in the front seat trying to act hardcore and shit. All I needed was for either one of them fake-ass chicks to bust a move, for me to cause damage.

Just as the driver was getting out, Shelly drove up in Ty's *Mazda Millennium:* "Kai, is there a problem?"

"Lil' Magic" damn near fainted.

"Why the fuck you driving Ty's car, bitch?"

I had to interject, "Because that's her man, bitch!"

"Lil' Magic" proceeded to call me all types of names, so I put my black Dolomites to work on the door of the *Dodge Neon,* before knocking off the side mirror. The driver sped off down Guy R. Brewer Boulevard.

crooks & angels

Six weeks later, Tony went missing, and I was free. At that point, I was involved in *too* much of his business. Tony managed to introduce me to all the heavy-hitters in Queens; I was always with him while Tony 'put in work'. While that was good for my pockets and popularity factor, I didn't want to end up becoming his co-defendant.

Tony changed my vocabulary, lifestyle habits and way of thinking. No longer was I scared to roll up to South Side, or to do anything else for that matter. I regularly took the dollar van up there and strolled through; like it was *my* neighborhood. I even carried the pearl-handled, .22 Tony got me for my nineteenth birthday on a regular basis.

Whatever happened would've been *his* fault anyway, and the fact that Tony hadn't called—*would* be my reason for breaking up with him.

Before we stopped talking, Tony asked me if I would put balloons in my pussy to bring up to *Metropolitan Detention Center* in Brooklyn, for his homeboy.

I said no!
I schooled myself on the drug laws and knew that I would face some serious time if I got caught. Besides, that's what the local squallys were around for!

I figured that Tony was mad at me for that, so I waited three days. No call, no show was official job abandonment. I figured that Tony was dragging me too deep, too soon, into his world, anyway! Although, Tony's drug money had me hooked, I desperately needed an out.

* * * * *

One day while sitting on the dollar van heading to work, I got my first dose of reality. The police had Linden and Merrick Boulevards blocked off, so the van driver had to make a detour. I was about to discount the situation as everyday hood-happenings, until I spotted Tony's red Civic sandwiched in between two squad cars.

I quickly hopped off of the van to try to see what was going on. I pretended like I needed to walk down Linden Boulevard, just to see what was up.

My knees got weak when I saw the cops put Tony in the back of one of their cars. As our eyes locked, Tony shook his head slowly. I knew that I had to double-back out of there, fast! Just as I turned around, I bumped into Rico.

He was one of Tony's business partners that supposedly had Far Rockaway on lock. Rico slipped me his business card and told me to call him if I needed anything.

* * * * *

Before classes were ending, I was back to being alone. With Tony locked up, I no longer had someone to answer my questions about the game, so I just watched every nickel-and-dime hustler; in an attempt to stay up with what Tony taught me.

Shelly was still with Ty. My main focus, now that finals were about to be over, was to learn about the business of drugs. I had to find out how *I* could get a piece of the drug game!

There was just too much money floating around these streets and I wasn't getting any commissions on it.

I needed that.

I needed a piece of what these young dudes were addicted to. I had a plan in mind and everything seemed to be running smoothly. That was until the last day of finals.

It was a hot day in May and I had just stepped out of *Gertz Mall*. Heading in the direction of my school, I heard someone screaming my name. It was "Lil' Magic" and five of her friends.

Shit!

Shelly was already on campus taking her finals and I didn't have the .22 on me!

"Is there a problem?" I said just above a whisper. You would think that college life would be so much different than high school...it wasn't.

I've been in that same type of situation since I moved to Queens and the bullshit *never* ended. I was already a hard head before Tony had instilled this "tough-as-nails" attitude in me. I thought that I *ruled* the world and tried to *prove* it, every chance that I got!

"Yeah, bitch! There is a problem! Where's Shelly?"

"Mira, ya no se donde estas mi amiga!" I replied.

"Lil' Magic" burst.

No one really knew that I'm half Spanish. It momentarily dazed her.

"I see someone has been taking 'Spanish 101'." Once again, "Lil' Magic" tried to play me.

"Look, Mama Beecho, I ain't got time for the bullshit! You and ya scary-looking friends can go fuck off!" I continued cursing like a sailor at "Lil' Magic", until this fine specimen of a man walked out of the barbershop.

We both stopped arguing.

He was about 5'11", with a light, pale complexion and honey-brown eyes. His curly brown hair was pulled back into a single braid that fell neatly down the middle of his back. The man must've just gotten a shape-up or something, because his face looked so smooth and fresh.

He and I caught eyes for a second, and then I kept it moving up to the school; never looking back. All I could think about while I took my final was his ability to diffuse the situation, with just his presence.

Dude didn't even have to say a word.

He was a very powerful man. In time, he would diffuse a lot more. Well, at least, try to…

"Honey-Brown Eyes" was an angel.

When I finally arrived on campus, I found Shelly and told her what went down with 'Lil Magic'. I made no mention of the light-skinned mystery man.

"Shells, kid, you won't believe what just almost went down on the bully!"

"Awww, damn, Kai! What now?"

"'Lil' Magic' and about five of her friends rolled up on me like they was jumping somebody."

"For real?" Shelly was in total shock. "When we going after her?"

"Going after who, 'Lil' Magic'? Man, fuck that bitch! We in college now and bitches *still* wanna jump somebody. Come on! That shit is for the birds. If she throws her fists, then I'ma *throw* mine, but if she doesn't, then fuck her! We gotta bigger thangs to worry about."

The bigger picture had started to unveil: drug money was calling. I couldn't waste my time on *petty* shit!

"Oh word?" Shelly asked. "Not too long, you was snatching off earrings and shit, and now 'Lil' Magic' got you shook! Ya getting soft on me?"

No. I was getting *HARDER!*

Shelly and I had nothing else to do that day, so we decided to go chill with my Godfather; Rashawn. Rashawn was only fifteen years older than me, so he wasn't my godfather through baptism. Rashawn always kept me out of trouble when I was on 'The Avenue'.

I used to have a real problem with them dudes that stood posted up in front of the Parsons Boulevard train station, until he and I became cool. Rashawn was cute with his freckles but, for a lot of reasons, things never popped off between us.

Just as we were walking up to Rashawn's spot, I peeped Jordan through the corners of my eyes. It was a year since I'd last seen him, and the feelings came rushing back like a tidal wave!

Shelly caught on quick and started to laugh.

"Kai, I *know* you're not still stuck on silly-ass Jordan! You've done pulled in serious ballers like Tony, and that red-boned fool still knocks you off your feet?"

"What are you *talking* about Shelly?" I couldn't lie though. Jordan still looked so damn good. I wanted to go up to him and tell Jordan that I was crazy about him, but my pride wouldn't let me. So I just nodded when he said hello, as we passed by him.

"Kai, you still ain't say nothing to him. It's like déjà vu. I don't know who you think you're fooling because you're *not* fooling me! You're in love with Jordan!"

Damn, was she ever right!

Just as I was about to deny it, Rippa came walking up to me.

"Hey gyal, wha' ya problem? I call you pon di phone an' you neva answer."

I really didn't feel like seeing him at that moment.

"I've been busy."

"It's alright. Busy gon' a party. I saw ya in *Club Liguenea* wit' dat *cooley* bwoy... It's alright...

37

"I've been missing ya still, ma. Why is it so *'ard* fi ya to give mi a try? I really want fi marry you…

"Mi nah ugly, mi ah go be seventeen in July, I soon finish wit' school. Wha' mi haffi *do* to get through to ya?"

"Rippa, this isn't the time or the place for this discussion. I'll call you later." I turned to Shelly and he grabbed my hand.

"Ma, mi know why ya *don't* wanna deal wit' mi. Mi know say, mi don't 'ave the type of money that ya used to. Money isn't everyting ya know! Mi have *so* much love inni mi heart fi ya. Ya *too* 'ard!"

I looked into his eyes. Rippa did really and truly love me, and on some strange level, I loved him, too, but, he didn't have the financial status that I needed to stand on.

"Rippa, I'll call you later." With that, I left him.

Shelly tried to resurrect my conscious, but it was no use.

"Kai, you are just *so* spoiled. That boy really loves you, and probably would give his *life* for you, and you standing here like Rippa's love is worthless! That's like the second time I done heard Rippa say that he wants to marry you. Give Rippa a fucking try, yo!"

"Yeah, yeah, yeah! If Rippa *really* loved me, he would get his weight up! My love is not cheap! I *refuse* to claim a dude that doesn't spend money on me like water. What am I going to do when I find him cheating, and I'm standing there empty-handed?"

That remark hit Shelly right between the eyes. Shelly rolled them and kissed her teeth.

"Shells, if Rippa wanted, he could easily start selling weed. It's simple, fast-easy money! From there, who knows?" I wish I had never said that. I wish that I looked around before that came flying out of my mouth.

"Ah, so ya want, Empress? Mi fi leave di honest life fi di drug money dem. I don't *come* to America for such FUCKERY! I come fi finish school an' try to make something out of myself."

Damn! Why didn't Rippa just walk away?

I tried to cop a plea: "No, Rippa, baby, it's not like that. It's not how you're taking it."

"Ah so ya say." Then he left.

Shit!

Just that quick, a monster was born.

* * * * *

About a month later, I found a manila envelope in my mailbox. It was in Rippa's pretty, English handwriting. I grabbed it and ran to my room. Inside the envelope: two thousand dollars.

I immediately called Rippa.

"Rippa, what is this?"

"Wha' ya mean?"

"The money, Rippa. Where did you get the money from?"

"Just hold it fi mi, ya hear? You can spend some, but save some, aight?"

"Rippa?"

"Listen, ma, I haffi go. Mi a go call ya lata."

With that he hung up.

For once in my life I did exactly what I was told. I took two hundred, and stashed the rest in my sneaker boxes.

We barely spoke on the phone, but every two weeks there was another envelope in my mailbox. It was like that for the whole summer, until Rippa got arrested.

It was his first offense, and the cops only found a nickel bag of weed on Rippa. His father was too pissed, and sent Rippa back to Jamaica.

Fuck!

At least I was sitting on six grand. Not much, but it was a start. I didn't feel no way about Rippa's father sending him back to Jamaica because of me. I actually found relief in the fact that I wouldn't have to own up to my feelings for Rippa.

School was about to start again, and I didn't have Ricardo
to pay for my tuition that year; I just took the money from Rippa's
stash. He was in Jamaica, Rippa would never ask for it.
Or so I thought.

I should've just filed for financial aid but, that would've
meant dealing with "Lil' Magic". I wasn't about to give that bird
an open opportunity to fuck me over.

Shelly was still with Ty, and I grew tired of their antics.
The millennium was about to happen and I was once again,
seeking a change.

I decided to call Rico.
Bad move, a really bad move.

Ring, Ring, Ring.

It was a home phone number and some broad picked up. I
didn't care.

"Yo, may I *speak* to Rico," I rudely replied after she said
'hello'.

"Who's dis?"

I sucked my teeth, "Can you just tell him that *Kai* is on the
phone!" I didn't have anytime for jealous girlfriends.

"Kai?" She paused, "...Girl, why are you calling my
man?"

Oh shit!

I recognized that voice. It was the ever so conceited,
Chyna Smith, a.k.a "Sticks". If my life were ever turned into a
movie, she would be labeled as ARCH-NEMESIS # 1 in the
script. Now come to find out, she was Rico's girl. "Sticks" also
worked in the mall.

It was a small world.

"Nah, Chyna, it ain't *like* that. Rico is friends with my
man, Tony. You know Tony, don't you?"

"Oh, you fuck with Tony? Ewww! Rico, pick up the
phone."

Ewww?

What was that supposed to mean? A little side note: "Sticks" swore she was the epitome of beauty at a size one.

Bitch, please!

Five minutes later, Rico finally picked up the phone: "Yo, Kai, where you at?"

Why did he even need to know? I entertained it anyway.

"I was just about to leave York, why? Wassup?"

"I'ma send my man, Diego to come get you because you and I need to talk. He'll be driving a black *Benz* truck."

"Um, ok—"

Click!

Rico hung up before I could even finish speaking. Less than five minutes later, a black Benz pulled up to the 160th Street side of the school playing *How to Rob* by *50 Cent,* at maximum volume.

I hopped in quickly.

"Wassup?" I said sweetly, trying to start a conversation. Diego never turned to me. He had his *Yankee's* fitted cap tilted so low that I couldn't get a good look at his facial features. I got that uneasy feeling again, but I decided to continue with the trip because of Tony. If these were his peoples, then I was safe.

* * * * *

First it was South Side, now, it's Far Rockaway, the sixth borough. Tony never took me out here, so if something popped off, I wouldn't have a clue on what to do or how to get back home. I only knew that we hit Far Rockaway because we drove passed *Red Fern Projects.*

Many stories came out of those projects...

Diego and I continued the drive down Beach Channel Drive in silence. It seemed like forever before he turned off a side street and parked in front of a pretty, bungalow-styled home.

"Get out!" he yelled.

Was Diego for real? I thought my affiliation with Tony alone would grant me the utmost respect everywhere I went. I guess that didn't apply out here because, this boy was straight disrespecting me.

41

I turned around, and before I could say 'excuse me?', I was snatched out of the car!

"Rule # 1: Do as you're told, no questions asked!" It was Rico.

Again, I tried to reply.

Rico put his index finger to his lip gesturing silence like I was a child. It had gotten dark and I wanted to go back to Rosedale. I should've just told him to bring me home then. I felt a bad vibe off of the situation. Instead of heading home, I just remained silent walking up to Rico's house.

We finally arrived inside. I could've *kicked* myself for forgetting to look at the street signs. I didn't know where I was.

Tony taught me better than that.

Despite my insecurities, I tried to act hard once when we were inside of the house: "Rico, what's really good?"

Rico grinned while stroking his goatee, "You tell me ma."

"You get 'Silent Bob' over there to pick me up from school, then wanna try acting all secretive. Fuck you bring me out here for?!"

I was *too* through!

"See, that's what I like about you, Kai. You're mad quiet and sweet on the outside, but tough. I *like* that shit, just as much as I like your fat ass!"

He couldn't be serious.

I cooked dinner for Tony and Rico before. He's supposed to be Tony's boy. Rico was with "Sticks", so why was he coming at me like that?

There was no need for the disrespect!

"Fuck you, Rico," I said between clenched teeth.

"I know you'd like to, and I'll prove it, too, but this here is about business, Kai."

Business my fat ass!

"Business? Rico, you and I don't have *any* business going on."

"Sure we do. I mean, sure we will. I want you to work for me. I already spoke to Chyna and she said it would be cool. Ya'll could lock down Valley Stream for me."

He already spoke to Chyna? What did that have to do with me? Lock down Valley Stream?

"What?!"

"I want you to work for me, comprende?"

As if on cue, "Sticks" came strutting into the room with two *Louis Vuitton* messenger bags. Rico opened them slowly. One had little white pills in it, and the other had crack vials with different colored tops.

As I tried to remember the price for each color, something clicked. "Sticks" always gave off an 'I'm a little rich girl with mad-money vibe', and I would have been mad-jealous of her if I wasn't prettier than "Sticks". Just then, I found out where all the *Coach* and *Chanel* goods came from.

She was a drug dealer.

"Sticks" used to try to clown my *Ralph Lauren "Polo"* wardrobe, but at least mine was attained in a more respectable manner.

I used to boost the shit before I got hip to hustler's money.

I *never* hustled drugs!

Never had to.

"Hey baby girl," "Sticks" said when I didn't address her.

"Sticks" could kiss my ass!

"Sup, 'Sticks'?"

Oops!

"Sticks? Who the *fuck* is you calling 'Sticks'? That *ain't* my name. It's Chyna Smith, bitch! Don't get shit twisted because you're up here by Rico's request! I'll *still* kick ya motherfucking ass for disrespecting me!"

Oh, my bad.

"Sticks" was my nickname for Chyna's little ass. She literally reminded me of sticks, so skinny and worthless.

"Fuck off!" I spat in "Sticks'" face. "As a matter of fact, *fuck* you, too, Rico! I works for *no* one! I say no to drugs, you little fucker. Please! Have 'Sticks' here put in work for you. I'm out!" I stormed out of Rico's house like I knew how to get the hell up out of Far Rockaway.

* * * * *

I stepped outside and the darkness enveloped me. Rage BURNED inside of me, as I walked off in search of Beach Channel Drive. After walking around in circles a few times, I found it. Just as I did, Rico found me.

Shit!

"Yo, Kai."

Rico pulled up in a black *Aston Martin Vanquish.*

Damn, I only saw those things in magazines.

Entering the drug game crossed my mind momentarily. I contemplated working for him for a second, then snapped out of it. Even though Tony was missing in action, I vowed that he would be the *last* dope man that I would ever deal with.

"Rico, just leave me alone!" I yelled from the curb. "I'm grown! I can find my way home! Thanks, but no thanks!" It would take me awhile, but I definitely could find my way home.

"Little girl, please! Hop in before you get hurt out here."

Hurt?

Rico did have a point.

My feet were hurting. I didn't know where I was. He was driving an Aston.

I had only one choice.

"Ok. But, Rico, please, just take me straight home! I already *tolerated* enough of your bullshit for one night. I don't think I can take anymore."

"Oh, it's like that, Kai? I will take you home, in a minute though. Let me just make a couple of stops and pick up a few things, ok?"

I agreed.

We went back to the bungalows, and then went to *Redfern Projects* for a little while. Before I knew it, Rico and I were in Dix Hills, Long Island. I hoped that this was his last stop, so I sat quietly and listened to *Jay-Z* spit on the *Reasonable Doubt* CD Rico was playing.

As he got out of the car that last time, Rico asked me to come along.

I wasn't ready for that.

"For what?" I replied with sarcasm dripping from my voice.

"Kai, you're one feisty bitch. Just come the *fuck* on! Dang, why does everything have to be a fight with you? Remember rule #1? Just come into my house for minute."

I glanced over at the beautiful white Tudor house with gold-trimmed French doors. The well-manicured lawn and the quiet neighborhood gave me a false sense of security, so I followed Rico into the house.

I thought Tony had money until I walked into Rico's house. His house made Tony's look like a half-way home. Rico's house was pure white, inside and out, with gold trim all around: the carpet, the sofa, the television and the walls.

Everything in the house was pure white, so I kicked off my *Dolomites* in the foyer before continuing further inside.

I started to get a little comfortable when instinct kicked in.

"Where's Chyna?" I asked, as my eyes darted across the room.

"Working," Rico said nonchalantly.

"Who else is here?"

"You."

"Ha, ha, real funny. I'm being serious, though."

I didn't trust myself with Rico.

I didn't trust Rico, period!

He was 6'1", Puerto Rican-looking with long jet-black hair that screamed to be braided. Rico was *definitely,* my kind of dude. He was more muscular and toned than Jordan.

I didn't think that was possible.

"Sit down, Kai. Make yourself at home," Rico said while pouring himself a glass of *Hennessy.*

I took one look at the white sofa, then at my dark-blue *Sergio Valente's,* and said, "I'm good."

Rico placed his glass on the coffee table then picked me up, and sat me in his lap. He smelled *so* good; I knew that trouble was brewing.

"Damn, Rico, ease up."

I didn't want to be alone with him any longer.

"Kai," he took a sip of *Hennessy,* "let me be honest with you. I know what Tony saw in you—I see it, too. I just wouldn't have gone to the extent that Tony did, until I knew for sure that you were dependable and faithful.

"That's why I asked you to work for me. I know if any chick out here could get the job done, it's you. Niggas is expecting other niggas to do my pick-ups. When they see two broads and think shit is sweet, I know you'll be able to handle that for me."

I immediately thought that this must have been a test of the "emergency drug-dealer boyfriend just got locked up system'. I tried to dominate the situation: "Rico, let me up."

If this was a test, I wanted to pass.

Rico held me tighter. "For once, chill-out, sweetie. If you're worried about Chyna stopping through here, you can chill. She doesn't even know about this crib."

What?

"Oh, for real? The way Chyna stays talking about how tight her and her man is, I guess you *ain't* him if you got houses that *she* doesn't even know about."

"You're right. I'm *not* her man. Chyna *thinks* I'm her man, and she puts in work, in exchange for pennies. She be thinking them three-hundred dollar *Coach* bags are the shit. On the real, a women's handbag *ain't* the shit, unless it's upwards of five grand."

Shit!

Back then I didn't even make three-hundred a week.

Dollar signs began to roll.

Insecurities dwindled.

Enter game.

I softened up my voice and gently caressed his cheek. "So, what you saying, Rico? You fittin' to buy me a five-thousand dollar handbag?"

Rico burst out laughing.

"Kai, you're wild. Why would I buy you anything? Unlike Tony, I don't *trick* in no shape or form. You can't get something for nothing!"

"Oh, really?" I tried to break free when I realized that Rico's 'little man' was at attention. "Damn, Rico, now you *really* gotta let me up now. I don't *play* them type of games!"

"What, lil' mama, you scared?" He whispered softly.

Tony said that I should never be scared of anything or anyone: "Nigga, please!" I replied while still trying to break free from Rico's grip.

"Kai, you and Tony never fucked." *Damn how did he know that?* "And, I know that you haven't been seeing anyone since Tony. A little fun and games won't hurt."

"How do you know that, Rico?"

"Same way I knew that you walk out on the 160th Street side when you leave York on Tuesday nights."

Oh Shit!

"Rule # 2: Keep both eyes wide open. Always be aware of your surroundings."

"Oh, so you been out pussy-watching?"

Rico laughed at me again.

"Nah, I just know that I like what I see. Kai, you're it, girl! Tony already schooled you on the game, you've got the right attitude, you've got a body like *WHOA,* you're smart, AND you can throw down in the kitchen? A-nigga-like-me would have it in his best interests to snatch you up!"

"That's all gravy, Rico but I gotta go. Snatch up 'Sticks'!" The conversation was heading in a brand-new direction that I did not like. I didn't want to continue with the game that Rico was playing.

"Aight then. I ain't gon' hold you hostage." I felt a sense of relief that was derailed when he started kissing me seductively.

After passionately kissing until my lips were sore, I came up for air: "Rico, what are you doing?" I half said/half whispered, knowing that I shouldn't have been there, but not wanting to leave.

"Nothing that you don't want, baby girl."

My breathing became hot-and-heavy as Rico's hands rubbed all over my body. He stood up with me still in his lap, and pinned me against a nearby wall, while I wrapped my legs around Rico's waist.

It was feeling so good, that I lost control.

He started to carry me upstairs.

"Rico, where are we going?" I guess the kissing and touching became too intense for him, because Rico just continued up the stairs.

"To Heaven," he whispered.

Oh shit!

I should have said 'no', but Rico's warm, soft kisses had hypnotized me to the point of no return.

I don't really remember how I ended up buck-naked on his bed with Rico's tongue in between my thighs… I do remember him feasting on me like a starved, wild boar.

It was incredible!

I forgot a-l-l about "Sticks" and Tony, when Rico slid his tongue deep into the *essence* of my femininity. Right then and there, I was in Heaven!

All of a sudden, Rico said, "I wanna fuck you, baby girl." I opened my eyes to see him standing over me, naked with a HUGE, erect pipe.

I wanted it…

I wanted it *so* bad…

I let him know it too: "Fuck me, Rico."

Then the unimaginable happened…

Rico started laughing really hard as he put his clothes back on.

"See, I told you that you *wanted* to, point proven! Now get dressed! We got some things to go over."

Rico played me.

I became extremely angry.

I don't know which was worse: being upset because I let myself go, or being horny like I've never been before.

"FUCK YOU, RICO!"

I was hurt and embarrassed.

"Settle down, Kai. For real, stop playing games and come work for me."

"Doing *what*, Rico?! Moving shipments?! Cooking?! Playing jester in your court?!" I couldn't find my things fast enough. I wanted to get out of there as quickly as I could.

"Let me set up shop at your house so we can supply Valley Stream with the finest 'E' pills. Trust, it'll be fast, easy money."

Now I saw the reason behind his seduction: Rico set me up for the kill. There was no way in *Hell* that I would bring product to where I lived! Everybody knows that you don't shit where you eat! Besides, I was surrounded by dealers on all sides and over the Bridge in Laurelton. I knew it would be a serious problem if I gave Far Rock access.

"Sorry, Rico. That's what 'Sticks' is for."

Rico shook his head in disbelief.

"I never knew a broad to pass me up."

I couldn't believe that he was for real.

"Well, I never knew a dude to pass up a fat pussy either. Rico, if you want me around you, that's cool. You're Tony's good friend, so maybe you can tell me where he's at. However, motherfucker, I will *not* move drugs for you!"

"Oh word?" Rico scoffed with anger in his eyes.

"WORD!" I replied sternly. "NOW TAKE ME HOME!"

"Take yaself home, you ungrateful bitch!" With that, Rico threw an empty *Heineken* bottle at me that barely missed my face. "Oh, and, pussy-is-pussy, bitch! Ya lil' ass twot can't do *shit* for the kid. See yaself out, little girl, oh, I forgot—you's a big girl, right? Find ya way home!"

"Aight, motherfucker!"

It was either then or never to prove that I was really tough-as-nails. As I jetted down the stairs, I immediately began a mental search for Rico's car keys.

STUPID LITTLE FAGGOT!

The car keys were on top of a table right next to my boots. He wasn't even running after me.

"Later, Rico!" I yelled.

No response.

Okay.

That night, I learned that the biggest hustlers were always careless in one form or the other. I shook my head at the irony of the situation, as I deactivated Rico's car alarm: *Chirp, chirp.*

I realized it was a 6-speed as I hopped in. That was why he didn't even bother to hide the keys.

WHAT A *DUMB* MOTHERFUCKER!

I started that bad boy off, popped the clutch, pressed the pedal and headed home. By the time Rico realized that I stole, I mean, took his car...I was already doing seventy miles per hour on the Southern State Parkway.

* * * * *

I ended up driving Rico's car into the lake in *Brookville Park*, and walked the rest of the way home that night. I didn't think about the repercussions or anything.

I did it to prove a point!

In my mind, I thought that everybody should respect me to the fullest of their abilities. If they couldn't, then I would do *anything* within my abilities to cause them serious harm, one way or another. I'd been through *too* much to take any more bullshit from anybody!

I knew an *Aston Martin* meant big money, I just didn't know *how* much money.

It didn't matter to me anyway!

All I knew was that Rico played me, so I played him.

Touché, Monsieur Pussy Cat!

get down or lay down

I was *really* feeling myself after I put Rico's car in the lake. That was, until I arrived at work the next day. As soon as I got there, I saw him reading the Dupont Registry of Fine Cars, right in the front area of the store.

My heart dropped into my stomach. I made a beeline to the backroom and pleaded with my boss to let me work back there with her, so I wouldn't have to face Rico.

Not even looking at me she said, "Kai, you're my only cashier tonight and Larry needs to take his lunch break. Sorry, but I need you out there."

I wanted to *punch* her in her face. I had a madman in the building and my boss acted as if it were nothing. She continued going through the paperwork on her desk, not even giving me the opportunity to express why I couldn't be on the sales floor that night.

I walked head on into Rico, just as I left the backroom.

"Where's my car, you little bitch?" he spoke loud enough only for me to hear.

I was about to lose my bladder.

"Um, in the lake."

My voice quivered nervously.

Rico's face turned beet-red.

"The lake? You put a $300,000 car in the lake? What lake?"

I smoothed out the imaginary wrinkles in my skirt.

"The one in *Brookville Park.*"

"You mean to tell me that you put my car into—" Rico stopped in the middle of his sentence. Nassau County's finest had just walked in. They frequented my store on a regular basis, and I was never happier to see them.

At that, Rico left and I thought I was in the clear. That was until the mall closed.

When I left the store that night, "Sticks" was waiting for me right by the escalators.

"Rico is going to kick your ass," "Sticks" sang. "How the fuck did you steal his car?" I guess Rico hadn't told "Sticks" that he left his keys in plain sight.

"And I should kick *your* ass for getting *all* up in *my* face 'Sticks'. Damn, go somewhere with yourself." I waved her off and proceeded towards the doors.

"Yeah, I will, bitch, and guess what? You're coming with me. Rico's outside!"

I could feel my dinner easing back up when "Sticks" said that. I still had to put on the tough-girl façade. "I ain't got *shit* to say to that nigga!"

"But I got shit to say to you, bitch!" It was Rico.

I held the façade steady as I replied, "Rico, I already *told* you where the car is. Now be a good boy and go fetch."

Just as I said that, Rico smacked me to the floor. Mall security pretended like they didn't see a thing.

"Get the *fuck* up, we going for a ride!" Rico snatched me up and dragged me out of the mall. He threw me in the back of a *Ford Explorer*. "Sticks" sat right next to me, and offered me some coke.

I didn't even know she was an addict.

"You're gonna need this. You better be grateful that I'm giving you something now to ease the pain that's about to come."

"Fuck you, 'Sticks'!"

This *bitch* thought I was junkie just like her. I'd spat in "Sticks'" beady eye, as soon as I began to recover from the sting of Rico's hand against my face.

I didn't know what he had planned. Whatever it was, I had psyched myself up to take it. I made a vow that night to *never* bow out without a fight.

Defeat would *never* be an option!

We weren't driving all that long when the truck stopped. Rico, "Sticks" and I were now back in Far Rockaway. It then took both Rico and Diego to get me out of the car.

"Sticks" watched on.

As the two men dragged me out kicking and screaming, I noticed that the street sign read: "Shorefront Parkway".

The four of us went inside one of the buildings, and they brought me to the roof. Rico had me by my hair.

"You and your funky, little attitude, like you can't get killed, bitch! Since you wanna *act* like you're untouchable and shit, stealing my car, I wanna see if you can fly, too, you fucking bird!"

He accidentally released his grip, Rico tried to grab me up again, but this time, I managed to break free.

"Oh word, nigga? You wanna *see* if I can fly?" Madness took over me. If I had to die, I wanted to die honorably. I started to back over to the edge of the roof slowly. "...Over some car that you ain't even buy, Rico? For real-for real, you gonna *tell* me that you got *that* off the lot? Nigga, please! Wanna *see* me fly? ...Aight then. *Watch* me fly!"

I wasn't about to plead for my life.

I spread out my arms and began to fall backwards off the rooftop; Rico then grabbed me by my belt.

"You're one crazy little bitch. But don't think ya little *stunt* got you off the hook, you're still going to pay for dumping my car in the lake."

I replied, "FUCK YOU, RICO!" as I tried to walk back to the doors that led away from the roof. I thought about mentioning the fact that Rico had eaten me out the night before in front of "Sticks", but then decided against it.

I was pleased that I hadn't been thrown off of the roof; my cockiness surfaced.

"In case you *need* me to say it, I ain't scared of you, pendejo sucio! You can kiss my ass!"

Rico scoffed, "Fuck you, Kai."

Then, a shot rang out...

"Sticks" screamed.

I displayed the ultimate cockiness: "You missed, bitch!"

Rico didn't miss completely.

He grazed my left arm and it stung like hell! I saw enough gunshot wounds among Tony's boys to know that I would live.

So I orchestrated my exit.

While everyone was recovering from the shock of accidental gunfire, I walked through the roof's doors, leaving a light trail of blood behind me. Rico must've been stunned because he didn't follow to finish me off.

Somehow, I managed to walk all the way up to a nearby park and called Shelly from a dirty pay phone.

Thank *God* she was available.

"Hey ma, it's me, Kai. I need you to come and get me, fast."

"Where the fuck you at?"

"Far Rock, nigga!"

"But, I don't know my way to—"

I had to cut Shelly off.

"Just hop on Snake Road. Take it to Rockaway Turnpike and make a left. You'll go through several lights before you see the sign for the Nassau Expressway. Take that. You'll end on Beach Channel Drive. Take it all the way down to Rockaway Parkway and make a left. Come quick, yo!"

About an hour later, Shelly finally showed up. I managed to stop the bleeding by tying the wound tight with a piece of my shirt that I ripped off. Shelly threw up as soon as she saw that I was covered in blood.

"What the *fuck* happened to you, Kai?"

"I fell. No time for questions, Shells. We need to *bounce* off The Rock, like now."

Shelly was scared as shit, so I ended up driving back to her spot in Cambria Heights with my one good arm. All the while, checking to make sure we weren't being followed.

Shelly's mom was a nurse, so all the first aid shit I needed was right there at her house. The amount of blood on my clothes made the wound seem a lot worse than it was. Shelly kept flapping her gums as I bandaged it up.

"Kai, are you going to tell me what happened?"

"Yeah, but not tonight."

I had so many things running through my head at that point that I didn't want to talk. I was shocked and amazed about what happened on the roof. Rico seriously began acting like a madman. Why didn't he just kill me for his stupid car? I showed heart in spite of fear, and that caught Rico off-guard.

* * * * *

Just about a month later, I found out that Rico was indeed a madman. Rumor had it that he murdered people for the fun of it. I couldn't understand why Rico didn't kill me, until I saw him parked in front of my school one afternoon. I played it off like nothing ever happened.

Rico didn't forget.

I walked up to his car fearlessly: "Que pasa, papi?"

Rico looked over at me, slowly, while sipping a Heineken.

"Kai, when did you learn how to drive?"

We were in broad daylight so I knew nothing would pop off.

I played along: "I've been driving since I was twelve."

"And you drive stick?"

I replied with a cocky smirk that became my signature: "Like the best of them."

"Oh word? Funny, I've never seen you even drive before, but yet you managed to get the *Aston Martin* out of my sight in less than a minute."

I shrugged my shoulders.

I needed to get away from him before shit got ugly: "Rico, my class is about to start. I'ma have to holla at you later." I walked off in attempt to dominate the situation.

"Kai, what time you get out?"

"I'm surprised you don't know."

"Yeah, I *do* know. It's now, so lets chill or something."

The nigga tried to *kill* me and now he wanted to chill?

"Nah, Rico, I'm good."

"Oh, so you gonna make me beg?"

I walked right up on him and said: "Rico, you're fucking crazy."

"So are you."

He had a point.

"If you too scared to chill with me today, why don't you spend New Year's Eve with me? I wanna start my year off with a bang."

Going against my better judgment, I agreed. Rico started to pull off, and then reversed.

"Yo, listen. Just because I ain't kill you on the roof that night, doesn't mean that I *won't* kill you." He sped off before I could respond.

an angel watching over me

Rico started calling me on a regular basis, checking to see if I needed anything. I would always tell him no, yet, Rico always managed to leave something by my job, or at my house.

I felt kind of funny about the love/hate relationship that started to grow between Rico and I. I knew "Sticks" would *lose* her mind if she realized what Rico was up to. I decided it would be best if "Sticks" and I didn't cross paths. That thought was derailed when she got a job at my store.

It was right before Christmas. I walked into the workplace and there she was, being trained by my manager. I clocked in and braced myself.

"Hey Kai, you look cute today."

Bitch, please! I look cute everyday!

"Hi Chyna. How long you been working here?"

"Today's my first day."

I played nice for the whole day while I racked my brain, trying to figure out why we were now co-workers. *Did Rico put her up to this to keep an eye on me?*

I was on my break chatting with Shelly on the phone, when "Sticks" snuck up on me: "Fuck Rico been calling you for?"

"Whoa, whoa, whoa, ma, be easy..." I hung up with Shells. I had to think of something fast. "...Mainly to give me info on Tony."

"That's it?"

"That's it, Chyna."

I held back on calling her "Sticks". That surely would have pissed her off, and I didn't want to bring Rico any unnecessary drama. I just played it off.

"Aight, bitch. I got my *eye* on you...I don't see why Rico ain't just kill ya *stupid* ass on the roof."

I didn't say a word and "Sticks" stormed out. When she was gone, I ran into the bathroom and turned the water on as I dialed Rico's cell number.

After the first ring: "Sup, Kai?"

"What's up, Rico? Why is 'Sticks' working with me?"

"What?" I could hear tires screeching in the background. "Fuck you mean Chyna is working with you?"

"Rico, ya girl's first day here was today. She got *all* up in my face asking me why you be calling me. I told her it was about Tony, and she left it at that. Tell me you know something about this."

He paused. "Aight, give me a minute."

Within ten minutes, "Sticks" came running back into the back room with a nervous look in her eyes.

"What's the matter, Chyna? You looked like you just saw a ghost or something."

I giggled to myself.

"Yeah, bitch, I did. Diego is out there."

Damn that nigga, Diego could move.

"Fuck you running from 'Silent Bob' for?"

"'Cause, Rico don't know that I took a job here."

"Oh, girl, please, so what you working here. What's the big problem? You're acting like Rico was never going to find out."

"Shut the fuck up! You don't understand."

"Sticks" reached for her *Prada* bag, pulled out a small yellow envelope and disappeared into the bathroom. Ten minutes later, she reappeared, with white dust sticking to her *MAC* "lip glass".

"Yo, Chyna, you might wanna wipe that off."

"Sticks" nodded and kept it moving while she rubbed voraciously at her lips. My break was over so I followed behind "Sticks", to find Diego and Rico standing at the back of the store.

"Chyna, come here for a minute." Chyna went to Rico and they exchanged words quietly, as I returned to the front of the store; never acknowledging him or Diego. When Chyna finally came up to where I was, I had to pry.

"Everything cool?" I asked.

"Yeah."

"Sticks'" high must've kicked in because she stood there, glassy-eyed, going on and on about her and Rico; telling all of their business. I made a mental note to tell Rico about her running her mouth before prying further.

"So, what ya'll got plan for New Year's Eve?" I just had to know.

"Oh, Rico said he's taking me on a shopping spree in France."

"Sticks" went on about Rico this and Rico that.

I became pissed!

How was *I* going to spend New Year's Eve with Rico if he was going to be with *her* in France? Rico must've been psychic because just then, the lady that sells flowers in the mall, walked in holding a beautiful bouquet. Chyna immediately approached her and the lady asked: "Are you Kai Toussaint?"

Chyna looked hurt.

"Oh, that's me."

I walked over to the flower lady while the other girls at my job kissed their teeth.

They could kiss...my...ass!

Just as I started to read the card, Jordan walked in.

My heart leaped!

Why couldn't the flowers be from him?

"Sup, Kai."

"Hey Jordan, how's it going?" He was with Day-Day's loud ass, who stared at the flowers.

"Hey Kai, pretty flowers. Your boyfriend gave you those?"

I replied while looking dead in Jordan's eyes, "No, Day-Day, I don't have a boyfriend." For the first time, Jordan smiled at me. Then the vibe that I was trying to build got broken up by this short, Asian-looking chick that started hugging all over him.

"Lata fellas. I have to go and find out who these flowers are from." I turned to see "Sticks" shooting evil looks at me, as I read the note that Rico wrote:

> *Mira, Sexy, No escucha La Bruja. Hasta pronto. Mucha besos y abrazos. Te amo, mami, Te amo mucho. No olividas eso.*
>
> *Tu Nuevo novio.*

Rico was crazy! My new boyfriend? He loves me? What about Tony? Even though he and I haven't spoke since Tony got locked up, I wasn't about to call Rico my man. I quickly put the note in my pocket and laid the flowers on a desk in the backroom. When the manager wasn't looking I called Shelly—her voicemail picked up.

"Hey Shells, it's me. Shit is getting mad-crazy around these parts. We gotta talk so meet me at *Bickle's* tomorrow around three."

* * * * *

I strolled into *Bickle's* a little after 3 PM, to see Shelly and Ty hugged up at a table. He would *have* to go because I wasn't about to share my personal business with Ty.

"'Sup Shelly? 'Sup Ty?"

Ty sucked his teeth. Shelly shook her head, pleading with her eyes for me not to cause a scene. They hadn't ordered anything yet, so I pulled up a chair and sat down with them. I had to be *real* slick to get rid of Ty.

"Shelly, you won't believe this, kid. I've been on my period for like, ten days, with all types of *clots* coming out."

Ty's face became flushed.

"Damn, don't nobody want to hear about that! I done lost my fucking appetite. I'm out, yo!" Then he left. I harbored hatred in my heart for Ty. I knew one day I would get him back.

"Finally!" I said with relief.

"Damn, Kai, it's been a hot lil' minute. What you been up to?"

"Shell's, what *haven't* I been up to?" I didn't know where to start. I never did tell Shelly about Tony getting locked up, and she knew nothing about Rico. The only thing Shelly did know was that me and "Sticks" did *not* get along. "I'm seeing this dude, Rico on the low."

"Here you go again. What happened to Tony?"

"Tony got locked up a few months ago. You can say that Rico is sort of like, one of his business partners. He's a little crazy, but got *dough* for days!"

"Kai, you're seeing one of Tony's boys? What are you stupid, or just begging to get your ass killed?"

"Actually, you can say that Tony and I stopped talking before he got collared. The only reason I even know that Tony's locked up was because I saw it happen. I kinda got caught up in Rico's world, and now he got me 'playing' by his rules. I must admit, it's kinda cool and shit."

"Wait a minute," Shelly started shaking her head, "not Rico from Far Rockaway?"

I nodded with a smirk.

"Kai, are you crazy?! Rico Santana? The same nigga who had crack heads merk his parents for the insurance money? How the *fuck* did you link up with a killer like him?"

"I decided to call Rico up one day and it snowballed from there. Oh, and by the way, 'Sticks' thinks that she's his girl."

Shelly gasped. "Are you losing your mind? Every time I turn around, you're getting deeper and deeper into some shit. Kai that bitch can't *stand* you, and now, you're seeing her man?"

"Yep." Indeed I was. "'Sticks' is also working with me at the mall now, too. That shit was too funny when Rico sent me flowers. That dumb bird didn't *even* know they were from him. And to think, just a month ago, Rico tried to kill me. Now, he swears he's in love with me—"

Shelly cut me off before I could continue boasting. "Kill you?! Now I get it! That night I came to get you from Far Rock, you were shot? Why did he try to kill you? Wait. Rico don't pull out his gun without finishing off the job."

"So I've heard. Well, that night I went to The Rock, Rico was like he wanted me to work for him. He got 'Sticks' pushing Ecstasy pills and crack. That bitch is a *serious* cokehead by the way. Anyhow, I said, *'NO,'* I tried to leave, but then Rico scooped me up in his *Aston Martin*—"

"What the fuck is an *Aston Martin*?"

"I'll show you a pic one day. Just know that it costs more than both of our parents homes put together. After he scooped me up, Rico went around the town doing whatever, and I chilled in the car. We ended up back at his house in Dix Hills—"

"Was 'Sticks' there?"

Shelly could not stop cutting me off.

"Aight, to make it short, since you're all anxious. Rico played me, so I drove his car into the lake." I then told her about what happened in the bedroom, and Shelly started laughing so hard, that we caught the attention of the entire restaurant.

"So now Rico's like, he wants me to be his girl and shit, and I'm like whatever. This fool *stays* throwing dollars at me. What do I have to lose?"

"Your life… Rumor in the hood is that Rico's losing his touch." There was nothing that I hated more than strangers putting their two cents in. I turned around slowly to the rich voice.

"Excuse me, mister—" I stopped mid-sentence, and my whole body went numb. It was "Honey-Brown Eyes" from the barbershop! He continued.

"Do you even know who Rico really is? You better mind how you mention his name out here, because it could bring you some serious problems. Rico's trying to rule the city with his dirty money.

"Just mind yourself. I know that my advice may be unsolicited, but I only have your best interests at heart. Rico is a very dangerous man. Just be careful before you're next in line for the 'one-shot'."

I looked at Shelly and she was hypnotized. I didn't know what to say. I looked back at the guy, and he locked his honey-colored eyes with mine. I tried desperately to hide the fear that started creeping over my heart.

The man then ran his fingers through my hair while continuing to stare at me: "You're such a beautiful person. Don't waste yourself on stupid decisions."

I finally mustered up enough courage to speak to him: "Thanks, mister. Your advice is greatly appreciated and all. I will take it into consideration, but why do you even care? You don't even know me." I turned back to Shelly.

He kneeled down beside me and whispered, "I do know that you seem to attract a lot of drama. Whatever did happen to that short Spanish chick...Maritza?"

Shit! He remembered.

Shelly rolled her eyes when the guy mentioned "Lil' Magic" by her real name.

"That situation is done and over with, mister."

"Just keep yourself out of trouble, little lady." Then he left. Shelly waited until the man was out the door before she quietly asked about him.

"Fuck Rico! Kai, who was that? And *how* he know about 'Lil' Magic'?"

I tried to play it off as I wondered that same exact thing. How did he know about Maritza?

"Oh...that's just some dude that I peeped coming out the barbershop that day me and 'Lil' Magic' was about to get into something."

"He's gorgeous, Kai! Now, *that's* the type of man you should be checking for. Why didn't you flirt with him?"

I must admit, Shelly *always* asked the right questions.

"I already have a man, ma-ma."

Actually, the light-skinned guy was fine. *That day, I should have just slipped him the digits to stabilize my life, before all hell broke loose...*

Shelly then pulled me from an impending daydream.

"Nah, bitch. You got 'Sticks'' man!"

We both laughed.

rico's slave

Unfortunately, New Year's Eve came and went without a call from Rico. As a matter of fact, he hadn't called in a few days. "Sticks" tortured me on a daily basis with her stories of her and Rico in France. Sometimes, I wished "Sticks" would just drop dead, or get hit by a truck!

Rico returned some time during the middle of January. I didn't want to see or speak to him, but somehow, I ended up doing just that. Rico arranged to pick me up one day, saying that he wanted to make some collections, and needed me as his driver.

Rico pulled up to my house in a black *Porsche Carrera*. I was too pleased to think if the car was legit or not. All I cared about was giving my nosey neighbors a show, as I strutted to the driver's side.

"'Sup, Rico?" I kept a stoic face showing no emotion. I didn't want him to know that he hurt me.

"'Sup, Kai? You might wanna slide back over to the passenger side where you belong."

Played once again.

I hissed at him as I got in the car: "I thought you said that *I'd* be driving, Rico? You and your *fucking* games. Understand that I want a piece of *everything* we collect today."

"We? ...Kai, I know you speak French, but I don't, so this *'we'* shit, ain't gonna happen. I'm driving and you ain't getting a piece of nada. Who says I'm even collecting?"

Words could not explain the intense anger I felt towards Rico. I wasn't about to argue with him, so I just laid back and enjoyed the ride. I made sure to make a mental map as Rico drove.

Before I knew it, we were on the New Jersey Turnpike. I had never been out of New York City, and became really nervous.

"Rico, where are we going?" I guess that must've been the straw that broke the camel's back. Or maybe I said it too softly, because Rico flipped out, and within seconds, he had a .357 Magnum pointed at my temple.

"Why can't you just shut up? Shut the fuck up, Kai!" I got so scared that my nose started to bleed; tears streamed down my face. "For the last time, SHUT THE FUCK UP!" Rico was screaming at the top of his lungs, and I did just that.

I didn't say another word.

I didn't even move...

All I could think about was "Honey-Brown Eyes".

* * * * *

I must've fallen asleep because I didn't realize that Rico and I were in the parking lot of the *Short Hills Mall*. I jumped when he called my name.

"Kai, I cleaned up ya face, sleeping beauty, so you're good. Let's go."

I did just that, never uttering a word.

That day, Rico took me on a shopping spree like none other. He picked out everything from the shoes, straight down to the thongs. Fearing that Rico might kill me, I pretended to be his "dress-up doll", while adding up the receipts in my head.

After four hours of non-stop shopping and learning about the buying power of an *American Express* "Black Card", I was exhausted mentally and physically. Rico made another attempt on my life, but yet spent somewhere around twenty grand on me.

Now I was locked to him.

Rico and I drove straight to my house when we got back to Queens.

"Put the bags in the house, sweetie and come straight back to the car," Rico ordered.

I just wanted to go to sleep. I turned to his direction with the intent of saying so. As my lips parted, I envisioned the .357 pointed at my temple, and decided to just do as I was told.

When I returned to the car, Rico didn't hesitate to tell me his plans for the rest of the night. Chuckling to himself, Rico said, "So, you finally decided to just do as you're told. Good girl."

I was heated!

Why did he have to be so condescending? I was young, but I was *not* a damn 'girl'!

Rico continued, "Listen, we're heading back to The Rock. It's Sunday, which is payday for the kid, so I'ma need you to drive Chyna around to make my tri-borough collections." *Great, just great.* "Oh, and I have another little gift for you back at the spot."

The gift was a .45 caliber handgun. When he presented it to me, I had to laugh to myself. Sure, I had the .22, but I never used a gun before. Rico wanted me to use it to protect "Sticks" in case of an incident.

That night, "Sticks" and I put in about four hours of work, and came back to the bungalows with three laundry bags filled with money. Rico had me drive to all of the boroughs with a curfew. I had to be back on The Rock no later than 4 AM.

I was there at three.

"See, Kai. That's what I like, timeliness. Keep up the good work."

"Ain't nothing, but I really need to be heading home because—"

Whack!

Rico smacked me for the second time and said, "Rule # 3: speak, when I *say* you can speak. I don't need to hear you respond to everything I ask or say, or whatever."

I tried to stare Rico down, as I wiped the fresh blood from the corner of my mouth.

Whack!

This time, it was with his fist. I lay where I fell.

"Stand the fuck up, Kai!"

I couldn't.

"Understand, that if you continue tryna act like a man, I'ma *beat* ya ass like a man ya heard?!"

I nodded and immediately flinched, anticipating more physical abuse. "Sticks" made the mistake of trying to help me get up. Rico lost it.

"Damn, Chyna! You of all people should know better!" "Sticks" barely mouthed Rico's name, before he started pummeling her with fevered punches and kicks.

I said a silent prayer, hoping that I wouldn't be next...

That night, Rico almost put "Sticks" into a coma. I now understood the science behind Diego's silence. He too, was conditioned to accept Rico's madman ways. "Sticks'" coke habit was just her way of coping with the situation.

* * * * *

It went on like that for two years. I dropped out of college, but still managed to keep my job at the mall. "Sticks'" behavior became more erratic, and she still bragged about how good Rico treated her. The only good I saw, was our weekly shopping trips in Jersey.

That was bullshit though.

Rico *always* bought Chyna and me the same outfits.

I contemplated getting caught by the cops, but Rico warned me about what would happen if the cops ever picked us up. He would bail us out, kill us, and then dump our bodies in the Hudson like trash, because that's what "we were" to Rico.

However, I was convinced that he had loopholes in his operations. Every day that I put in work, I noted what happened, with the hopes of having some type of revelation. The only thing that wasn't solid was "Sticks".

Her coke habit made her loose at the lips and careless. Just before we would return to the bungalows, "Sticks" would beg me to stop under the elevated A-train tracks, so she could get high before dealing with Rico.

It was like clockwork.

We usually hit that part of town at exactly 2:46 AM, just as the last patrol car of the hour passed by. We had a fifteen minute window to do whatever before the cops would be back around.

Finally, relief came. It was a hot night in July and Rico was in a very bad mood. The crack game had practically come to a halt, and his money flow slowed down considerably. Somehow, for whatever dumb-as-fuck reason, one of the bags came up short after our collection. It could have only been "Sticks" because I *never* touched the money.

Rico didn't understand that because he came at me first.

"Kai, can you tell me why the fuck is the Queens bag short by three grand?" I learned the hard way not to speak unless he told me I could, so I just looked at my shoes until he said, "speak."

"Rico, I don't know what to say. I just drive, I never—"

Whack!

He slapped me.

"Kai, I'm asking you why is the bag short, so why is my name in the mix? Try again. Speak!"

"I just drive. I never touch the money."

Rico shook his head like he knew I had three grand stashed on me somewhere. "Sticks" was nowhere in sight.

"You only drive? You've been doing this for about two years, and you only drive? What, you think I'm stupid? Fuck is the money, Kai?!" Rico made sure that he was in my face when he said that. He didn't say "speak", so I continued staring at my shoes, hoping that Rico would just *drop* dead and leave me alone.

He didn't.

Instead, Rico grabbed me by my ponytail and *slammed* me to the floor! All I could feel was the heat from his kicks and punches. By the time I felt Rico's *New Balance* sneakers buried in my stomach, I was slipping in-and-out of consciousness. I started to smirk, anticipating death. That ticked Rico off.

"Fuck is you smiling for? You think this a joke?!" He was about to kick me in the face when, out of nowhere, maniacal laughter overtook the room, jolting everything to a halt. I cringed at the sound and gasped, that's when I realized that the sound was coming from me.

I was laughing like a maniac.

I laid on the floor of the bungalow, twisted and contorted, laughing hysterically, as blood spewed from my nose and mouth.

My little act of defiance enraged Rico. I don't even remember when he ran to the back of the house to get his infamous "one-shot" *Smith and Wesson*. Rashawn told me that it was called the "one-shot" because, that was all it took for Rico to kill somebody.

For the last time, Rico tried to kill me...

He looked down at me and aimed the barrel directly at my face. Rico was breathing heavily as he said, "You '730' alright, but bitch, I'm about to make you '187', for real!"

Pop!

Only one shot...

Rico actually did miss that time. Strangely enough, the bullet hit the floor right next to my head, and ricocheted past Rico's leg, grazing him slightly.

There was a knock at the door.

I was still on the floor laughing. Rico limped over to the door, "Who the *fuck* is it?"

"Santana, nigga, it's Tony, open the *fucking* door."

I passed out when I heard Tony's voice. When I came to, Tony and Rico where standing over me, shouting at each other. Tony was too pissed.

"Fuck you got Kai in here for? Why is she bleeding like that, son?"

"Tony, man listen, um...it's a big misunderstanding; really. She'll be fine. When did you get out, man? Welcome home, dog. Let's go get some bitches and forget the whole thing. Come on." Rico was talking faster then a fiend trying to get some crack without money.

What? Was Rico trying to cop a plea?

Tony wasn't *hearing* it.

"Don't worry nigga. I'm here and ya bright ass better hope that Kai's fine, because if she ain't, it's your ass. Nigga!"

Then everything went black.

* * * * *

67

Gasp...
Breathe.

"Where the *fuck* am I?"

"You're at *Long Island Jewish Hospital,* sweetie, I'm glad to see that you're finally up."

Finally up?

It didn't register until the nurse said that my boyfriend had found me badly beaten at a club in Far Rockaway. I slowly tried to piece things together on my own before asking her any more questions. There was only one thing I just had to know though: "How long have I been here?"

The nurse reached for a chart nearby.

"Oh, let's see. Six weeks. I'm going to get the doctor and let him know that you're no longer comatose. I *knew* you would come to any day now. You're such a strong little girl!"

I didn't know if was my foot recovering from atrophy or reflex but, when she said 'little girl', I kicked over the nurse's medical tray.

"Oh my, Ms. Toussaint! Those muscle spasms can really be unpredictable."

They *weren't* muscle spasms.

* * * * *

A week later, the hospital discharged me. I was seeing about the medical bills when Tony popped up behind me.

"Hey Kai, you ain't gotta worry about that. Santana took care of everything." *Wink.*

"Is that right? Rico paid my hospital bills?"

"Yeah, ma. We'll talk about it when we get home."

I smiled and nodded.

When I got inside of Tony's brand-new *Cadillac Escalade Ext.,* I reached for the vanity mirror. My body was still aching, and I knew my face had to be fucked up after the beating I endured from Rico.

Surprise, surprise.

My face was just a little swollen; all of my teeth, still intact. Good! ...The only bad thing was that my hair was in need of a touch-up.

68

Tony was thrilled too: "Don't worry, Kai, you're good. That nigga, Santana is a lucky motherfucker. I swore that if you never woke up, or if your wounds hadn't healed properly, I would torture his punk ass for the rest of his life."

It was nice that Tony had saved my life, picked me up, tried to avenge my honor and-all-that-good-shit but, where was he before?

"Tony, where the *fuck* you been, huh? You go missing and six weeks later, the jakes got you in the back of a squad car. If it wasn't for me *trying* to see about you and ya whereabouts, I would've *never* have worked for Rico." That was one of the few times in my life that I was completely honest.

"Work for Rico? …You was working for Rico?"

"Yeah, for *two* years, Tony! TWO *MOTHERFUCKING* YEARS, TONY!"

"Wait, he ain't tell me no shit about you working for him. The only broad on his team is Chyna!"

"That's a *motherfucking* lie Tony! I've been Chyna's driver while she went collecting. That night, he fucked me up because one of the bags was short and he tried to pin that shit on me!"

"Did you take the money?"

"Did I take the money? NIGGA! I neva even *seen* the money! 'Sticks' had to take that shit. For two years, all I did was drive and make sure we rolled on schedule."

Tony then fell silent for the rest of the ride back to South Side.

So did I.

* * * * *

After letting me into his house, Tony disappeared for a few hours. When he finally came back home with bags from the pharmacy, I told him everything I could remember about Rico. Tony just kept shaking his head as I spoke. He finally couldn't hold in his curiosity any longer.

"Kai, just tell me this, how did you even link up with a nigga like Rico?"

"That day you got picked up over there on Linden!" I then told him about the incident in Dix Hills, Rico's first attempt on my life, and how I had to put up with "Sticks'" *bullshit* for the past two years. Tony put two and two together.

"You mean to tell me Rico was there when the cops came for me?"

"Yep. Just as I was leaving the scene, I bumped into him. It was almost as if he expected me to be there or something."

Tony raised one of his eyebrows.

"Funny you should say that, Kai. I hadn't heard from Rico in a hot-minute at that time, but yet he manages to be around when 'One Time' snatched me up. As a matter of fact, I ain't heard from Rico until six months into my bid. Let me find out he a snitch."

"He made it seem like you guys talked on a regular basis."

"Not at all, Kai. That nigga, Rico only came up to see if I would let him take over Queens while I was in. He told me to consider it babysitting."

Tony became quiet again. Tears formed in the corner of his eyes, and his creamy, light skin was now the color of strawberries.

"Babe, what's wrong?"

Tony remained silent, as the tears streamed down his face. Ashamed, he turned away from me before answering: "Kai, I need you to listen and listen good."

Hearing Tony's voice crack and seeing him tremble made me misty eyed.

"Tony, baby, whatever, I'm listening—what's up?"

Tony turned back to me: "I don't want you to feel sorry for me or nothing. If you don't wanna be with me, I'll try to understand and shit."

"BE WITH YOU? Tony you *saved* my life! That nigga, Rico would have *killed* me if you hadn't come through that night!" I couldn't figure out where Tony was going with this.

"The only reason why I came through that night was to check that nigga, yo! He called the jakes on me, Kai! I always had a hunch it was Rico, but now, I know for sure. Shit! Baby girl, I was looking at life. The only reason why I'm even out was because my lawyer got the state on a technicality."

I was trying to understand what Tony was saying, when I realized that he began to stand up.

"Kai, that nigga wasn't too pleased when I wouldn't let him take over my territory. That night, I had a big accident coming out of the showers. Some *Latin Kings* approached me as I was getting out. Rico had me fucked up real bad when they had me at *Five Points*, ma."

I looked over his face and didn't notice anything different, so I remained silent. Tony then took a deep breath and started unfastening his belt.

Nothing could have prepared me for what I saw...

Tony dropped his pants and boxers shorts slowly, to reveal a small tube extending from where his penis *used* to be. Curiosity caused my eyes to follow the tube all the way down to the bag filled with urine—that was strapped to his thigh.

I gasped...Tony shook his head.

"That nigga, Rico is one fucked up dude. Everyone thinks that he ain't scared of nobody, but truth be told, he's scared of me! I *killed* his parents, not some crack heads like the hood believes!"

I was taken aback.

"What?" That was the only word I could manage.

Tony continued, as he put his pants back on: "I killed his parents over some money Rico owed me. Simple. But I guess taking my dick was the sweetest revenge. And now, he tried to kill you, too?"

Tony shook his head, as he walked up the stairs to his bedroom with the bags from the pharmacy. I waited for a few hours, and then joined Tony.

When I got to his bed, Tony was fast asleep, and didn't budge when I slipped in. Before I fell asleep, I vowed to make a name for myself, by not only *killing* Rico, but also taking at least some of his money.

Rico Santana would *have* to pay!

If not for Tony, definitely for killing my psyche.

The next day, Tony got up and went about his business as usual. I made no mention of what happened to him; neither did he.

delusions manifested

Tony and I lived as happily as a non-sexual couple could. I tried being his backbone and honestly, began falling in love with him. Tony continued teaching me about his lifestyle, which only fostered my plan to kill Rico. What was even better was that Tony took me out to the firing range three or four times out of the week.

Within six months, I became a top-class marksman with sniper status. By my twenty-third birthday, there wasn't a firearm on the street that I couldn't use with the grace of a ballerina. The firearm of choice, however, became the Government issued Kahr K-9, which I named, "Khara".

With a little time and strong-arming, Tony had managed to get Queens back under his influence, but I still needed to pay Rico back. I was in a good enough position co-partnering with Tony, in one of Queens deepest secrets—but I wasn't satisfied.

Rico haunted me constantly in my sleep. I'd get flashbacks of the beatings that I got from him on a regular basis. I remedied that with daily trips to the firing range. It was right there by *Roosevelt Field Mall,* out on Long Island, so it was convenient.

One day, after a couple of hours at the range, I decided to go shopping for a little while. After the whole Rico fiasco, I really didn't need to shop for clothes. My dad actually had to build me a walk-in closet to fit all the clothes that Rico bought for me. Many were from designers I could not even pronounce.

Most I had yet to wear.

That day, I ended up buying some sneakers, and was about to call it a day. As I was leaving the mall, Jordan and Day-Day came walking in. I initiated the conversation.

"'Sup, Day-Day? 'Sup, Jordan? How ya'll fellas doin' today?"

Jordan looked me up-and-down, admiring my tight-fitting *Gucci* outfit. I *hated* when people *only* saw me for the clothes, assuming that I had money.

I wish I had on a pair of fitted jeans and a t-shirt.

Jordan started to beast: "Damn, Kai! Time has *definitely* been good to you. Look at you looking all Hollywood and shit!"

Day-Day added to the mix: "Jordan, you better hook up with her, seems like someone got new money."

I started to get upset.

That was the first time I thought about using "Khara". I seriously was going to clap them where they stood, but then I remembered that murder one in Nassau County would get me put away for a long time.

I put on fake smile and said, "Gentleman, whether I'm in a fifteen-hundred dollar outfit or one for fifteen dollars, I'm *still* 'Kai' regardless. Money *isn't* everything you know."

Money wasn't everything to me.

A lot of people thought that it was the money that drove me. Actually, I was after the power all along.

Jordan didn't agree. He dangled his *BMW* keys in front of my face and said, "Ya absolutely right! Money *ain't* everything, but it damn sure makes the world go around! Kai, I gotta hand it to ya, I really thought you was ready."

He threw me off with that comment. I replied, "Ready? Excuse me, but I fail to comprehend what you mean."

Ever so smoothly, Jordan took off his *Gucci* shades and looked into my eyes. I thought I would die being so close to him.

"Kai, I really thought you was ready to be with a man like me. Step outside for a second." Jordan's arrogance broke the mood.

"Actually, I'm good. I really need to be heading home." I just wanted to get away from him as quickly as possible. Jordan wouldn't let me.

"Look, just for a hot-second. I wanna show you something that'll help you understand *exactly* what I mean." We began walking outside and "Mr. So Damn Fly" became "Mr. So Damn Conceited".

"Kai, I'm that type of dude that needs a *certain* type of gal, ya know…and I knew that you had a crush on me for years but, I ain't neva approached you like that. That was because, you're a *fucking* pauper; you're a loser, ma. Pretty looks, done.

"You need much deeper pockets to even *get* a date with a *nigga-like-me* because, I've got expensive taste. Shit, I'm closer than you know to being inducted into the *Billionaire Boy's Club*. My cousin knows Pharrel and shit. I can't be seen with you!"

At that point, I became infuriated like never before. It was a strange feeling. I was able to stand up to Rico, but I couldn't put Jordan in his place.

All I could do was shake my head as he continued, "You ain't ready, Kai." As Jordan said that, I realized that we were standing in front of a brand-new, gray, *BMW Z-4.*

I gasped.

Jordan laughed, as he and Day-Day walked away.

I gently caressed "Khara".

* * * * *

I ran to Tony's *Cadillac* and immediately regretted coming out that day. When I got back to the truck, I started crying. I was twenty-three years old with grand delusions of murder and being the most feared person in New York.

Who was I fooling?

Jordan, the only dude I was ever crazy for—just played me like I was nothing. Rico played me that night in Dix Hills and Tony, Tony couldn't *fuck* me if he needed to, so he played me *every* night I laid in the bed next to him! I needed to get away from everybody for a minute.

I put the truck in gear and hopped on the Meadowbrook Expressway. After getting off of a random exit, I ended up at a huge park in the middle of nowhere. I parked the truck and started walking through the park like I had a particular spot that I wanted to go to. After about ten minutes, I did.

I saw a beautiful lake in the distance. Water always had a calming effect on me, so I walked straight towards it. While walking, I noticed that there was a guy with a slight tan following me.

I didn't care.

I didn't even bother to turn around to get a good look at his features.

When I finally got to the lake, there was a bench, so I sat down, closed my eyes and let the tears flow. Someone had sat down right next to me, but I didn't bother to open my eyes—until he started wiping my tears away.

"Mamacita, why are you crying? I know it's not Rico giving you trouble, so what's the problem?" I couldn't *believe* my eyes or ears. It was "Honey-Brown Eyes" from Jamaica Avenue! I

74

looked at him deeply and realized that Shelly was right. Even with his tan, "Honey-Brown Eyes" was gorgeous.

Yet, I felt that he was probably here to make me feel worse than I already had—I became defensive.

"Look, mister, every time that I'm down-and-out you seem to pop up! What are you FBI or something?! WHY DON'T YOU GO *FUCK* OFF?!"

Tears began to flow uncontrollably.

I was mad that "Honey-Brown Eyes" was invading my personal space, but I was even madder that, I, not only let him, but I also allowed myself to break down in front of him. Just thinking of it made me cry more, but "Honey-Brown Eyes" was so understanding. He held me in his strong arms.

"Whoa, listen...like I said before, you're a nice woman. Don't let dumb decisions ruin your life. Look, you're young, and beautiful. You should be a model."

"A model? Me?" I always knew I was beautiful...but to actually hear someone else proclaim it, soothed my hardened heart.

"Kai, you're perfect."

I shook my head and laughed. "I'm perfect, huh?" *If I really was, Jordan and Rico would've been much nicer to me.* Then I realized that this was the third time I saw "Honey-Brown Eyes", and I didn't even know his name. "Mister, I don't even know who you are, and you *don't* know me!"

He blushed.

"Kai, I know that you need to stop getting into trouble. You need security and protection. You're like a baby lamb that *thinks* she's a lion. Oh, by the way, my name is Arturo Jesus, but please, call me 'AJ'."

Then he left.

For the entire ride home, I fantasized about AJ like I used to fantasize about Jordan. Something inside was urging me to listen to AJ, but my pride wouldn't let me. I was stubborn and had a point to prove to Rico, "Sticks", "Lil' Magic" and now, Jordan. They a-l-l needed to be taught a lesson!

fuck you, pay me

When I finally arrived back home, Tony was heated. I didn't even realize I was out that long.

"Where the fuck you been, Kai?!" he yelled as I walked through the door.

"I went to the range and then shopping. I had a lot on my mind to clear and I just needed to get away. Damn, is there a law against that?"

"Nah, ain't no law, shorty! Just watch yaself, cuz if I finds out different, we gonna have major problems."

Tony was taking on a "Rico" tone with me that I did not like whatsoever.

"Who the *fuck* is you talking to, Tony? I *know* it ain't me. Ya better keep that *shit* in ya back pocket before you come at me with it."

I had never seen Tony like this before, and it made me very upset. I knew I had to calm down, before I said something that I would live to regret.

"Oh word? It's like that, Kai? Fuck you forget or something? This here is *my* house! *I'm* the star, baby girl! You *used* to be the co-star, but now you just another *fucking* spectator! Show over, get the *fuck* out!"

Just when I thought things couldn't get any worse!

"Get the fuck out? You get mad over some *bullshit* and now it's 'get the fuck out'? Tony, think about that shit for a minute." I started talking slowly and softly. "I'm ya 'co-star' alright, but do you *know* what that means? ...It means, everything you own, *I* own. All the work you put in, I put in, too.

"You forget who sees over the cooks and make sure ya deliveries are made on time? That's me, *motherfucker*. You *sure* you wanna have me running the street with all ya info, baby boy?"

That weird laugh echoed out of me again. This time, it set Tony off. He grabbed me by my throat, and *threw* me into the hard brick wall! When I hit the floor, Tony started to strangle me as he screamed, "BABY BOY?! BABY BOY? HUH? YOU FUCK THAT NIGGA?! HUH?! DON'T YOU *EVA* IN YA LIFE CALL ME 'BABY BOY' AGAIN, YOU FUCKING SLUT!"

Tony let go, and I hit the floor again. It took all the air I had in me, but I managed.

"Tony-I-ain't-fuckin'-nobody!"

"Oh word? You come in here acting brand-new, and you ain't *fucking* nobody? We'll see!"

Tony then picked me up by my waist and ripped my jeans off. He proceeded to remove my panties. I didn't know what Tony was up to, until he threw me onto the couch. Tony then spread my legs wide-open, as he stuck three fingers in me at the same time.

I screamed in pain...

Tony bowed his head in regret.

"I'm sorry, Kai," was all that he said, before Tony left the house for the night. I laid there until he came back early the next day. When Tony walked in the house, I'd pretended to be asleep, as he started to play with my hair.

"Kai, I hope you're listening to me. You know shit's been kinda hard since *Five Points*. You know it's hard knowing that I can't make love to you. I be seeing how dudes look at you and shit. I know your type, ma, you got the sex drive of a 18-year-old man."

I stifled a giggle.

"I just be thinking when you're gone, you out there getting the only thing I *can't* give you. I know you've been on my side since I came back home, but I still be bugging. You're a trooper, baby and that's why I love you. Please don't leave me—I need you. All this shit, is 'cause of you. I know that, ma-ma; I love you."

That became my driving force. The man that ran Queens *needed* me. It's true that behind every great man, was a great woman. I wanted to go down in history as being the greatest.

Tony would be my link to the city. I already had him in my back pocket, so that meant I had Queens in my back pocket! All I needed was the other four boroughs to fall in line.

Sure, I would step on some toes, but I would stand to be retired at twenty-five—with enough money to finance my life, for the rest of my life. AJ was right, but I had a point to prove, and money to make! After that was done, I would be game to anything else.

I started stashing away as much money as I could. I told Tony that I would no longer sleep at his house, since he put his hands on me.

Tony begged for me not to.

Instead, we came to the "agreement" that, I would *only* sleep over two or three nights out of the week, and I *had* to be on his payroll.

Tony agreed.

Every Friday morning, I got five-thousand in cash.

I *never* put it in the bank.

I used some of it as pocket money, and had my checks from work directly deposited in my bank account every Thursday. I used my work money to pay my bills and other expenses. I didn't want to give "Uncle Sam" a reason to start sniffing up my ass! Instead, I hid the money that Tony gave me in my bedroom closet at my father's house.

My game plan was clear: I would be the Queen-of-the-NYC drug empire.

I had Tony do all of the dirty work, and I stopped managing the cooks. I became his silent partner, so to speak. With a little coaching from me, and a lot of strong-arming, Tony could definitely have a heavy hand in the other boroughs.

In case the Feds were watching, I had a sound-proof alibi:

I was a student...

I worked full-time, and I lived at home with my pops. Technically.

The only way I would be fucked was if they ever wanted to search my father's crib. Tony *never* came to my house, so I doubt that would ever happen.

mafia connection

By the beginning of 2003, Tony and his goons became the number one suppliers of pure cocaine, and the most elite firearms in the city. He supplied most of New York City directly from Columbia. In order to keep the Mafia and other high-powered societies happy, Tony only dealt with certain neighborhoods throughout the five boroughs.

I helped Tony not only reclaim his turf, but build an empire that hasn't been seen since the late eighties, when crack first hit.

That was good enough for me.

It wasn't good enough for Rico though. After all that happened, he was still trying to knock Tony off of his hustle. I knew the day would come, but I sure as hell wasn't prepared for it.

It was early May, and classes were wrapping up for the semester. This was my first semester back since Rico had me drop out three years ago. As I was walking towards the parking lot, Rico and Diego pulled up in a black, tinted-out *Mercedes Benz-CLK 450.*

It seemed like everyone had an expensive car except me.

I needed one quick.

I then took my anger out on Rico: "FUCK YOU WANT, RICO?" I wanted so bad to reach for "Khara" and *take* his life!

Thankfully, I waited.

"Oh, so now you think you free to talk to me any which way 'cause Tony saved ya little, dumb ass. Don't be a bird and get *clapped* right in the heart of ya man's bullshit turf!"

Money made me delirious.

Despite what Rico had put me through, I still thought that I was untouchable. I walked around to the his side of the car, put one foot on the hood, as I leaned in through the window to get in Rico's face. He and Diego had a clear view of my crotch.

"Look, motherfucker, you don't scare me. What, you gonna shoot me again? Do it, Rico!"

I hadn't forgotten that I was wearing a mini-skirt. What I did forget that I wasn't wearing panties underneath my shear stockings. Rico and Diego just stared at my pussy.

79

Dumfounded.

Rico licked his lips, "Kai, the older you get, the bolder you become. Damn, girl. You gonna start a war. I just hope you're ready to go back to work when the smoke clears. I promise next time, not to fuck you up too badly."

I let my leg rest on the hood of his *Mercedes* like I was doing a standing split. I nibbled at Rico's bottom lip before I whispered in his ear, "If you want a war...bring it. I'm *m-o-r-e* than ready, honey. And, um, Hell will freeze over before I *work* for you again."

Rico just smiled, as I swung my leg around and walked off. I didn't realize that my little "freak show" brought Guy Brewer Boulevard to a halt. Slowly, I was coming into that power I was seeking, and I *loved* every minute of it!

By the time I arrived at Tony's truck, Shelly was waiting there for me. It was an unexpected surprise. I hadn't seen her since before I started working for Rico.

"Wassup, Shelly?" I crossed my arms in front of me and leaned up against the Cadillac. I hadn't had much time for her since Tony came home. I was busy trying to get my "retirement fund" up.

"Ain't nothing. I'm about to graduate, kid and wanted to see what was up with you and all."

I would've been graduating too if Rico hadn't made me drop out of school. For the first time in my life, I felt envy.

"Shells, I really gotta go."

"Come on, Kai. I haven't spoken to you since the winter of '99. It's a lot of shit that I've been going through. I wish that you could've been there for me, but you out here *running* the streets like you're untouchable. There's talk in the hood, ma... Real talk, about some broad stirring up trouble. Nobody knows who the fuck she is but, why I got this *funny* feeling it's you?"

Friend or foe, Shelly didn't have the authority to *approach* me like that! I'd decided that I was going to *kill* her, right then and there...

I kept a low profile. Sure, everyone knew that I was Tony's girl, but no one in the hood knew just how heavy Tony's hands were. Somehow, Shelly had caught on, and she'd have to *pay* with her life!

"Step inside the truck for a minute, Shells, so we can talk."

No questions asked, Shelly just hopped into the truck.

DUMB BROAD!

As soon as she made herself comfortable, I pulled "Khara" out, and pointed it right in between Shelly's eyes.

"Shelly, I *knew* you was never my homegirl! That day Rhazza came after me, you punked out and hid! YOU *FUCKING BITCH!* FUCK YOU THINKING?"

Shelly started crying hysterically.

"Oh my God, Kai, what are you doing?! Look, I call you, you don't pick up the phone! I got this nigga, Ty telling me Maritza be telling him something about these three brothers, and one got this crazy bitch, and they making mad loot and shit! Now tell me that shit ain't you, cause if it is, ma, you're *gonna* get killed!"

I couldn't *believe* what Shelly was saying. I wanted to *kill* her, but Shelly's voice was wrapped in honesty.

I then put "Khara" away.

"Aight then, if it is what you say it is, then I'ma find out about this three brothers bullshit and that bitch, and guarantee, us both to be sitting pretty by the fall."

Shelly acted surprised.

"Kai, what are you saying? You throw a *gun* in my face, and you say you *ain't* that bitch?"

I wasn't about to blow my cover to Shelly. After all, I didn't know what her intentions were.

"Nah, Shelly, I heard about the couple, too. Ain't nothing though. I'm strictly out here for the dough. Wanna be down?"

"Huh?"

Shelly was forever dumbfounded.

"Look, bitch! Either you with me or *against* me! Get back to me, a week from today. And if you say no, I will *kill* you, personally."

I didn't mean to say that last part.

It just flew out of my mouth effortlessly. Shelly left the car, and I headed to South Side.

* * * * *

When I got to South Side, Tony's block looked like a funeral procession had stopped there. There were black stretch

81

Hummer limousines and black *Lincoln Navigators* all over the place. I had to park Tony's truck around the corner from his house.

I slowly approached Tony's steps, and saw two huge Italian men standing in front of his door.

Italians in South Side?

I turned to the parked cars and dialed Tony's house phone number. As the phone rang, I read the license plates. One stood out: "Omerta". I started to panic when I realized that I was standing in the midst of Mafia henchmen. I was about to hang up when Tony finally picked up the phone.

"Babe, whatcha doin' outside? Come inside, there's some people that I want you to meet."

Then he hung up.

I turned around, and the two men by the door hadn't budged. I knew if I didn't go upstairs, there would be a problem. Despite my racing heart, I went pass the guardsmen and into the house.

Poor Tony.

His house was filled with men in fine designer suits, and a few women that looked like they just walked off of the set of *Sex and the City*. I felt out of place in my *Gap* mini-skirt and *North Face* jacket.

When I was a child and my father had surprise guests from Haiti, I would just go up to them, say "hello" in French, and kiss them on their cheeks. I'd hoped this worked for the Italians.

It did.

Except, I saw that they kissed me on both cheeks. I remained quiet and didn't speak, unless I was spoken to. Of course I had plans to run the city, but I was no dummy. The Mafia was in Tony's house, and I *wasn't* about to disrespect anybody.

I just sat there and looked at everyone. I was surprised to see that Tony knew how to speak Italian. He spoke quietly to this man who looked just like him in a corner of the living room. I swore the nervousness was sending me on a mind trip. I excused myself, and hid in the bedroom.

After about an hour, Tony called up to me: "Babe, our guests are leaving."

I walked downstairs slowly and kissed everyone goodbye. The man that Tony was speaking to before hugged Tony and looked my way while saying something in Italian. Then he walked over to me.

"You have to excuse me but, you have the most exquisite eyes... Tony has told me a lot about you. I told him that he better take good care of you. If he doesn't, here's my card. I'm his father."

His card simply read: *Niccolo Cartagena, Waste Removal Specialist.*

My heart hit the floor.

Tony was black. How could this Mafia-looking dude be his father? I smiled, "Thank you, Mr. Cartagena. I will keep that in mind."

Tony's father then left.

Just as the last truck pulled off, I let Tony have it!

"Um, Tony, you want to tell me what's going on?"

Tony looked at me like I lost my mind.

"What do you mean, Kai?"

"I mean, you have the fucking Mafia sitting up here like it wasn't anything. What's up with that?"

Tony put his finger on my lips. I caught an instant flashback of Rico and passed out. When I came to, I was lying in Tony's bed.

"Tony," I said softly.

He was lying right next to me: "Yes, sweetie?"

"Please don't do that again. You know I get flashbacks and shit."

Tony pulled me into his arms. "Sorry, Kai, I don't be knowing what sets you off. No worries, one day Rico will get his."

Little did Tony know that, I was already planning that out.

"Tony, how come you didn't tell me your father was a mob boss?"

"What difference does it make? Look, we'll talk about it in the morning, just get some rest."

"But Tony—"

He cut me off.

"Get some rest, Kai. Goodnight."

queen b.

The next morning, Tony woke me up at 5:30 AM. I got dressed, and threw on my regular tight jeans and t-shirt ensemble.

Tony looked at me and disapproved.

"Damn, Kai, don't you have anything else to wear? Today isn't the day for that shit." He was dressed in a black *Armani* suit that I never saw before.

"Um, nah. Come on, baby, you know that I don't like all that 'next' bullshit. I'm comfortable."

"Kai, you're a grown-ass woman. I've never see you get dressed or in high heels."

"That's because I'm not *comfortable* in that shit. This is how you met me, so *don't* expect me to change any time soon." I started walking towards the kitchen.

"Kai!" Tony was getting upset. "Listen, you saw how the other wives were dressed yesterday. You claim you some type of femme fatale, but won't dress the part? Where we're going this morning, that shit *won't* rock, so you better find something else to wear!"

I was pissed, but he was right. Those women from the night before were fierce. I looked at my *Reebok Classics* and said under my breath, "I'll be back in twenty minutes."

I took Tony's truck and dashed back to my house in Rosedale. Rico had gotten me a lot of chic clothing and shoes that I rarely wore. It always reminded me of him, so I only wore it every now and then.

Everyone in my house was still asleep when I quietly walked in. I grabbed a black *Chanel* A-line skirt, and a white button down *Donna Karan* dress shirt. As much as I hated them, I also grabbed a pair of black *Stephan Kelian,* T-strap, three-inch heels, and a cropped Chinchilla jacket.

I was just about out the door when my father called me. "Kai."

"Oh, good morning, daddy, I didn't mean to wake you."

His eyes were full of concern.

"You also didn't come home last night."

84

"Daddy, I'm sorry. It's just that after school, I was tired, and I fell asleep at Tony's house." I told my father that I had been seeing Tony, but I never told him what Tony did, or about the money that was hidden in my bedroom.

"Why haven't I met this Tony man before?"

I told Tony I'd be back in twenty minutes, and my father was stalling me.

"Daddy, I have to go. I will bring Tony home tonight." He then grabbed me by the hand. "Dad, I promise." I gave him a kiss on the cheek and dashed out the door.

When I got back to Tony's crib, he informed me that I had ten minutes to look presentable. I'd stepped out of the bathroom and Tony's mouth dropped.

"Damn, baby girl, this is what I'm *talking* about." For my first attempt, I must admit that I was looking mighty fierce. I pulled my hair back in a tight chignon bun. The only makeup I needed was the "Satinette" lip gloss by *Chanel*.

"Anything for you, Tony." If that was what it took to make Tony happy, then I'd have to do it. I didn't have to worry about him sleeping around, but if Tony ever did leave me, before I came into power, it would be the end of my pipe dream.

* * * * *

We drove to New Jersey in a brand-new *BMW 745*, compliments of Tony's father. I was pleased because it seemed my wish of dominating New York City would be much easier to achieve; with Tony's dad behind me.

During the whole ride, I contemplated how I would get his support. Though Tony hadn't said it yet, I already knew Niccolo admired black women. Tony's features showed that he had African-American blood running through his veins, so I knew Tony's mother was black.

It would only be a matter of time before the entire story came out.

I was snapped out of my daydream when Tony and I pulled up to a huge mansion. Since I was with Tony, I ignored all highway and street signs.

I had no clue where we were.

The driveway into the mansion was very long. When we finally arrived at the front door, Tony and I were greeted by a man and two maids. He parked the car for Tony while the two maids escorted us inside.

I walked in and nearly fainted when I saw the white and gold decor that the mansion had. It was strikingly familiar to Rico's place. I quickly popped an *Altoid* in my mouth to steady my queasy stomach.

Niccolo greeted us with his fabulous looking wife whom he introduced as "Donia Cartagena". Tony left with his father and I was left alone with her.

"Donia" had a look of disdain in her eyes.

"You *fucking* mooley! Understand that you are in my house as a guest, but I'd much rather have you as my foot servant." "Donia" then pulled out a pack of *Virginia Slims.* I pretended like I didn't hear her. "You little black *bitch*—I know you hear me!"

It was the middle of 2003 and racism was still rampant. Green was the *only* color that mattered to me, so I continued ignoring "Donia". My father always said that was the best way to get at people.

She started rambling something in Italian, then let out a slight chuckle, "Don't think that your clothes change my perception of you either. You looked like a *slut* yesterday, and you look like a *slut* today.

"You're ghetto-trash! Understand? Trash! As a matter of fact, I shall call you 'little black trash', because that's what you are! I don't know what Nicky was thinking, inviting *you* here. It's obvious that you *don't* fit in."

Then "Donia" let her tongue slip, "If Tony wasn't Nicky's only son, you wouldn't be here, either! Thank *God* he's at least light-skinned. Did Tony tell you about the inheritance?"

I continued with my poker face, as my heart leaped out of my chest. Still, she noticed.

"Yes, 'little black trash', the inheritance! Tony could *never* take his father's place, because of his tainted blood. Don't worry, just as soon as *I'm* pregnant with a son, you can kiss that inheritance goodbye. Take a good look at my lovely home. This will be the *last* time that you will *ever* get to see it, you little black bitch!"

I was one of the most envied women in Queens, and here "Donia" was talking to me like I was worthless. I was in shock at the audacity of this woman, to divulge her ruthless plans within ear shot of Niccolo.

Even I knew to keep my plans to myself.

"Donia" then flicked her cigarette ashes at me. They burned a little hole through my *Chanel* skirt.

Enough was enough!

I had to show this *BITCH* that I was as versatile as they came. I gently cleared my throat, "'Donia Cartagena', I will not disrespect you in your home. However, I implore you not to disrespect me either. Though, I am impervious to your insults, I feel that it's not very lady like to speak in such a manner towards me. Indeed, you do have a lovely home..." I paused for dramatic effect, "however, do not take that for granted. After all, nobody is promised tomorrow."

I ended it with my signature smirk.

"Donia" became enraged.

"Is that a *threat* you little black bitch?! How *d-a-r-e* you threaten to kill me in my own home?!"

I continued just above a whisper.

"Actually, the issuances of threats are for those who are weak...and insecure... Rest assured that if I wanted to injure or harm you in any way, shape or fashion—I would do just that."

I immediately regretted leaving "Khara" at home.

"Donia" continued to scream: "Bitch, I've been here five fucking years. Tony just met you yesterday! I will *not* tolerate you fucking up my meal ticket! Do you understand?! Don't even *think* of having no babies for Tony. I want that inheritance money! I'll kill the both of you to get it!"

I sat there, seemingly unfazed by her comments though my blood was boiling, and said: "Donia". Money isn't everything. Perhaps, you might want to see Niccolo for who he is, and not for what he has." I giggled to myself at the bullshit that came flying out of my mouth, ever so eloquently. "Killing for inheritance money? Woman, do you have a heart?"

"Donia" scoffed!

"Hearts are for the weak and insecure. Let's see how you feel the first time when Tony cheats on you!"

I thought, *Tony could never.*

It was physically impossible.

87

"Let's see how calm and collect you are when you find him screwing the help!" As she said that, "Donia" threw a vase filled with tulips directly at me. I guess the bullshit I was feeding her, started to affect me, because I didn't budge. The vase broke right in front of my feet.

I didn't move.

The sound caused the servants to come running into the living room.

"You see what happens when you invite *NIGGERS* over?! They simply do not know how to behave."

"THAT'S ENOUGH, ELIZABETH!" Soft spoken Niccolo, sounded like a lion. I don't know when he and Tony walked in, but there they were at the entrance way, as the servants cleaned up the mess.

"Niccolo! Darling, how long have you been there? I was just—" Niccolo then put his finger to her lips.

Damn.

"ENOUGH! YOU HAVE DISGRACED ME IN MY OWN HOME. HOW DARE YOU PLAN TO KILL MY ONLY SON IN MY HOME?" Nicolo smacked his wife to the floor.

Elizabeth then pleaded, "Nicky, it's a big misunderstanding."

Something about that situation felt "painfully" familiar...

Niccolo ignored her and walked towards me.

"I apologize for Ms. Angeletti's remarks."

I guess she wasn't the "Donia" anymore.

He then reached into his vest pocket and pulled out a neat stack of money—placing it in my hand.

"Please accept this for your ruined skirt and as my humble apology."

I looked to Tony for approval.

Tony nodded.

I bowed my head graciously and accepted the money.

Niccolo gently pulled my chin up and looked into my eyes.

"My child, remember one thing. Though you bowed to me as a sign of respect, you never bowed to her. Very, very good. Never forget that. Never bow your head in the midst of your enemies."

I smiled.

"A man like me would be *proud* to have you as my daughter-in-law. You're tactful, respectful and beautiful. Tony, you better be good to her."

* * * * *

As soon as Tony and I got back into the car, I switched back into ghetto mode: "Tony, what the *fuck* was that?"

"A test," he said curtly.

"A test?" I quizzed.

"Yes, a test."

I folded my arms across my chest. Tony laughed.

"Babe, I told my dad all about you and all of the work we've been putting in. He invited us up here to see if you would fit into the family. I guess your homegirl was being tested, too. What was that stunt you pulled, ma?"

"Tony, what are you talking about?"

"My dad and I saw the whole thing. You sounded like you came straight out of one of those old Mafia flicks. I'm proud of you. You held your own without being ghetto. I *had a feeling* you was smart-as-hell, I just didn't know *how* smart you were."

I was insulted!

"Tony, you forget? I'm in college—a straight-A student. You ain't *find* me in the streets! Just because I *act* hood on the block, don't mean that I *can't* switch it up if a situation calls for it.

"I'm saying, we're in a very diverse business. You got the bottom-feeding savages who'd *kill* their own mamas for a dollar, to the multi-billionaires who order hits on other mob bosses over steak and lobsters. You gotta have that type of versatility to woo both of them motherfuckers, and everyone in between."

Tony smiled. "That was the first lesson my father taught me. Damn, girl, my father was right! I was a little scared to have you tested, but it had to be done; to see if we could go on like this. He did say you were a gem though."

I could not believe what Tony had said, but it all made sense. I was just tested by a mob boss, and I passed. I hid my excitement, as Tony delivered another surprise.

"Kai, I also told my father that I want to marry you!"

I didn't know what to say...

How could I marry someone that I couldn't have sex with?

It was cool for now because I had school that I focused on, and a job to keep me busy. Between that and my "seduce the city" scheme, I had *no* time to fuck around!

I did love Tony, because he sincerely cared for me. However, I was *only* in this for the money, just like Elizabeth! Sure, Tony was nice and all, but we had no sex life. If I'd said 'no', he'd leave me. If I'd said 'yes', I'd be stuck in a sex-less marriage.

I tried to change the subject gently, "Oh, really? I'm glad you mentioned that. We're going to my house after this."

"What?" Tony looked perplexed.

"Yep, honey, we're going to my house, to meet my family."

He paused for a minute. "Ok. I have to make a stop first."

I agreed.

We stopped at an unfamiliar mall while we were still in New Jersey. I waited in the car. I took the time to think about how to fine tune my plan.

Evidently, the clothes *did* make the woman. Elizabeth and Jordan both showed me that. I decided that day that I would always dressed nicely. Even if I wasn't sporting expensive clothes, I would definitely dress the part of the femme fatale. I would also mind how I spoke, and attempt to refrain from cursing as much as did.

I was lost in my thoughts when Tony finally came back to the car. He was gone for about two hours, but returned empty handed.

"Um, Tony, where did you go?"

He grinned like he had done something really bad and got away with it.

"To the store."

"And this store has no bags?"

Tony replied, "Nope," before he started kissing me deeply. Tony and I have kissed before, but never so passionately. It was deep and intense…stirring up wicked heat in between my thighs. I wished he would stop, because I had become extremely horny, and I *knew* that Tony couldn't finish the job.

I gently pushed him away, "Damn, Tony, sweetie, we gotta get going." I didn't want to make Tony feel self-conscious about his accident, so I made sure not to look down at his waist as I pulled away.

I thought I was in the clear, until Tony said: "Babe, just bear with me. I know this cosmetic surgeon that says he can help me out—"

I cut him off.

"Baby, sweetie, understand that your power doesn't resonate from between your legs. It comes from within your mind. Look at how quickly your empire developed." I held his chin and stared deeply in his eyes before continuing. "Tony, I love you. Not for anything else, except for loving you. You have a pure heart, and you love me just as much as I love you. No matter what, remember that I love you so much."

I fed Tony bullshit with grace and no remorse.

That evening, my consciousness died and my heart hardened completely. That was the only one way to seduce the city.

trouble on the homefront

The drive from New Jersey to Rosedale seemed exceedingly long. *Is Tony trying to devise a plan to impress my father?* Little did he know that my father could see *bullshit* from a mile away.

"Tony, why are you so quiet?" He gazed off into the distance. "Tony!"

"I'm just...you know...thinking."

I always found quietness to be upsetting.

It bugged me out not to know what someone was thinking. Tony didn't speak to me for the rest of the ride.

* * * * *

When Tony and I arrived at my house, everybody was home. I braced myself for the questions.

"Dad, this is Tony. Tony, this is my father."

That was the first time that I ever saw Tony nervous. He looked my father dead in the eye: "Bonsoir, Monsieur Toussaint."

As I was getting over the shock that Tony knew a little French, my father said the unthinkable.

"Ah, so *you're* the one who's been *fucking* my youngest daughter." Tony's face turned strawberry-red as my father continued, "At least I can say that you're able to dress her in fine clothes, and keep my daughter's pocketbooks well-stocked. But, Tony, tell me, *what* do you do?"

I could not believe my ears.

Then again, I shouldn't have been surprised. My father was *always* straight-to-the-point! He didn't even give us a chance to sit down before coming out of his face like that. Tony's face showed no expression, but was still very red.

After a few, very tense moments, Tony pulled out a business card.

"Mr. Toussaint, it seems as if you think that I'm going to hurt Kai. I love her. I love her very much."

My father took the card from his hand.

92

"Antonio Jesus Cartagena. Waste Removal Specialist. Mr. Cartagena, what are you, some type of Italian? You look black to me."

Tony finally smiled.

"Actually, I'm half Italian." He then cleared his throat. "My mother was black."

My father looked perplexed.

"Your mother was black? What happened, she turned white?"

I snickered.

Tony wasn't smiling anymore.

"Um, my mother died about five years ago."

My jaw dropped...

I was about to ask Tony why was this the first time that I'd heard about his mother, but realized that we needed to have a private conversation.

"Oh, I'm so sorry to hear that. Did Kai tell you that her mother is also deceased?"

My father was being sympathetic.

I made a note to myself to tell Tony what really happened to that "lady" who gave birth to me.

I killed her...

Not intentionally, but I did; right there in Prospect Park.

Remembering what happened in that Brooklyn Park, damn near seventeen years ago, caused me to space out for a minute... When I snapped out of it, Tony was bending down in front of me.

"So, will you?"

Will I what? I thought.

"Kai, monsieur ap pale avèk ou," my father replied.

Yeah, I knew Tony was talking to me, but about what?

I didn't have a clue.

That was, until I saw the brilliant, seven carat, heart-shaped diamond.

I gasped!

It was even set in eighteen carat yellow gold, and *not* that platinum bullshit!

Tony really wants me to marry him?

What the hell!

Being married to the mob would *definitely* help me conquer the Big Apple!

93

"Yes." I tried to sound confident and sure, but it ended up coming out like a question.

"Yes? You sound unsure."

"Tony, I said 'yes'. Now hurry up and put that ring on my finger before I *change* my mind!" Thoughts of a sexless marriage then ran through my mind...

I became nauseous.

* * * * *

Tony started to explain everything to me, as soon as we got back to South Side.

"Kai, understand that I will *only* tell you that she died five years ago."

"But how?" I just had to know.

"Little mama, that topic right there, *ain't* up for discussion. She's dead, and that's *all* you need to know!"

"Can you at least tell me her name?"

"Donna Blake. Classic rags-to-riches story, died for her stupid decisions. Are you *happy* now?"

"Damn, Tony, was that so hard?" I should've been able to put two-and-two together, but didn't.

"Now, let's talk about your mama."

A wicked smile danced across my face.

"She had an unfortunate accident when I was seven-years-old. She fell into the lake at Prospect Park, over in Brooklyn."

"Kai, we talking about dead people. Why are you laughing?"

He was laughing, too.

Yet, another hint.

"Because, Tony—" I was interrupted by his cell phone. I started to undress as I listened to the one-sided conversation. It was pretty much business related, until Tony shouted a few "no's" followed by a "FUCK YOU, SANTANA!" He threw the phone across the room. It hit the wall and smashed into pieces.

"What the hell happened, Tony?" Tony stormed off in the direction of the basement. That only meant one thing: he was going for his guns.

I raced after Tony.

"Tony, you wanna tell me what the *fuck* is going on?"

He picked up a sawed-off shot gun and loaded it.

"That nigga, Santana, yo, always wanna start some shit. He's like, make him my business partner, or he gonna *kill* me. Aight, nigga!"

I tried to play the situation off.

"Tony, please! You said it yourself, Rico is *scared* of you! He's only talking—" I got interrupted again by another ringing cell phone that was not mine. Tony picked up the phone which was on top of one his safes.

"Yo...yeah...WHAT? You fucking shitting me...How the fuck? ...Get the fuck off the phone and come down to South Side...NOW NIGGA!" With that, Tony flipped the phone shut.

"Tony! You need to start talking and talking fast—what the *fuck* happened? How many *damn* cell phones do you have?" He didn't even look at me, as Tony had left the basement.

I stared at all the guns in the basement and tried to piece the situation together. Whatever happened to piss Tony off would end in murder. I welcomed the thought, and decided to chill out in the living room until Tony calmed down. When he finally came into the living room, I was livid!

"Tony, I ain't gonna ask you again, what the *FUCK* is going on?" He was about to answer me when, Rashawn let himself and two other goons in through the front door. Godfather or not, why did he have a key to Tony's place?

"Yo, son, m-a-n, niggas came through and started shooting like *crazy,* yo! They clapped the doorman, took the work and the dough!"

Tony looked at Rashawn with fire in his eyes. He took a deep breath: "What time?"

Rashawn was shook!

"A half hour ago."

That was around the same time Rico called.

The war had begun.

Shit!

"A half hour ago? Hmmm." Tony was eerily calm. "A half hour ago would mean that the work was already packaged up. Hmmm."

One of the goons spoke out of turn. "Yo, Tony, it ain't our fault niggas came through—"

Whack!

95

Tony knocked the kid out cold.

"Yo, Rashawn, tell ya little flunkies to keep their *fucking* mouths shut!"

Rashawn started to stutter.

"T-Tone-lis, listen, man. His brother was the doorman. He, he got killed, yo."

"Him and who else?"

"About five of ya workers."

"Did you see any faces?"

"Nah, man, niggas came through in fucking ninja suits and shit."

"Oh word?" Tony then pulled out one of his twin nines, cocked it, and aimed right at Rashawn's face. "Tell me, nigga, what the *fuck* did you do? What part did ya ass play in tonight's mayhem?"

Rashawn threw both of his hands up.

"Cartagena, listen, I was watching the spot like I always do. I would never—I"

"Never what? Betray me?" Tony started shaking his head. "NIGGA, YOU *KNOW* BETTER! The game is filled with punk-bitches that wanna be big time! How I know that you ain't set me the fuck up? HUH? HUH, NIGGA? Ten-thousand dollars worth of cooked crack is a good start for any little nigga like yaself!"

"Tony, man, ain't no need for name calling. We caught one of the niggas. Now, I may not be as heartless as you, but I thought you would try to put this on me, even though I had ya back from when you was in diapers. Gimme a second." Rashawn went outside and returned with a garbage bag in his hand.

"Now Kai, you might wanna go into the kitchen or some shit, 'cause this ain't pretty."

I didn't move.

"Alright, ma-ma, have it your way." Rashawn put on latex gloves and reached into the bag. Tony looked on with curiosity in his eyes.

"Kai, this is your last chance."

Tony was anxious: "Rashawn, just hurry the fuck up!"

Rashawn slowly pulled his hands out of the bag. Nothing could have prepared me for what he was holding in them... Weakness overcame me, and I threw up right next to Tony.

Tony threw up, too.

I wiped my mouth my bare arm, turned back towards Rashawn to confirm what I *thought* I saw.

I was right.

Rashawn was holding Diego's head—the first casualty of war.

"I told you, Kai!" Tony didn't miss a beat. Things became too real. "Let's go find that nigga, Santana!"

I had to think fast!

"Whoa, whoa, whoa; hold up! You already killed Rico's number one man. He knows you're going to come after him. So he's either going to hide like the little bitch he is, or he's gonna stand in plain sight, wait for you, then call 'One Time' to lock ya'll fast asses up! We get that nigga on Sunday."

Rashawn looked at Tony and nodded his head.

"She got a point, yo."

Tony agreed.

The goon that Tony knocked out came to, and started running off at the mouth again: "Fuck is this *bitch* talking about, yo? Them niggas done killed my baby brother! Nah, fuck that, we going tonight!"

Tony was too far away from him to knock him out again, so I took matters into my own hands.

"Excuse me?" I looked at the goon and smirked.

The goon continued, "Who the fuck is the *bitch* anyway? Shouldn't you be somewhere cooking or working the track?"

The track?

...He must've thought I was a prostitute.

I had to show the goon who was the boss! Tony and Rashawn just stood there letting the situation play out further.

"Um, are you talking to me?" I asked.

"You the only *bitch* in here, right? Be glad I don't sit here and make you suck my—"

He shut up quick-fast when I pulled "Khara" out! I licked my lips slowly.

"Little man, you want me to suck on something? How about this?"

Pop!

One shot tore off the goon's left ear lobe. He screamed out in pain.

"Who's the bitch now?" I walked up to him, pointed "Khara" to the goon's temple and whispered into his good ear: "Now be a good boy and clean up this vomit. And if you get blood on my floor, I will *kill* you so you can join your *fucking* brother in hell!"

I then tucked "Khara" back into the waist of my skirt, and walked upstairs to the bedroom.

Tony came rushing behind me.

"The fuck was that about?"

"He came out his face and I *dealt* with him accordingly. Is there a problem?"

"Yes, there's a fucking problem! I don't appreciate you shooting in my house! There won't be any—"

"There won't be any what?" I spoke softly. "Any what, Tony? You thought you were the only one with surprises?" I then went to the bathroom and soaked in the tub for a couple of hours.

When I got out, Tony and the two goons were gone. The vomit was cleaned up, and there wasn't a spot of blood anywhere. Rashawn was asleep on the couch. I gently nudged him.

"Where's Tony?"

Rashawn jumped to his feet.

"Whoa, ma, don't shoot!"

I sucked my teeth.

"I'm for real, where's Tony?"

"He said he'll be back soon."

I glanced at my watch. It read "2:47 AM". "Sticks" crossed my mind.

"When?"

"Calm down, Kai." Rashawn pulled out a box of *Black & Mild* and lit it.

The aroma entranced me.

"What you smoking, Rashawn?"

He offered me one. I lit it, and relaxed a little bit. I was never fond of cigarettes, but the miniature cigar worked its magic.

"Thanks, man."

"I knew it!" Rashawn then caught me off-guard.

"Knew what?"

"The kind of female that you are. Don't let anybody tell you no fucking different, ma! You're unbelievable! You're smart, you're gorgeous, and you're handy with a burner! I should've

wifed you up a long time ago. Look at you, pulling on a *Black &
Mild* without even choking. Let me find out you burn trees, too!"

"Ewww, Rashawn. Come on, you know you're like my
Godfather and shit."

"Ewww my ass! Only reason why I stood around and kept
you safe when you was younger was because I wanted you for
myself. A chick like you comes around once in a lifetime. If it
wasn't for you, Tony would not be sitting pretty right now. The
entire hood knows that."

Then out of nowhere, Rashawn kissed me. I pulled away
from him.

"RASHAWN, WHAT THE *FUCK* IS ON YA MIND?"

"Damn, ma, I was totally out-of-line. I'm sorry." Rashawn
then shook his head and went back to sleep on the sofa. I decided
that it would be best that I waited for Tony in his bedroom.

A couple of days later I returned to work. "Sticks" was in the back room gossiping as usual.

I was in no mood for her bullshit!

I clocked in without acknowledging anyone, and was about to leave when "Sticks" called my name.

"Yo, Kai, looks like somebody just got engaged."

I had totally forgotten about the ring on my finger. I replied smugly, "Oh shit, look at that," and then walked away. "Sticks" wasn't finished with me yet.

"Sure is pretty though. It would've been prettier if it was platinum or white gold. Who rocks yellow gold anymore?" I stared at her expressionless as she continued, "My, my Kai, you're moving up in the world. Got ya little *Coach* shit on with the bag to match. I'm glad to see ya finally stepping up ya game. But peep this, shorty."

She then pulled out car keys that were unmistakably from *Mercedes Benz* and dangled them in front of my face. I rolled my eyes.

"Yeah, bitch. A cherry-red *Mercedes Benz CLK.* I'm sure you peeped it in the parking lot with the vanity plates that say 'BigChyna!'"

I tried not to let "Sticks" get to me, but she did.

"Oh word? And what's that supposed to mean to me?"

"Sticks" laughed.

"Oh, nothing, I mean, especially since Rico had an extra fifteen-thousand lying around after what went down a couple of days ago."

That comment tore through me!

I was about to plunge at her neck—but then remembered that I could easily walk onto any car lot and buy any damn car I wanted with the money I had stashed. I played it cool.

"So, Chyna, let me get this straight. Rico bought you the car in cash?"

"Yep, ain't I fly?" "Sticks" replied. I smirked.

"You sure is." I started laughing to myself.

"Sticks" was a *dumb* broad!

She should've just *smoked* the money, instead of giving Uncle Sam a reason to investigate her and Rico. Who doesn't know that ten grand and better gets reported to the Feds?

"Lady Luck" was on my side that day because, as soon as I reached the sales floor, two detectives walked in: "Ma'am do you work here?"

"Yes, sir. How may I help you?"

One of the detectives pulled me to the side. "Does a Ms. Chyna Smith work here?" He pulled out a photo copy of her driver's license.

"Why yes she does. Let me go and get her for you." I went to the back room and yelled: "'Sticks', some people are here to see you!"

"Sticks? Who the fuck you calling 'Sticks'? I done told you—" The detectives walked in.

"Ms. Smith?" Chyna turned pale.

"Yes."

"May we talk to you in private?"

I cleared out the back room and left Chyna alone with the detectives. Five minutes later, Chyna was escorted out of the store by them. Although she wasn't cuffed, I was never happier in my life.

I kept my excitement to myself.

Everyone had questions, but I acted nonchalant about the situation.

That day continued going well until I went on my lunch break. As soon as I stepped out of the store and into the mall, I was greeted by Rico.

"Baby girl, look at you. Damn, you get finer and finer every time I see you. Let me get a hug."

I put my hands out and stopped him dead in his tracks.

"Rico chill." I flashed my engagement ring in front of his face.

"What's that supposed to mean? I know you really ain't going to marry him." Rico locked me in his arms. "Besides, he can't *fuck* you. I know you still wanna fuck me... Let's go fuck!"

My face burned with anger, as I tried to break free from hiss grip.

"Rico, what the *fuck* is your problem? Don't you *ever* come out of your face like that."

101

"Or what? Ma, you don't get it do you? The war is just beginning. I'ma have the whole NYC on my fucking payroll before the smoke even clears."

I shook my head.

"Rico, you actually think the odds are in you favor, huh? Diego is dead and 'Sticks' is probably getting booked at Nassau County Correctional as we speak."

"And what that mean? 'Sticks' knows the deal. Rashawn killed Diego and I'm a kill—"

"Kill who? Me? No, no, no. Not me. You done tried twice."

"...Third times the charm." With that, Rico pulled me against his chest. The bulge just below his waist was not his nature rising. It was a Desert Eagle. "I'ma kill Tony." Rico let me go and walked away.

I sent Tony a "911" text message.

* * * * *

Tony never called me back that night. When I got off of work, I headed straight to South Side. Just as soon as I walked in, Tony grabbed me up by my neck.

"Fuck was Rico hugging up like that on you for?" I closed my eyes and stopped breathing, in an attempt to make myself pass out. Then I thought about just killing Tony right then and there.

I'd had enough of his violent outbreaks!

"Answer me, Kai!"

That was the last thing I heard.

I was successful in passing out. When I came to, Tony was in tears.

"Tony...Make that the *last* time you put your hands on me."

"Kai, I'm so sorry. I just seen you with him and I lost it."

"Well, since you wanna jump to conclusions, let me be the first to tell you that Rico's going to start a war, and will not stop until he runs New York City. I sent you a text message and you never responded. Instead, you *fucking* strangle me until I pass out! FOR WHAT? FOR WHAT, TONY?"

I was about to make a sly comment about his manhood, but remembered that I needed Tony until I had the power that I was after.

102

"Tony, I'm out! Call me when you learn how to keep ya *fucking* hands to yaself."

I left!

The first person I called when I got home was Shelly. She answered the phone after the first ring.

"Kai! I'm so happy you finally called me. What's up?"

"Struggles, baby girl, struggles. Listen, I'm gonna need to see you ASAP. Can you meet me at *Junior's* tomorrow? Early, like at noon."

"Sure, Kai, no problem. I'll just have Ty drop me off."

I hung up without saying goodbye to her. Hearing Shelly mention Ty's name turned my stomach.

* * * * *

It was going on one o'clock and Shelly still hadn't showed up. I decided to call it a day, and was about to leave when she came strutting in. Shelly looked haggard!

"You're late!"

"I'm sorry. It's just that Ty had to go to work, he wouldn't drive me up here and I had to take a train—"

"Time is money, ma-ma."

I thought about it all night. My plan now needed a car, my own business, a lawyer on demand and a scapegoat. Shelly's sister just started practicing law, and Shelly could be my scapegoat.

"I need to talk to your sister Michelle."

"For what?"

"Just in case."

"Well, I don't know if—"

"Listen, Shells, let me just put her on retainer, starting next month, and both of ya'll could work for me."

Shelly wasn't feeling my offer.

"Work for you? ...I'm trying to stay clean and you want to involve me in your *dirty* work. Nope! Try somebody else! I'm ya best friend and all, but I ain't going to jail for you!"

Little did Shelly know that she would.

"Dirty money, huh? A little yayo money ain't hurt nobody. Please! This country was *built* with dirty money." I flashed my ring in her face. "See. Beautiful, ain't it? Let me show you how dirty money makes you Queen in the land of peasants."

With that, Shelly and I left *Junior's* and headed back to Rosedale.

* * * * *

When we got to my house, I told Shelly to wait for me in the living room. I went to my room and locked the door behind me. I took twenty-thousand dollars out, and placed it neatly in my vintage *Gucci* doctor's bag.

"You ready to rock?"

Shelly looked dumbfounded.

The first thing that I needed to get was a car. Jordan, Rico, "Sticks" and Tony, all had nice luxury cars.

I needed something different.

I didn't want the hood to know how deep my pockets were, so I decided to get something practical, nice and fast.

We went to Hillside Avenue and bounced from dealership to dealership, until I found my starter car. It was a black, t-top *Mazda RX-7*. I called the salesperson over.

"Excuse me, sir, how much is this car going for?" The salesperson then nearly pounced on me.

"This car, um, I'll sell it to you for eighty-five hundred dollars." The car was a rare find, and that price meant that there was something seriously wrong with it.

"I'll give you sixty-five hundred in cash for it."

"I'm sorry, miss but—"

I was in no mood for games!

"I'm sorry, but we're talking about a 1997 *Mazda RX-7*. You could easily get upwards of ten grand for this car, gimme the damn keys!" I snatched them out of his hands and hopped into the car.

The interior was a disaster and it had a stagnant water smell to it! I started it up and watched blue smoke billow out of the exhaust pipe from the rear view mirror.

"My friend, what we have here is water damage which means electrical damage, and the blue smoke, hmm, looks like engine trouble."

I then popped the hood and saw a rust inflicted engine.

"As a matter of fact, my friend, I take back my previous offer. Thirty-five hundred dollars in cash. Tax, title and registration included! And that title *better* be a clean one and not a salvaged one either!"

The salesman just shook his head as we headed to his office.

That's how business gets done!

Again, Shelly was dumbfounded.

"Kai, how do you know so much about cars?"

"Shells, remember when they used to tell us knowledge is power back in school? As you can see they weren't lying. The more you know, the more power you have. Get it? I just got this man to drop five grand off the price."

"Yeah, but if you got dough like you *say* you do, why you buying a used car?"

"Because, I don't need everybody knowing how fat my purse really is. See, if they do know, they'll make me a target. I don't have time for that."

"But the car is a piece of crap!"

Shelly was too much of a girlie girl for me.

"Enough with the questions! Let's see how you feel about the car in two months."

me & mrs. jones

I still had a little over fifteen grand in my bag.

"Shells, where did you say Michelle worked?"

Shelly didn't want to be bothered.

"Listen, do we *really* have to go up there? You know me and my sister haven't spoken in years."

"And what does *that* have to do with me?" I needed someone who I could trust on my legal team. I figured that Michelle would work for me, being that I was her sister's best friend. If Michelle wanted to try to fuck me over, I could always use Shelly as a bargaining piece.

Either way, I was secure.

"I'm sure she'll forget a-l-l about whatever beef you two have, once she hears me out. Nobody walks away from money! I don't care who you are or where you're from, dough is dough! Everyone out here is looking for that extra dollar."

* * * * *

Michelle's office was situated in Forest Hills, not too far from the *Queens County Court* houses. Shelly was still very skeptical about seeing her sister. Just as soon as we got off of the bus, Shelly wanted to get back on and go home.

"Kai, I'm not sure my sister even works out here anymore."

"Relax, ma, we'll go up to the spot and see what's what. If she ain't there, oh well. We'll catch up with her sooner or later."

For the rest of the walk up to Michelle's office, Shelly remained quiet. That gave me enough time to think of an offer that Michelle *couldn't* refuse. I'd give her fifteen grand, just as the start-up, and five-thousand dollars every two weeks.

I wasn't sure if it was too much or not enough. Just as I was doing the math in my head, Shelly spoke: "Well, we're here."

The outside of the office was ordinary. However, once we stepped inside, it was a different world. Michelle definitely had more taste than Shelly! She even had a personable secretary that greeted us as soon as we walked in. Nice.

Shelly asked the receptionist if she could tell Michelle that we were there. The receptionist responded with no questions asked. Much to Shelly's surprise, Michelle gave the okay for the receptionist to let us into her private office.

Shelly walked in first and I followed behind. As soon as Michelle laid eyes on me, our eyes locked.

I was totally mesmerized.

Even though she had at least two decades on me, Michelle had a body of death. She was around my height with hips that spanned for days. Her waist was even smaller than mine. Michelle's deep mocha skin tone looked as smooth as silk.

She looked like a goddess.

I was completely floored by Michelle's beauty, which *never* happened before! Just as I opened my mouth to introduce myself, she showed her ugly side.

"Get the *fuck* out, Kai! Get the *fuck* out, now!"

Holy shit!

I frowned as I tried to figure out where I knew Michelle from. She continued, "Shelly, how *d-a-r-e* you bring this *tramp* into my office? Get the *bitch* out of here before I *fucking* cut her!"

I didn't know how to respond: "Do I *know* you?" Michelle's voice did sound familiar. She then placed her right hand on her hip.

"Yes, bitch! You know who the *fuck* I am. Maybe you don't recognize me, maybe you thought I was some bag lady with nothing better to do than—"

"Look, you might be Shelly's sister, but you really need to calm the *fuck* down before I curse you the *fuck* out. Who the *fuck* are you to come at me like that? You don't *fucking* know me! I came here on business, so calm the *fuck* down now!"

"Calm the fuck down?" Michelle snorted. "How about you get the *fuck* out of my office before I *fuck* you up? BITCH!"

I couldn't believe that Michelle was coming at me like that; Shelly couldn't believe it either. A good fifteen minutes had already gone by and Shelly was still standing in the same spot. I casually walked pass Michelle and headed straight to her desk. I sat on top of it.

"My, my, Michelle, I'm a bitch, huh? Well, hear this, I got fifteen grand to retain you as my lawyer. Every two weeks—"

"Retain me? ARE YOU OUT OF YOUR MIND? ...As a matter of fact, give me your driver's license and social security

number. I'm going to report you to the Feds my *damn* self!
Young-ass girl...can't even afford the shit you have on! Why the
fuck should *I* have to work so hard, while *bitches* like you live it
up?"

I giggled nervously.

"Yo, Shells, tell your sister to relax. She *too* can live it up
on my payroll." I turned back to Michelle. "See, now I know you
really don't *fucking* know me, because if you did, you would've
been asking me where to sign to making our agreement binding,
ya dig, Miss Jones?"

"IT'S 'MRS. JONES', YOU STUPID BITCH!"

"Whatever."

I noticed a set of pictures on her desk through the corner
of my eye. I picked one up.

"Cute kids... How can someone with a fucked up attitude
like yours, make such beautiful babies?"

"Put that shit down, Kai and get the *fuck* out of my
office!"

How did she know my name?

"I'm growing tired of you yelling at me—I'm leaving." As
I got up, I managed to knock everything off of Michelle's desk.
"Oops, I'm sorry. Maybe if you were nicer to me, I wouldn't have
to *fuck* up your office."

"Fuck you, you home-wrecking son-of-a-bitch!"

Why was Michelle so angry at me? I honestly didn't know
her. The heel of my boot then cracked the glass on one of the
picture frames that had fallen to the floor. I looked down to find
the reason behind her anger towards me. It was their wedding
picture.

"YEAH, BITCH!" Michelle yelled, as I looked at the
picture in disbelief. Her receptionist then came running in.

"Mrs. Jones, is everything alright?"

"Yes, Ms. Katz. Please let callers know that I am out of
the office for the remainder of the day," Michelle replied softly.

Shelly finally snapped out of her daze.

"Michelle what's your problem? You don't know Kai to
be coming at her like that! Can you just chill?"

"Chill? Chill? This trick-ass bitch wrecked my marriage
and now you want me to chill? Fuck that and fuck you! Get your
loser friend out of here!"

"What is you talking about, Michelle?"

"Fuck that! I'm no *fucking* loser," I interjected. "You're a loser, Michelle. A big, *fucking* loser."

"Fuck you, Kai," Michelle spat.

"No, fuck you! Now, maybe you're mad because you *think* that this is Ricardo's money."

"Ricardo?" Shelly asked.

"Yeah, Ricardo Jones, my summer love. The dude that put me onto the fly clothes and paid for my tuition. I tell you what, Michelle, this ain't Ricardo's money. I still have that stashed but, he did get me this bag." I looked at my right hand, then at Michelle's left hand and laughed. "And since you're such a *fucking* loser, bitch, I'll let you have the four carat friendship ring your husband gave me, because your tiny excuse for an engagement ring is pitiful."

Shelly gasped.

"You was fucking her husband?"

"Fucking?" I waved my pointer finger in the air. "No, baby girl. Trust, if I fucked Ricardo, Michelle would have gone through a divorce, a long time ago. I ain't have to fuck him for the outfits."

Tears then streamed down Michelle's angelic face.

"I hate *bitches* like you, so damn—"

"So damn powerful? It's a beautiful thing. I'm not going to stand here and take the blame for your fucked up marriage. That's your fault, loser. I'm sure you had to see a credit card bill or two. Come on! *Zales, Neiman Marcus, Bloomingdale's, Dior, Gucci*...need I say more? How much of that shit was for you?"

Michelle bowed her head in defeat.

"Nah, ain't no need to put your head down. Just face the facts, Ricardo got two women pregnant at the same time, the last I saw him. That was over three years ago. I'm out!" I retorted, before I grabbed my Gucci bag and walked out the door.

Just as I was exiting the building, I bumped into Ricardo.

"Hey sugar, you sure look sweet today. How you doing?" I gave him a tight hug and a deep kiss, right in front of the receptionist. Shelly and Michelle saw, too.

I didn't *fucking* care!

aj on the brain

A month later, I decided that I needed to start speaking to Tony again. I still handled a lot of his business for him, but we weren't on speaking terms, and I hadn't been in South Side. Tony did continue to leave me messages and send flowers every so often.

I'd called him early one Friday afternoon, but Tony never answered his phone. I didn't see the point in leaving him a voicemail, so I left it at that. I then went up to Richmond Hill to check on the progress of my car.

Before meeting with my friend, Sonny from *York College,* I went window shopping on Liberty Avenue. I was about to walk into one of the jewelry shops, when someone tapped my shoulder from behind.

"Hey Kai." It was AJ. I hadn't seen him in months. Something about AJ was warm and refreshing. I don't know why I was so excited to see him, but I kept calm anyway.

"Hi AJ. How's it going?"

"Good, good."

"Seems like I'm bound to bump into you anywhere I go, huh?"

"Funny, I was just about to say the same thing. It's like it's fate that we always bump into each other like this."

"Fate? I thought that you were stalking me!"

"No, Mamacita, I'd never."

I guess on some subconscious level I was pissed that Tony didn't pick up the phone when I called, and I needed to get back at him. AJ was a good choice.

"So, what are you up to?"

"Actually, I was just taking a little breather from school."

"School?"

"Yeah, I have this computer school where we teach all types of certification classes."

That sounded boring.

"Cool. What else do you do?"

"I'm a computer technician, as well as other things. But enough about me, what brings you out here?"

"What else? A little shopping before I go pick up my car."

"A car? From where?"

"A friend of mine is working on it not too far from here."

"I tell you what, let me go with you. I gotta see how you, of all people, would hook up a car."

I saw no harm in that.

"Sure."

AJ and I arrived at Sonny's crib twenty minutes later.

"Sonny, where's the car?"

Sonny was working on somebody's engine right in front of his house.

"Round di back, gimme one minute."

It was a warm Friday afternoon and all eyes were on me. I could hear the fellas asking Sonny about me, and my motive for being out there. Thank God AJ came with me.

The three of us walked into Sonny's backyard where the RX-7 slept underneath a car cover. I knew what laid beneath the car cover would say 'Kai', one-hundred percent. I held my breath as Sonny pulled the cover off.

"Tada!" Sonny was going to get an extra five-thousand dollars for his efforts.

The car was immaculate.

"Midnight black paint ever so delicately flaked out. Nice. Lexani rims? Did you lighten up the car some place else?" If this car was to be the getaway car, chrome rims would add to the weight.

Not a good thing.

"Kai, you insult me right inna mi own yard? Tsk."

"Chill out, Sonny. Let's see what else you have going on here."

The outside of my car had chrome accents, and the super-bright blue headlights with the fog lights to match. The interior was in white, butter-soft leather.

"Sparco seats and a short-shift knob? Very, very nice. Let's see how the engine looks." No cost was spared when fixing up my dream car. The engine itself was brand-new and imported from Japan.

I stood there admiring the car when AJ asked the wrong question: "Damn, Kai, how much did you spend on this?"

I was never big on divulging my financial status outright to anybody, especially men. I squinted my eyes and replied, "Does it even matter?" Sonny took that as his cue to exit, and had left me alone with AJ.

"Yeah, of course it matters. What you plan on doing with a car like that? You don't even have to start it up to see that it's dripping with power and speed. Aren't you afraid that you're gonna wrap yourself around a tree?"

I wasn't afraid of anything!

The thrill I got when I drove Rico's *Aston* was unlike anything I knew at the time.

It was euphoric!

Speed was my drug!

"If I do, at least I'll die happy."

"I'm not too sure you even know how much…"

"Oh, so you think you're the only one with a fast whip?" We'd drove up to Sonny's crib in AJ's tricked-out '92 *Mustang*.

"Nah, I'm just—"

"Just what? Just about to see how your pony rides against my kitten?" The comment sounded a lot more sexual then I intended it to. AJ blushed.

"Ya'll can settle that over there on 120th," Sonny interjected when he returned.

Sonny had a good point.

* * * * *

"AJ, you ready?" I hopped into the *RX* and started it up. I eased down Sonny's driveway, and was greeted by his entire neighborhood. I turned on the *Alpine* sound system and Soca music came blaring through the speakers. That was all the proof that I needed to know that Sonny had been driving my car.

I continued listening to the CD all the way up to 120th Avenue. We got lined up and Sonny walked up to the car.

"Kai, don't *fuck* around and get ya'self killed! Ya see, dis button is for the *NOS* tanks. You arm it first wit' dis switch, an' den you push di button only if you need it."

"Tell me something I *don't* know." I knew nothing about *NOS,* but was willing to give it a try.

Sonny waived us off. AJ and I were nose-and-nose speeding down the avenue. By the time I switched gears from 4th to 5th, AJ was way behind me.

Damn.

I wished I could've used the *NOS*.

ain't that a bitch!

I broke the car in for about a week before I went to see Shelly. I still hadn't spoken to Tony, and I needed backup for when I approached him.

I called Shelly from my cell phone: "Come outside dressed."

"But Ty—"

"It's ya first day of work, ma-ma. Come outside, now!"

Ten minutes later, Shelly came outside in tight Capri pants and sneakers.

"Took you long enough," was all I said as we headed to South Side. Shelly and I drove there in complete silence, as I thought of the reasons why Tony was, all of a sudden, not answering my phone calls.

"When did you get this car?" Shelly stole me from my thoughts.

"You don't remember? You was right there with me when I bought it."

Shelly's eyes widened.

"Oh word? This is the *RX-7?*"

I beamed like a proud parent.

"Yep!"

We talked about her and Ty as I approached Tony's block slowly. I thought my eyes were playing tricks on me when I thought I saw AJ and "Lil' Magic" drive by in his Mustang.

Time later revealed that I was right.

I knocked on Tony's door, there was no answer...

His cars were around so I knew that Tony had to be around, also. I tried my key, but it didn't work... I had to take a step back and make sure that I was in the right place.

Shelly became nervous.

"Um, Kai, what's going on?"

"This nigga wants to play games, that's all."

Tony left me no other choice...

I had to break in.

"Shells, come on." She hesitantly came around to the back of the house with me. "Here's what I'm gonna do. I'ma go in through the kitchen window. I want you to go sit in my car on the driver's side and wait for me. Don't talk to anybody and don't *look* at anything but the magazines in the car.

"In exactly seven minutes, I want you to come to the front door and knock. I'ma have you wait for two more minutes, then I will open the door. If you see anybody coming towards the house, you *fucking* call me ASAP."

Shelly started to tremble.

"But what if—"

I pulled "Khara" out.

"What if nothing. Time is money; now *do* as you're told."

Shelly returned to my car, and I went to work on the kitchen window of Tony's house. I didn't even have to break it because it was left unlocked. All I did was lift the screen from the outside and push the window up.

When I got inside of the house, I noticed that the alarm system wasn't activated. More proof that Tony had to be around somewhere. I tucked "Khara" gently back into the holster and took my shoes off. I decided to check the basement first.

Nothing.

I went upstairs, and there Tony laid like a baby, sleeping in his bed.

I glanced at my watch.

I had another six minutes before I had to let Shelly in.

I stood there admiring Tony's features, when I heard the toilet in the bathroom being flushed. My heart broke as I pulled "Khara" out, and aimed it at the bathroom door.

An older woman came out, naked.

I gestured with my finger for her to be silent. I didn't know who she was. I signaled with "Khara" for her to get in the bed. I glanced at my watch and saw that, only four minutes remained until I had to let Shelly in.

Elizabeth was right...

Tears began to cloud my eyes, as I yelled at the top of my lungs: "ANTONIO, WAKE THE FUCK UP!"

The lady jumped.

Tony slowly opened his eyes.

"Kai—"

"Oh, so *n-o-w* you know me?" I turned away from Tony and aimed "Khara" back at the "Jane Doe". "Who are you? And what business do you have coming outta Tony's bathroom?"

115

She started crying.

"Please, don't kill me. I used to go to school with Tony and I came—"

I started to giggle.

"I bet you did cum, you *fucking* bitch!"

"Kai, this is uncalled for. Let me—"

"Let you what? Speak? Nope. You just lay right there while I take out the garbage." I then looked at the woman. "Come on, get out of the house—let's go."

"But my clothes," she then whimpered.

I let "Khara" fire right next to her left ear. The sound of gunfire was loud enough to pop her ear drum.

The lady winced in pain.

"Now that I have your attention, you're going down those stairs and directly out the door. There's a car waiting for you, my dear. Bye-bye." She started walking slowly down the stairs. "Oh, and miss, if you turn around, I *will* make you a 'Jane Doe'."

I followed behind her.

By the time we got to the door, Shelly was already walking back to the car. I called out to her: "Shelly, come here for a minute."

When Shelly came back to the door, she took one look at the naked lady and laughed. I whispered into Shelly's ear: "Take 'Jane Doe' to 110th and Guy R. Brewer and drop her off. Then come back here and let yourself in."

I then turned to "Jane", "You will walk up-and-down Guy R. Brewer Boulevard until we come to get you. If you call the police, I will find you, and then *kill* your entire family in front of you before I kill you, comprende?"

The woman nodded yes.

I went back into the house to find Tony still lying in his bed.

"Get dressed, Tony."

He didn't move.

"Why did you come back?"

"Why did you think I was gone? The last thing I said to you was for you to come and find me when you learned how to *keep* your hands to yaself. I needed to speak to you, and all of a sudden, you're not answering my phone calls, or returning them for that matter."

Tony sucked his teeth.

116

"Whatever, lady. What do you want now?"

Tony had pissed me off!

I then decided to launch an impromptu business plan. The more he tried to hurt me, the further I'd dig into Tony's pockets.

"Tony, I need fifty-thousand dollars. I want to start a titty bar over in Hempstead. I figure I can get the best girls and push "E" pills through the bar as well."

"You're not going to get into my ass about—"

"About what, Tony? Strictly business, nothing personal. Speaking of business, I've noticed that there's been an increase in munitions demands, as well as cocaine from your elite customers. I need my weekly allowance increased to fifteen grand a week, as well as an additional three-thousand dollars for my partner."

"But—"

"But what, Tony? I just broke into your home and revealed key business information. You should know better than to *fuck* with me!"

"You're supposed to be my wife!"

"And you're supposed to be faithful! Now that *we* both know that the other is fucked up, *we* can move on. You have until the first of the month to meet my demands!"

I turned to walk away from Tony, and he hugged me from behind.

"Why did you leave me?"

Again my heart broke.

I was hurting on the inside.

I always thought that Tony would never cheat on me, but somehow he managed to.

Without turning around to look at Tony I replied: "I never left. I was just away, since you like putting your hands on me so much. But it's whatever. I mean, I know we wasn't talking, but we still got business to take care of. Dough is dough, REGARDLESS of ya bullshit!"

He squeezed me tighter.

"I'm sorry."

I turned around and smirked.

"Save your sorrys for someone who cares. Don't think for a moment that you hurt me."

He had.

117

Shelly returned a few a moments later: "Damn, Kai. What the *fuck* is going on? That bitch got out the car and just started walking down the street like she wasn't buck-naked."

"I hope you ain't fuck up my car."

"What car?" Tony sounded surprised.

"My little hooptie."

Tony went to the window, looked at the *RX-7*, and then looked at me.

"The *fuck* you get a car like that from?"

"Oh, while you was out here *disrespecting* me, I was doing the things that you *should've* been doing for me."

"Come on. You know niggas is gonna start to see you around and make you a target, especially in that shit! That's why I didn't get you a car from jump."

Shelly silently excused herself; I called to her: "Wait for me in the car." I turned to Tony. "When money wasn't coming in fast enough, who was the one who devised a plan to knock out the small-time hustlers? Me! Who was the one who managed all twenty of your cook houses? Me! And who was the one who stood by you through thick-and-thin. ME, GODAMMIT!

"Niggas already know that I'm *not* one to fuck with! If they wanna try and put a price on my head—let them try." I walked away and joined Shelly in the car.

"Is everything cool, Kai?" Shelly asked.

"Yeah, yeah. Look, we rolling out to Hempstead for a minute. I need to check out some real estate."

Just before I hit the South Conduit, I saw AJ and "Lil' Magic" arguing in front of one of the corner stores.

Rage burned inside of me!

I turned to Shelly.

"Yo, ain't that *fucking* 'Lil' Magic'. She still *fucking* with Ty?"

Shelly rolled her eyes.

"Bitch please! You know that's her. Why you asking me stupid questions? *Fuck* her and *fuck* Ty!"

I turned down the radio.

"Just a little while ago, you was telling me how good shit was between you and Ty."

Shelly then started crying.

"They still fucking, Kai! Ty says that he only sells to her, but I know it. I just know they still be at it like rabbits."

The only thing I heard was 'sell'.

There wasn't a pusher in Queens that wasn't on Tony's payroll or his shit list. Either way, I knew about them!

I didn't know Ty was pushing weight...

I started to think that paranoia was getting the best of me, so I asked: "Shells, *fuck* you mean Ty sells to her?"

Shelly bit her bottom lip.

"Oh, I didn't tell you? Ty sells crack every now-and-then."

Oh word?

Pushing cookies was a very territorial business, and I was just finding out about Ty stepping on my toes.

He would *have* to be dealt with...

My luck felt like it was running out. There, I sat in my car, watching my "supposed" guardian angel with another one of my archenemies. Then I find out there's dudes out here pushing weight without my consent or knowledge.

I pulled over to the curb, slid the transmission into neutral and pulled up the e-brake.

"Let's go put 'Lil' Magic' in her *fucking* place. Just follow my lead, baby girl."

Shit!

Somebody had to feel my wrath.

I walked straight towards AJ.

When he saw me approaching, AJ put his head in his hands.

I turned on the charm.

"Looks like you need some help."

"Lil' Magic tried to pull me away from him.

"Nah, bitch. Don't even *play* yourself up here!"

I heard it in her voice and had to turn to "Lil' Magic to confirm it. The nervous twitch, the bugged out look in her eyes— "Lil' Magic" was *definitely* on something. I turned back to AJ.

"Listen, since you're *always* coming to my rescue, it's only fair that I come to yours." I slid my business card into one of AJ's front pockets. "Call me when you want to talk."

My work wasn't done. I walked up to "Lil' Magic".

"You're still fucking with Ty, huh?"

Before she could answer, AJ cut her off. He looked at me with disbelief.

"You know Ty?"

119

I looked at Shelly, Shelly turned to AJ. I needed to break the tension.

"Um, well, you know the hood talks." I didn't want him to know that Ty's girl was Shelly, and that we all knew what was going on. Before I could think of something else to say to AJ, he stormed off.

"I work too hard for this bullshit! Find your own way home, Maritza. It's over."

"Lil' Magic" started crying.

"Well *fuck* you then! *Fuck* you, you no good piece of shit! I hate you! Puerco sucio!" She then walked up to me. "Are you happy now, bitch? Are you *fucking* happy?"

By that time, we were the main attraction on the block. All eyes were on us. I knew it would be a bad look if anything else popped off, so I started walking back to my car.

"Lil' Magic" wasn't having that!

She ran behind me, yelling so loudly that her voice became hoarse and shaky.

"NAH, BITCH YOU GET HERE SO I CAN *KICK* YOUR ASS! I'MA *KICK* YA ASS!"

Then "Lil' Magic" did.

She literally kicked me in my ass!

The fellas that were hanging around watching us started laughing.

I DIDN'T FIND ANYTHING FUNNY!

I turned to "Lil' Magic".

"Now, now, little one, settle down. AJ isn't here to stop me this time." She muttered something in Spanish and I snapped!

Both of my hands were around "Lil' Magic's" neck when I lifted her up off of the ground.

She was little, so it wasn't hard.

I slowly squeezed both of my hands together.

"Mira, I said, I will *kill* you and I meant it. Now you die bitch!"

"Lil' Magic" grabbed at my hands, but I had no intentions of letting go. It wasn't until an awful stench had filled my nostrils was when I'd dropped her.

Poor "Lil' Magic"...

She'd shitted on herself!

Just as I turned around and headed back towards my car, I'd noticed that familiar procession of Mafia cars driving by. They were going in the direction of Tony's house. At the same time, my phone started to ring. It was Tony.

Shit!

"Hello babe," I causally said as I took off the e-brake.

"I need you to come back to the house, right now."

I was in *NO* mood to deal with Mafioso type pressure that day.

"For what? I'm sorry, but I have other business to attend to today. I'll swing by another time, and we can get our business in order."

Niccolo then took the phone away from Tony, and was now on the line.

"Bella, I ask that you put your plans on hold, and pay your father-in-law a visit."

I had no choice!

I did a U-turn and headed back to Tony's house.

When I got there, I left Shelly in the car and headed straight in. Only Niccolo and Tony were in the house. I greeted Niccolo first: "Good afternoon, Mr. Cartagena."

Niccolo gave me a hug.

"Kai, I think that the three of us really need to have a talk." I was in no position to tell him to "go fuck himself" like I wanted to, so I obliged.

"Yes. I believe you are absolutely right." I cut Tony with my eyes as I said that. We then sat together on the couch. Niccolo began softly, "Kai, don't fuck up a good thing by letting your emotions get the best of you."

My eyes burned and a knot formed in my stomach.

"What do you mean, Niccolo?"

He then lit a Cuban cigar and took a long pull before answering me.

"What do I mean? I mean the car. What you did to that girl that was here, and how you were behaving in the streets earlier."

I kept an emotionless expression on my face as I stared into his eyes. Niccolo continued.

"It's just not lady like. You're putting a face to the name, and soon there's going to be a lot of heat on you and Tony. That means heat on me, and I don't like heat... It gives me a rash.

"The Feds are already looking for a reason to lock me and my son up for life. Kai, I know you don't want that to happen."

I shook my head.

Niccolo proceeded.

"Listen, all that I ask is that you lay low like you used to. If you have a problem, let me know. I have henchmen for every design. There's no need to put yourself on front street."

Niccolo did have a point.

However, I had a point to prove my damn self! Long before there was a Tony, there were people out here trying to bring me down. The *HARDER* they tried, the *HARDER* I became!

I already had made a vow to return the favor. I smiled.

"Sure, no problem."

We smiled. We hugged. We kissed.

Everything was smoothed over by Niccolo's and Tony's standards.

I had other things in mind...

I had to rule the city, one way or the other!

When I drove by or walked by, I needed every *MOTHERFUCKER* to stand still and hold their breaths! That wouldn't happen if people didn't know that it was *ME* behind the madness.

How could I instill fear in the hearts of people, standing behind two of New York's top players?

freaks come out at night

For months, I sat quiet like Niccolo asked, all the while, I'd schemed the execution of my plan. I needed a calling card, a signature of sorts that would string together the murders that I had planned. I bought several decks of tarot cards, and decided that I would leave "THE EMPRESS" and the "DEATH" cards near every dead body.

My first victim was Ty.

First of all, I hadn't forgotten that he was out selling crack without me knowing. Secondly, on some level, I felt that I owed Shelly that. I did some surveying and found out that Ty was selling crack out of a house off of Farmer's Boulevard.

One night, I decided to drive by the house and sure enough, fiends were pouring in and out that house like running water. There were three cars posted up, watching the house as well.

Damn.

I drove up to the nearby *Dunkin Donuts* on Merrick Boulevard to devise my plan, when AJ walked through the door.

AJ saw me before I saw him.

"Hey," he replied, sounding tired.

I pretended to be excited to see AJ.

"Oh my God. AJ, how are you? You look so tired."

AJ then rubbed his eyes.

"You don't even know the half. I'm just gonna get some coffee and catch a cab home."

I jumped at the opportunity.

"A cab? No, no, no. AJ, let me buy you some coffee and I'll take you home."

He looked at me and smiled.

"I couldn't—"

"I won't take no for an answer." I slowly rose out of my seat and lightly rubbed my body against AJ's, as I walked up to the counter to get his coffee.

Then we left.

Once the two of us got comfortable inside of my car, I asked AJ where he lived. I was shocked when AJ said that he lived in Rosedale. Thank God he lived on the other side, and not the same side as my father.

When we pulled up to AJ's house my mouth dropped! It was the most beautiful house in Rosedale, one that I'd drove by a lot. It was three stories high and had the most beautiful translucent, glass doors.

AJ had caught me admiring the house.

"I take it that you like it. I built it myself."

I turned to him.

"What do you mean you built it yourself?"

AJ gave me a shy smile.

"I also own a couple of construction companies, but I stopped working. I don't need to be out there in the sun like that. I'm at that point in my life where I need to just settle down and have some babies or something."

Silence filled the car.

AJ and I both gazed into the night while Cupid worked his magic. AJ threw me for a serious loop. He had me hypnotized by the way he spoke, and there was something about that last comment that tugged at my conscious. That's when I first realized how fucked up of a person I had become.

A speeding car had whipped us out of the trance. AJ opened the door and got out. For one reason or another, I silently followed behind him.

That night, AJ told me everything about himself. I was surprised to find out that he and "Lil' Magic" had hooked up—right after that day he'd seen us about to fight in front of the barber shop. That meant that they've been together for four years.

I couldn't figure out why I was so mad at AJ for being with her. He knew that "Lil' Magic" was still seeing Ty, and AJ also told me that she had a serious cocaine habit that she couldn't shake.

AJ just couldn't shake her!

He'd claimed to have loved "Lil' Magic" so much. I had enough of hearing about it, so I got up to leave.

"Wow, sounds like you really love her. Well, hopefully, with some rehab, she can leave the pipe alone. I wish you the best." I'd then turned to walk away, when AJ pulled me by my waist.

"Mamacita, por favor, stay the night."

I stopped in front of his door with my hand on the gold door knob. I felt AJ gently breathing on the back of my neck, and all of the hairs on my body stood up. He must've felt it happen because, just then, AJ started slowly kissing me down the back of my neck and across my shoulders.

I immediately regretted wearing the halter top that I had on... He continued kissing me down my back, and I gave in.

This was nothing like what I experienced with Rico.

It felt too real.

It felt *too* good!

When I couldn't take any more of AJ's tongue caressing the naked skin of my back, I turned around and started kissing him on his neck.

When our lips met, my whole body shuddered and I quickly pulled away from AJ. He had the most succulent lips I had ever kissed!

"Damn, boy. So that's what Heaven feels like."

AJ bit gently on his bottom lip and picked me up effortlessly. As we went up the winding staircase, he started kissing me again. I never knew I could reach such heights of ecstasy with my clothes on.

By the time we arrived at AJ's bedroom, my "Vickies" were saturated and I was completely light headed. AJ then gently laid me upon a white, down comforter covered sleigh bed. He placed kisses on every piece of exposed skin which made me yearn for AJ even more.

I couldn't remember the last time I had sex, and I was in desperate need of it!

Drowning me in his kisses, AJ softly whispered: "Mamacita, can we take it all the way?" My body screamed "yes" and I replied, "Toma!" Take it in Spanish.

At the point, AJ could've "taken it" in e-v-e-r-y language for all I cared, just as long as he "took" it good!

Within seconds, AJ was almost naked standing over the bed. The only thing that remained was his *GAP* boxer shorts.

Muscles ripped through every inch of his body...

Seeing the light, thin film of sweat glisten across AJ's yellow skin, made my pussy PULSATE uncontrollably! I wanted to tell him to hurry up, but I didn't want to seem needy, and I *definitely* did not want AJ to pull a Rico on me!

After letting me admire his body, AJ gently started taking off my clothes. Starting with the sandals on my feet, he took the left one off first and gently nibbled on my toes that had a fresh, French pedicure. No man had *e-v-e-r* done that before, and it sent a brand-new sensation, running up-and-down my spine. AJ then did the same thing to my right foot, as I softly moaned.

Slowly, he let his fingers dance up my legs until they reached my pink paradise. AJ fondled my clit and noticed that I had soaked through my jeans.

He grinned in delight.

Soon after, AJ's fingers unfastened my belt, then the button on my *Marc Jacobs* jeans. He unhurriedly eased my jeans off while placing juicy kisses all over my thighs.

Just as AJ got my jeans past my knees, my cell phone rang. The ring tone that played signaled that it was Tony. Surprisingly, AJ took my phone, which was still on the belt clip on my jeans, and handed it to me. I sat up slowly and answered: "Yo, yo...hello?" I tried sounding like I had just awakened.

"Ma, listen...I miss you, I know what I did was fucked up—"

It was going on two o'clock in the morning and I was about to get my world rocked! AJ had laid me back down, as he continued to take off my jeans without any hesitation. I needed to get off the phone with Tony.

"Whatever man, you did what you did. It's late and I really want to go—"

My voice escaped me when AJ began removing my *Victoria Secrets* thong with his mouth. I closed my eyes and steadied my voice.

"Tony, listen, I'm going back to bed; we'll talk about that tomorrow or whenever—'cause it ain't important. You know good and well that things could *never* be the same with us."

"Oh word? We supposed to be getting married and now it's whatever? Okay! So you wanna start acting brand-new? You *fucking* do that, and see what can happen! I still love you—remember that! Shorty, if it wasn't for me, you'd be dead! Remember, I FUCKING LOVE YOU, MA! Me, Antonio Jesus Cartagena!"

AJ's tongue was buried deep within my pink paradise, and I was moments away from climaxing. Breathlessly, I whispered: "Yeah, Tony, you love me, prove it you sorry motherfucker." Just

126

as I turned my phone off, AJ pulled his face away from in between my thighs. I still managed to squirt my love juice, as I climaxed like never before. Some of my nectar hit AJ's chin, while the rest trickled down my butt cheeks.

That had never happened before—I immediately became embarrassed. AJ quickly sensed my discomfort and licked every last drop of cum from his chin with his fingers. He then ran both hands under my butt cheeks and licked his fingers.

"Waste not, want not," AJ said between the licks.

I laid there mesmerized.

Just as I thought the foreplay intensity couldn't increase, he ripped off my halter top and began sucking on my thirty-four double Ds like he was thirsty. All the while, AJ let his fingers continue to hypnotize my clitoris.

The grand finale!

He reached over the side of the bed and pulled out a box of *Magnum* condoms. I *died* right then and there as I watched AJ take off his boxers and put a condom on.

AJ was H-U-G-E!

The state-of-ecstasy that I was in meant that it would be a first-round knockout, guaranteed!

As he stood over me, I slowly got out of the bed. I let my hands rest on AJ's chest and looked into his eyes.

"Take me from the back, papi."

A wicked smile then played across AJ's face, as he swung me around so that my back was facing him. I pushed my butt out and bent over, eagerly anticipating penetration.

AJ took his time putting it in…

Slowly, he let himself ease into my drenched kitty cat, stretching my walls, as AJ ascended further and further into paradise.

For a few minutes, I was in agony. I was tighter then a virgin on prom night! Even though AJ went in slowly, it still hurt like hell!

It was a sweet hurt though.

Just as my kitty cat got adjusted to his pleasure pipe, AJ commenced to ram inside of me like he was trying to get the demons out. AJ had pumped in-and-out of me so hard and quickly.

My neat bun unraveled itself, and my hair was *all* over the place. I swooped my long mane to the side so AJ wouldn't pull on it! As I did so, I accidentally arched my back and AJ lost it!

His legs started to quiver, as AJ began to scream my name; muttering something in Spanish.

I couldn't make out what he was saying.

It really didn't matter.

He could've been calling me: "dirty whore", "queen-of-the-faggots", "trifling tramp", and I wouldn't care.

It felt *so* damn good!

AJ's legs gave out from underneath him as he climaxed. I turned around and found AJ drenched in sweat. He collapsed onto the floor.

"Damn, AJ, it's like that?"

He could barely talk: "Yeah, Kai, damn, girl... Shit... You deadly."

I didn't know what exactly he was getting at, but seeing AJ laid out on the floor, drenched in sweat, meant that I did the damn thing!

I noticed that I was also sweaty, and my natural juices were still flowing down my thighs.

"Um, AJ, where's your bathroom?"

He simply pointed to the bedroom door. I ventured out to find it for myself.

Just as I stepped into AJ's shower, reality kicked in. The cold water against my hot body brought two things into mind. The first being: where is "Lil' Magic?" The second: Tony never called me at that time of night...

The latter really got to me because just then, I remembered hearing an echo coming from Tony's phone when we had spoken; just before my sexual escapade.

I closed my eyes and envisioned Tony standing up against my car as he called me. In my lucid vision, I saw Tony shake his head back-and-forth—while he stared up at the house; screaming into his phone.

Tony then stared at the phone for a while before putting it back on his hip. He would continue to look at the house for a little while longer, before speeding off in his Beemer. Just as I thought I heard tires screeching, AJ stepped into the shower with me.

I nearly *leaped* out of my skin!

"Boy! Don't be *scaring* me like that!" Goosebumps rose all over my body.

AJ looked just as surprised.

"Sweetie, what's wrong? You look like you've just seen a ghost."

A.K.A. my conscious.

I didn't answer AJ. My vision of Tony felt surreal, and I was a little afraid.

Afraid of what would happen next.

Afraid of AJ's mystique.

Afraid of what I had just envisioned in my mind.

I let the water fall over my head in an attempt to regain my composure and mental stability. I couldn't.

Tears rolled down my face freely, as the weight of everything came crashing down on me. I had dealings with the mob, I already had one murder under my heart—with the intent for at least another, and, I stayed with a man *only* to end up ruling the NYC drug empire.

I began to wonder if the power I was seeking would compare to the intense love and passion that AJ gave to me. That was my *last* opportunity at making a clean break from the game, and starting a fresh new life.

I should have taken it then.

I was so lost in my thoughts, I didn't even notice when AJ began to wash my hair and my body. He was in the process of drying me off, when I snapped out of my daze.

"Thank you," was all I could manage. AJ smiled and nodded his head.

Again, he picked me up and this time, sat me down on the bed.

"Babe, I know you have something to tame that thing on your head, somewhere in your bag."

I took a quick glance in the mirror and noticed that my hair curled up so wildly, that I looked like Diana Ross.

I lunged for my hand bag!

AJ then let out a small laugh.

"Don't worry, you're still beautiful. Let me help you with that though." He stood behind me and dried the excess water in my hair with a towel. AJ then gently brushed my hair and pulled it back in a neat, but puffy, ponytail. He dressed me in one of his t-shirts. When AJ was done he said: "Come on, time to go mimi."

I looked at him and asked, "Go mimi?"

AJ kissed me gently on the lips.

"Yes, baby, go to sleep. My mama used to use that word."

I smiled a little and allowed myself to lie down in his bed. AJ laid right next to me and quickly fell asleep. I let the scenes of that night play over-and-over again in my head until I fell asleep. I had never been babied like that by a man before, and I wanted that moment to last forever.

the beauty of medical technology

The next morning, I'd awakened to a continental breakfast in bed, another sentiment that I have never experienced. Just before I finished eating, AJ started his plea.

"You haven't said a word all morning. All I can say is please, just come and stay with me. You don't have to be out here ripping the town to pieces. I can give you everything you want and need, Kai, if you just let me."

I gazed into his beautiful eyes and saw sincerity dripping from them. AJ was in love with me, and I was torn. Torn between the streets and the cozy lifestyle he was trying to make for me.

"AJ, I gotta go. I have to check on Tony, and then be at work at three o'clock."

A frown formed on AJ's face.

"Okay. That's fine, but at least take this." He'd handed me a small yellow envelope. As I went to drop it into my handbag, AJ stopped me. "Kai, it's the keys to my house and the security code for the alarm system. The keypad for the alarm system is to the left of the light switch that's by the front door."

AJ had further complicated the situation. I'd opened the envelope and there they were.

"AJ, why?"

"Because, just because." He then kissed me on my forehead. I'd tossed the envelope in my bag and proceeded to get dressed. I was just about to walk out of the door, when AJ asked me, "Kai, are you coming back?"

"AJ, you've shaken everything up. You've got my mind so twisted, I don't know whether *I'm* coming or going. Am *I* coming back?" I stopped to think about it. "Yeah, eventually. When I can sort everything out in my head, and make sure that the decision I make is the right one."

AJ then gave me a tight, long hug.

"Okay, mamacita. Whatever you want. I'll be right here waiting for you."

"You promise?"

"I promise."

AJ then watched me walk down his cobblestone walkway towards my car. I gasped when I saw something stuck to the windshield of my car, being too small to be a ticket. The post-it simply read: I LOVE YOU KAI!

My heart broke...

Tony was there that night when AJ and I first made love.

I checked out the car, making sure everything was intact before driving into the early morning sun. I didn't even bother to call Tony to ask him why he was following me around. I decided to just drive straight to his house.

During the drive, I turned my cell phone back on. It was filled with messages from Tony. I let my voicemail play on speakerphone, while I drove towards South Side.

"Today, at 1:53 AM: Babe, you ain't even let me tell you goodnight."

"Today, at 1:58 AM: Come on, you're not even gonna talk to me?"

"Today, at 2:15 AM: Okay, so I'm back on South Side. Some next shit just went down. Call me, please."

"Today, at 2:31 AM: Ma! ...Ma! Come the fuck on! Turn on ya damn phone!"

"Today, at 2:32 AM: I'm sorry for yelling. Just please, call me back."

"Today, at 3:03 AM: Kai? ...Kai? Alright, fine!"

I hit the end button on my phone after that last message. *Tony sounded desperate...* I sped the rest of the way to his house.

When I got there, everything looked fine on the outside. When I walked up to the door, I noticed that it was left open. I pushed it in slowly and saw Tony passed out in the middle of the living room. I shut the door behind me and walked slowly towards him, while trying to see if anybody else was around.

Tony had passed out in a sitting position. There were bottles of *Bacardi Apple* and *Jack Daniels* all over the coffee table. Anticipating the worse, I rushed to check his pulse.

Thank God he was still alive!

However, Tony did manage to pee all over the couch and floor while he was passed out.

My initial thought was that Tony's urinary bag broke. I went to the kitchen and wet a hand towel to clean him up. When I unbuttoned Tony's jeans, I found the shock of my life...

I swore that there was a lump in his boxing shorts where the catheter used to be. I didn't think it was so.

I continued pulling Tony's jeans down, and then his boxers right off. There was no catheter or urine bag.

Tony had gotten a prosthetic penis!

What tripped me out even more, when I was cleaning him up, Tony managed to get hard. I shivered in disgust, but finally saw why "Jane Doe" was here. Whoever he went to did an *excellent* reconstructive procedure for Tony.

If I hadn't known he had his real one *chopped* off, I would've thought it was natural.

It even felt real...

The early morning "wood" woke Tony up. He stared at me seductively as I continued to gently clean Tony up. Finally, he said, "I love you, Kai."

"I love you, too, Tony. Now let's try to go upstairs and get you bathed."

"Can I make love to you?" Flashbacks of AJ flooded my mind. "Come on, Kai, let's make love."

"Tony, you know that I can't sleep with you after you had that broad up in here. I don't know how many broads you've ran through. You ain't even tell me—"

"I can't *fuck* my own wife?" Tony became enraged. "I CAN'T *FUCK* YOU? FUCK YOU MEAN? HUH? But then you expect me not to *fuck* other bitches! Get the *fuck* outta here with that bullshit! You know better."

I was waiting for him to throw AJ in my face, but Tony didn't. I saw no point in arguing with him, so I continued pushing him up the stairs. Tony called me every name in the book on our way to the bathroom.

It wasn't until the bathtub was filled with water and bubble bath liquid when he'd shut up. Tony finally had let me finish undressing him, and then he got in.

Tony remained silent as he soaked in the tub. I took that opportunity to make him some coffee, figuring that it would calm Tony down. I brought it to him and Tony didn't say anything, until he found that there wasn't any sugar in the coffee. Tony tried to spit it out.

"Nope. You gotta drink it just like that if you want your hangover to ease up."

Then I went to go lay in his bed. About an hour later, Tony came and laid next to me smelling like *Bath & Bodyworks* "Cucumber Melon", and fell asleep.

Around one in the afternoon, I woke up and started to get ready for work. I had just stepped out of the shower when Tony walked in the bathroom, naked and at attention.

No words were exchanged.

I let him kiss me until passion took over. Tony then picked me up and I wrapped my legs around his waist, as he held me up against the wall.

I thought I would *vomit* when Tony entered me!

Much to my surprise, it felt like the *real* thing. I began to think of AJ, as I climaxed all over Tony's prosthetic penis.

Just as he put me down, Tony started telling me about Ty.

"Ma, yo, these Jamaicans done got the green light from me to push weed only over on Farmers. Can you believe these dudes are also serving crack heads? Dudes in the street say them fuckers are now grossing twenty grand a week, which I gets no percentage from.

"Can you believe that shit? So, I send that nigga, Rashawn to go tell dudes to fucking close up shop, or pay me my cut, and this little ferret looking asshole was like, *'Nah, nigga, we ain't paying you shit!'* I should've never let them fools sell trees out here in the first place!"

I knew Tony was talking about Ty and his crew.

"So what you gonna do, honey?" I asked, already knowing what the answer would be. Tony then smiled.

"We rolling up on them dudes tonight!"

I shook my head.

"Just know that there are three lookout cars. A blue *Toyota Camry* that's parked in the driveway of the house. A black *Ford Explorer* across the street from the house, and a silver *Nissan Maxima* up on the c9orner facing the house. They all have *Nextels* and stay on the lookout."

Tony shook his head, astonished.

"Baby girl, how you know this?"

"I really found out about it yesterday. That ferret-looking motherfucker with a limp—that's Ty; Shelly's boyfriend?"

"Is Shelly involved?"

"Nope, she won't go near the crack house. Shelly barely wants to work with me."

Tony then stopped and thought for awhile.

"So what's the plan, ma-ma?"

"Gimme two days."

*****

The two days never came. That night, while driving home from work, I decided to swing by Shelly's house before heading to Tony's. I was on Brookville Boulevard, about to turn left onto the North Conduit, when I noticed Ty's car parked in the dirt, right before the bridge.

It was close to midnight and no street lights were on. I turned my headlights off and drove slowly pass his car. I peered in and saw that Ty was getting head from a dirty-looking chick. I continued driving a few yards, checked for other cars, and did a quick U-turn.

I drove back up to his car so that my window was facing Ty's window. I looked into the back seat to make sure there weren't any witnesses, before letting my tinted windows roll down.

"AIN'T THAT THAT NIGGA, TY, LOOKING *FLYER* THAN A MOTHER FUCKER?" I said loudly while popping my chewing gum.

Ty slowly opened his eyes while keeping the girl's head in his lap.

Excellent.

"Kai? Fuck you want?"

I'd *never* get an opportunity like that again in a lifetime!

"Damn, why you always so *mean* to me?" I reached under my seat and pulled "Khara" out. Ty was thoroughly enjoying the oral sex he was getting, because he couldn't keep his eyes on me.

In between breaths, Ty said: "Because…you're a…stupid bitch…Fuck off…and if you tell Shelly…I'ma kill you dead!"

That was the last thing Ty said…

The girl never even saw it coming.

I cocked and aimed "Khara" right at Ty's left temple.

"No, you dead motherfucker!"

Pop! Pop!

Two shots.

135

One through his temple.

The other through the back of the head of the girl.

I put a latex glove on and got the tarot deck from the glove compartment.

I tossed out the two cards and drove off.

rippa's return

Days after the shooting, I still hadn't said anything to Tony about what happened. It was, however, the talk of the town. The local news reported it as a *"drug deal gone wrong."* There were no witnesses, and both occupants of the car died.

The reporters even talked about the tarot cards. They figured the meaning behind the "DEATH" card, but couldn't understand what "THE EMPRESS" stood for.

I became drunk with power again!

I'd promised myself that I would retire, just as soon as I got *everything* that I wanted.

Shelly was distraught over Ty's death. I let her mourn for a week on her own before paying Shelly a visit. Tony picked up the entire twenty grand, shortly after Ty died. Rashawn now served up the fiends on Farmer's.

I honked my horn when I got in front of Shelly's house. She didn't come to the door. Just as I got out the car, I noticed an undercover detective parked further down Shelly's block. I continued to Shelly's door, knowing that I was clean and they didn't have a thing on me.

I didn't have "Khara" with me that particular day.

Shelly was asleep on the couch when I walked in. She *smelled* as if she hadn't bathed in a week! I leaned over Shelly. "Wake up, sleepy head."

Shelly had simply turned her back to me. I gave her a nice firm slap on her ass, and Shelly rose to her feet immediately.

"Damn, Kai, *fuck* you gotta hit me for?"

"Because, you're in here *smelling* like shit! Go wash your *ass* so we can go get you some fresh air."

Shelly then folded her arms across her chest.

"I don't wanna go anywhere."

I pulled a wad of money out.

"Oh, so you gonna t-e-l-l me that I got nobody to spend this money on? Come on, stinky beauty, its payday."

Shelly looked hard at the money.

"Fine, I do smell funky don't I?"

I put a finger under my nostrils.

137

"Girl you about to *knock* me out with that funk."

For someone in mourning, Shelly did manage to pull herself together rather nicely. We were walking out of her house, when a car rolled down Shelly's block blaring *Serve Jah* by *Luciano.*

Shelly tried her best to name the car: "Ain't that a *Bentley,* Kai?"

I had only seen the front of the car.

"Probably not. It's most likely a tricked-out version of a *Chrysler's 300 M.* Ain't *nobody* 'round here got dough-like-that."

Nobody would have a *Bentley* on this side of the Hudson without *me* knowing!

As I walked towards my car, I made a mental note of the Florida tags. By the time I got up to my car, I realized that it was indeed a *Bentley.*

"Yo, Shells, you right! Check out the tail of the car. You see how the lights sit? It's a *Bentley.*"

Just as I said that, the driver lowered the music and put the car in reverse. I knew he'd seen the parked undercover detective car, so it couldn't have been a drive by.

I continued walking towards my car.

Just as I opened the driver's side door, the driver of the *Bentley* yelled, "Wh'appen, pretty?"

I stopped dead in my tracks, as I tried to put a name to that familiar voice. He continued.

"Yes, pretty. Lookin' pretty as eva'. Time been good to ya, gyal."

I still hadn't figured it out.

"Mi a go call ya lata. Number still the same, right?"

"Excuse me, but do I—" My mouth dropped when I turned around and saw Rippa!

Jamaica was *really* good to him!

Rippa was no longer the short, skinny little pushover I knew four years ago. I slowly removed my *Chloe* shades.

"Rippa, is that you?"

Rippa then got out of his car and smacked his muscular chest with both hands.

"Ah, mi girlfriend."

He now had a sun-kissed, honey-brown complexion, and stood tall at 6'7". Rippa towered over me when he hugged me. He was *dripping* in canary-yellow diamonds and rose gold. Rippa's *Lacoste* cologne swept me off my feet.

I then called to Shelly: "Shelly, ma-ma, look—it's Rippa!"

Shelly did a double take.

"Oh my God, Rippa you look so damn good! Boy, what you been doing with yourself?"

Rippa never took his eyes off of me.

"Ah, ya know, a likkle dis, a likkle dat. No-ting major."

Our little reunion vibe got disrupted when his passenger stepped out-of-line. The *bitch* actually got out of the car, looking like who-did-it-and-ran! She walked right up to Rippa.

"Rippa, ah, who dis, eh? A wha' di bumba clot a gwan?"

Rippa still had his eyes locked with mine.

"Birdie, ya cyan do mi a favor? Eh? Gwan catch a van over deya on Merrick Boulevard, an' get di *fuck* outta mi face."

Birdie wasn't having it!

"Ah, so ya forget who a give ya a good *fuck* last night, dis morning and fill ya belly, eh? Ya wan' tro' me away fi dis *Yankee* gyal wit' her fake ponytail an' eyes."

Rippa stepped in front of me when I attempted to lunge at her.

"Jus' cool na', baby" he said smoothly. Rippa walked up to Birdie and whispered something to her. Whatever he'd said must've put fear in Birdie's heart, because she took off running in the direction of Merrick Boulevard in three-inch heels. Rippa then turned back to me.

"Kai, ma-ma, tonight you an' me gon' a party, alright? Be ready fi nine." He gave me a kiss on the cheek before returning to his *Bentley* and driving off.

I stood there in shock for a good five minutes.

"Oh boy, now you want Rippa, don't you?"

I turned to Shelly with a devilish look in my eyes.

"Of course I do! Apparently, he's still in love, so I'ma hop on Rippa's paper train for a hot minute. Make it my grand finale. Besides, he and I have unfinished business." *I wonder if Rippa would ask me about the six grand...*

Shelly and I had driven to *Roosevelt Field Mall,* reminiscing about old times and when I first met Rippa. Our whole time out, my main focus was Rippa. He had become so sexy, and apparently very wealthy.

Besides, I saw no harm in seeing Rippa and working for Tony, too.

*****

Rippa picked me up from my house at nine o'clock on-the-dot. I was going to meet him somewhere, but Rippa insisted on picking me up. I opted for a short and tight black halter dress with black stiletto heels, both by *Michael Kors*. Rippa wore a nearly sheer, white linen suit, and had his hair loose.

I knew it was too early to go to the club, so I asked Rippa, "Where to, sweetheart?"

He opened the passenger side door of the *Bentley*.

"It nah really matter. Jus' as long ya deya by mi side."

I smiled and bit my bottom lip.

"We a go check my uncle, then we a go to *Club A*."
I agreed.

Rippa's uncle lived in a huge house in Elmont. It was almost hidden on a side block that ran parallel with the Long Island Expressway. Rippa and his uncle talked for about two hours straight.

AJ had called a few times, but I just kept sending him to voicemail. He left me a message telling me how much he missed me, and how he needed to see me that night. AJ was my salvation...but Rippa, Rippa was my "golden dream" come true.

"Baby," Rippa had finally blessed me with his attention, "where's mi money?"

I could hear my dream *shatter* in my head when he said that!

"I have only two-thousand left. After you bounced, I had problems and I used the money for school."

"Eh heh." Rippa paced back and forth in front of me. "Is two reasons why mi come back to New York. Daddy tell me say: *'Dat idiot bwoy, Tyrret dead. Police bwoy find 'im in Rosedale wit' a shot to ' im head.'* Mi say: *'Nah, daddy, it nah true.'* Daddy say: *'Ah, yes, it true.'* So mi say: *'Good fi him; ras clot!'* Is him who mi used to work for."

Rippa then sucked his teeth and poured himself a glass filled with *Wray & Nephew* over-proofed rum.

"Baby, ya know di second reason?"

I shook my head no.

"Ah, you, mami."

"Me?" I said coyly.

"Yes, baby love. Everywhere mi turn around, mi 'ear about some gyal wit' some funny-colored eyes and long, light-brown hair that's deadly-to-ras! Mi say: *'Nah, it cyaan be mi empress.'* Di one who tell mi say: *'Fi leave di honest life to make some drug money fi carry bring to her.'*"

"I never asked you to—"

"It nah matter. Mi link up wit' Tyrret an' drop off every *cent* mi make inna ya mailbox. I's vex-I-vex! If it weren't fi mi Daddy sending mi back to Jamaica, it would've been *MI* inna Tony's place!"

My mouth dropped!

"An' ya woulda put me deya, baby love. So 'ear wha', ya a go leave Tony. Him make enough money off of dis *blood clot* ting! Him can manage without ya. Ya can come back to Florida an' put *MI* in his position! Alright?"

Going out-of-state was not a part of my initial plan.

"But, Rippa, you forget, I still have school that I need to finish; and a family that will miss me."

Rippa laughed.

"Ya? Care about family? Ya are di most heartless *bitch* mi know. Who say it not *ya* who *kill* Tyrret, eh?"

My facial expression didn't change.

"It nah matter. Mi *still* love ya, and mi know ya love me! Maybe by next summer, we a go have a *BIG* wedding! Inna year or so, mi a go be di biggest drug lord. *Fuck* this *shotta* business! Is time fi mi to move on to bigger and better tings. Ya understand?"

I had to think fast!

"Rippa, I *can't* just up and leave Tony. If I leave so abruptly, a lot of people will be upset and wonder why."

Rippa guzzled down another glassful of rum.

"I'll make you a deal though, Rippa." My fingers traced along the sparkly band of his *Presidential Rolex*. "It seems that you are already making a lot of money on your own. So, I'll come down to Florida every other weekend or so, and we'll start from there."

Rippa stood there with his hands on his hips.

"Ya nah easy, ma-ma, but alright."

offer that couldn't be refused

Two weeks later, I found myself in Tampa, Florida at Rippa's request. He said it was urgent that I come as soon as possible. I'd arrived in front of Rippa's door with the clothes on my back and my *Christian Dior* saddle bag only.

I didn't plan to stay more than one night with him.

I *couldn't* stay more than one night with him.

Tony closed some deals, and I'd wanted to be back in New York to make sure he'd executed them properly. The drug game is *highly* seductive, especially on a larger scale. Once your operation is in place, and everyone is doing what they're supposed to, cash flows in lovely!

Rippa's estate was comparable to Niccolo's. I was extremely impressed, gazing at the stucco palace, as my white *Yves St. Laurent* stiletto sandals clicked against the cobblestone walkway.

I walked up one of the twin stairs and rang the door bell. A lady with a thick Jamaican accent quietly spoke into the intercom: "Who is it?"

It took me a minute or so to find where the voice was coming from. I pressed the intercom button: "Kai Toussaint. Rippa is expecting me."

As I was finishing my sentence, the front doors slid open automatically. I slowly walked into the marble foyer. There were six maids running back-and-forth in a frenzy. One of them pointed toward the back of the house.

I walked in that direction and stopped when I reached the pool area.

I *immediately* lost my cool!

My face twisted up in disgust at the amount of females that surrounded Rippa. I stopped counting after twenty-five.

I walked slowly onto the patio. Rippa jumped to his feet as soon as he saw me leaving a topless female behind.

"Baby!" Rippa then waltzed over to me with both of his arms opened wide.

"Fuck you, Rippa! You said you wanted me out here and *this* is how you living? This is what *I'm* supposed to leave Tony

142

for? This is what's so *fucking* urgent?" I turned and started walking away.

I had just reached inside of his house when Rippa caught up to me.

"Sugah plum, ya mus' understand say, a so mi live. Mi nah *'ave* no wife, no pickney, an' *plenty* gyal dem want mi! So, mi give dem wha' ya don' want." Rippa started gyrating his hips sexually. "Come on. Let we go back inna di pool an' talk."

"Fuck you, Rippa! I'm catching the first flight back to New York! Besides, I didn't come with anything—"

"Cha! So let we go shoppin'. Hold on; mi soon come." Rippa then turned to walk away when the topless girl approached him.

"Rippa, you said you would take *ME* shopping," she whined. I was surprised to see that the topless girl didn't have a Jamaican accent. Rippa didn't seem upset.

"A wha'? Ya nah 'ave nah home training?" he calmly replied. "Ya *see* mi wit' mi wife an' *dare* come wit' ya nonsense."

The girl must've thought that she was his wife or whatever.

"FUCK HER!" she said with her hands on her hips. "TAKE ME SHOPPING, NOW!"

I must admit, the girl had balls. She'd openly disrespected me without knowing who *I* was. Unfortunately, Rippa wasn't as understanding. He softened his voice.

"So sorry, I dunno wha' mi ah think! Cha! Come here, gyal." Rippa pulled her gently by the face and started kissing her. I was about to turn around when, I noticed blood trickling down from the corners of her mouth.

He then pulled away and I heard something that sounded like uncooked meat hitting a floor tile. It was the girl's upper lip hitting his marble floors.

My stomach turned.

Rippa wiped his mouth with his forearm and turned to me.

"See, a ya ah di wife. Come, lemme show ya *someting* else."

The topless girl went running back to the pool area with both of her hands covering her mouth.

Rippa then grabbed me by my hand and walked me back to the pool area. All the other girls pretended not to see that the one of them had been maimed. They carried on like nothing had happened. Rippa whistled loudly and got their attention.

"Mi will return in an hour. One *fuckin'* hour. Who so ever mi find *still* inna mi yard, mi a go kill. If mi wife say she find even so a likkle earring dat belong to one of ya, ya dead!" Everybody froze in their tracks, including me. I couldn't believe little old Rippa had turned into such a monster.

Fifteen minutes later, we arrived at a strip mall. The only thing I picked up was a bikini set.

"Is dat all ya want, baby?" Rippa said while he sipped on a *Guiness Stout.*

As if by some sort of premonition, I declined. At that time, I couldn't figure out why. I always got as much as I wanted. Instead, I looked at Rippa and simply said: "Yes, this is all I need. We're going to sit in the pool, talk business, and then I must head home."

Rippa then smiled devilishly. "Ah, so ya think!"

I countered in my best Jamaican accent impersonation: "Ah, so mi know!"

Rippa laughed a little. Just as promised, we took exactly one hour. When Rippa and I got back to his estate, the only people around were his maids and a man in a nice business suit. As soon as we walked through the door, the man immediately stood at attention and approached us.

"Mr. Everett, I've asked you to please consider my schedule at the hospital before you go around inflicting serious injuries on people. I cannot be on your every beck and call. I have patients to deal with you know."

Rippa cleared his throat and a maid came running with an unopened bottle of rum and two shot glasses. She poured the rum into both glasses and disappeared. Rippa took one after the other, straight to the head.

"Dr. Brown, wha' di problem, eh? Is mi who call ya? Nah! So wha' di fuck ya come 'round here fah?" Dr. Brown shook his head.

"Ms. Beverly called me about a girl bleeding from the mouth. You know she's going to need cosmetic surgery, right?"

Rippa shook his head.

"Fuck her. She can *stay* dat way. Doctor bwoy, mi a go call ya a likkle lata. Right now, mi have some *real* important business to attend to."

Rippa looked at me seductively and tingles ran through my body. Just as that happened, my phone rang. It was AJ.

I excused myself to speak to him in private.

"Hey," I answered nonchalantly.

"Kai, where are you?"

"I'm in Tampa taking care of some things. I should be back in New York by tomorrow afternoon." AJ paused for a while.

"Kai, when are you going to chill? When is it going to be enough for you? Now you're expanding to other cities? Baby girl, what are you doing?"

I was speechless.

"AJ, what are you *talking* about?"

"Don't even try to play *dumb* with me, Kai! I know you better than you know yourself. I'm begging you, don't do this."

"Do what, AJ? What am I out here doing?"

His tone made me panic.

Panic turned into anger.

"You know what, AJ, I don't know what the *fuck* your problem is! Who the *fuck* are *you* to accuse me of any damn thing."

"Cross him, and he will *kill* you, sweetie."

Just as AJ said that, Rippa had snapped my phone shut.

"Tell him fi *fuck* off. Ah, my time dis! Come, let we go inna di pool."

The urgency in AJ's voice and Rippa sneaking up on me like that, rattled my nerves. I needed to steady myself.

"Rippa, darling, gimme a minute to put this thing on." I dangled the bag holding the bikini in front of him.

"Alright, no problem." Rippa then escorted me to a changing room near the pool area. "You can leave all your stuff right in here." I nodded my head in agreement.

I took my time taking my clothes off and slipping into the bikini. All the while, second thoughts raced through my mind. I knew this situation wasn't right, but I couldn't stop. I must've lost track of time because, Rippa started banging on the door!

"Ay, gyal, time is money ya know?" I left all of my belongings in the room and hurried out to meet Rippa.

"Damn!" I screamed at him. "There's really no need for all of that *banging* and shit!" Rippa sucked his teeth.

"Just come."

We sat under a huge palm tree in his backyard, instead of getting into the pool. Rippa pulled out a dime bag of weed and emptied it into the palm of his hand.

"See mami, dis' bwoy, him name Ding-Dong. When mi father did send mi back a Jamaica, him jus' come to Florida. Back home, mi used to hear stories of how many police bwoy 'im kill inna Kingston, an' him not even Jamaican.

"Him ruthless! But him no *ruthless* like mi! Mi would've *done* him off a long time ago, but him is the *big* fish over here. Every chance mi a take fi done da bwoy, him surrounded by body guards an' ting. Dem say no one can touch him. But mi haffi touch him an' take way all him business, ya understand?

"So what do you want me to do?"

"Wha' ya do fi Tony?"

"This is not the same situation. Tony already had the city on lock, way before I came into the picture. I only helped him regain that, after Tony did some time."

Rippa thought about that for a minute.

"College gyal, how mi a go deal wit' Ding-Dong? Him a *nasty* rat; mi want him dead."

"If you kill him, Rippa, then what?"

"Then him customers will haffi come check mi!"

"What makes you think that *you're* the only person scheming on Ding-Dong?"

"Mi know. Everybody scared of him 'cept for me. Mi nah fear no one!"

"Five-hundred grand for his head, and fifteen percent of *every* dollar you make after."

Rippa started laughing.

"It's like dat, ma?"

"I figure this. You're going to almost triple your gross income, right?" Rippa nodded in agreement. "So, fifteen percent is not a lot. It's fair to me, considering that you will not have the additional income that you're trying to get, *if* I don't kill him.

"Besides, I'm just about the *only* person that you know that would even consider killing this Ding-Dong person. If he is holding a lot of weight down here, then Ding-Dong has to be known throughout the entire state, and the Caribbean. You'd be a *fool* to even consider hiring somebody else. They might end up *killing* you."

"Neva dat. Dem fear mi, too; understand?"

146

"But they fear Ding-Dong more, don't they?" Rippa's silence answered for him. "Look sweetie, give me some time, I'll think of something."

I eased up from the comfy lawn chair and headed back towards the room Rippa had me change in. He then grabbed me roughly from behind.

"Kai, mi a go *kill* ya if ya fuck mi over."

I turned around quickly.

"Why would I do that? I'm already sitting pretty in New York City. I know I owe you. You ain't got to *rub* it in my face every chance that you get. But fuck you over? Rippa please!"

* * * * *

Once I was safely on the plane heading to JFK, I smiled to myself. I couldn't believe that Rippa had just handed me a carry on bag with at least one-hundred thousand dollars in it. All I had to do was come up with a plan to knock out his competition, and I had another four-hundred thousand to look forward to.

the other woman

I'd arrived back in Queens sometime after midnight when I came back from Florida. I wasted no time driving to AJ's house. Tony would have to *wait* to see me! AJ's car was parked right in front of his house, but the lights weren't on. My heart leaped when I slipped my key into the keyhole.

I was surprised to see that it actually worked.

As I walked into AJ's house; I could smell jasmine incense burning. I thought about calling out his name, but the soft baby-making music in the background let me know that AJ was upstairs in the master bedroom.

I decided to sneak up on him...

I took off my sandals and gently tip-toed up the winding staircase. I began to think of *a-l-l* the wonderful things AJ would do to relax me.

As I got closer to his room, I could hear AJ breathing heavily. Stupidity had me believing that he was working out. When I reached the doorway, reality floored me!

There AJ was, easing in-and-out of "Lil' Magic" as she purred softly. Seeing him give her what *I'd* come for sickened me!

What happened to AJ waiting for me?

I stood there wondering what turned him on about "Lil' Magic". She was fat and sloppy! Even with the incense lit, I could *still* smell fish in the air!

Just as I was about to throw my keys at AJ, he looked up at me. Our eyes locked, but AJ continued pleasuring "Lil' Magic" as if I wasn't standing there. I motioned with my finger for him to come to me. He nodded his head slowly.

AJ then looked down at her, then back up at me. He started moving slower and slower, then AJ had stopped. I quietly walked away from the doorway and waited for him in the kitchen.

The first thought that ran through my mind was, *what would she do if she saw me?*

NOTHING!

I had "Khara" nestled in her holster that was strapped to my side. All "Lil' Magic" had to do was give me a reason to introduce them to each other. Then she and Ty could find their "happily ever after" in Hell!

I heard AJ tell "Lil' Magic" to take a bath.

Good! She *needed* it!

As she soaked in the tub, AJ had come out of his room. He then silently walked passed me. I followed behind AJ, fighting the itch to start a commotion, so "Lil' Magic" could come running out of the bathroom.

I followed him all the way down to his basement. AJ had locked the door before he started to speak. I was surprised that I was able to remain calm and rational up until that point. Yet, AJ took too long trying to gather his thoughts. I started the conversation.

"That's *fucked* up. That's really, really *fucked* up, kid. You wanna act all holier than thou and try to accuse me of some bullshit. But here you are, *screwing* "Lil' Magic's" brains out."

AJ finally got it together.

"Kai, you knew she was my girl."

"Ya girl?"

My body BURNED with rage!

"Oh, so *now* she's ya girl, but yet, you *give* me the keys to ya house with the security code! But yet, you *stay* calling me! But yet you always want to be around me. But yet—nah man, forget this! Fuck you, you *nasty* bastard!"

"But, Kai—"

I blocked him out as I walked towards the basement door. My brain could not register whatever AJ had said. I went on "auto pilot", and my *only* concern was getting out of his house! I turned the knob but the door wouldn't open. Remembering that it was locked, I turned to AJ.

"Open the door."

He looked up at me from the bottom of the basement stairs.

"Nah, Kai. Not until you come back down here and I can finish—"

"OPEN THE DAMN DOOR, YOU *FUCKING* LIAR!"

I was screaming at the top of my lungs, but AJ didn't move.

Pop! Pop! Pop! Pop!

149

I let "Khara" unlock the door for me.

As the smoked cleared, I walked through the door as AJ raced up the stairs behind me. I was just about to make my exit out the front door when, "Lil' Magic" came racing down the winding stairs.

She was hysterical: "AJ, AJ ARE YOU ALRIGHT?"

Just as "Lil' Magic" said that, she saw me standing there.

I politely smiled at the skank, "Hey bitch."

"Lil' Magic" then ran towards me. I pulled "Khara" out, and she stopped dead in her tracks.

"Now, now little bitch! You're not looking to die are you?" Tears rolled down "Lil' Magic's" face. AJ had stood there dumbfounded. "You guys enjoy the rest of your evening."

I walked out the front door and didn't look back. As soon as I got in my car, my phone rang. It was AJ.

"Um, there's *really* no need to be calling me," I retorted.

"Kai. I'm sorry. I'm so sorry; you have to understand that I never meant to—"

"Meant to what? Let me guess, hurt me? Hmmm? TOO LATE! And to think, I was just about ready to give up this life to settle down with you. For what, AJ? So you can sit there and *fuck* around on me? You got the w-r-o-n-g lady!"

"Kai, it's not what you think. Please, let's just get together tomorrow in the evening sometime so we can straighten things out."

"STRAIGHTEN THINGS OUT? WHATEVER!" I'd flipped my phone shut. AJ then called back and I sent him to voicemail.

The drive to Southside made me think. What was it all worth? Tony cheated, AJ cheated so why did I even want to settle down when I had a shit load of money to make?

ding-dong

A month had passed and I still didn't have a solution to Rippa's problem. Everything was good with Tony and I, but I was still very eager to have a piece of Florida in my back pocket.

I never responded to any of AJ's messages, but he kept calling like clockwork.

I didn't have the time to invest in his emotional issues.

The *only* thing that I was concerned about at that time was, keeping control of Tony's empire and attaining *my* piece of Florida.

That's *all* that mattered!

I didn't even stop to see my family since I came back from Tampa.

* * * * *

One day out of the blue, Rippa had called me.

I sent him *straight* to voicemail!

He left me a message saying that his "problem" needed to be "solved" by the end of the month.

I had no idea of what to do.

Rippa's only competitor was this half Indian, half Chinese, Trinidadian guy named, Ding-Dong. Rippa didn't even have a picture of this man. All I knew was that he also lived in Tampa and had a lot more clout than Rippa did.

I was at my wit's end when the solution came to me. One day, I decided to hit the *Jerk Hut*, which wasn't too far from where I lived. It was early in the afternoon so it wasn't packed. I had just paid for my lunch when, the most exotic-looking guy I've ever seen walked through the door.

All eyes, both men and women, were on him. It was like time had stopped, as he strolled into the restaurant with his entourage.

I was awe struck.

I gently glided towards the guy, letting our eyes connect. It was evident that he liked what he saw. Just as I was about to pass him and head out the door, our eyes locked. I could feel the eyes of the other women in the place, burn a hole through my back, so I continued towards the door.

Just before exiting I'd glanced back, and the exotic man still had his eyes fixed on me. I stared at him seductively, as I slowly pulled my hair out of the loose bun that hid its beauty.

One of his eyebrows rose in admiration, as my hair cascaded down my shoulders and past my waist. Pleased that I had him hypnotized, I continued out of the restaurant; smiling.

I looked in the direction of my car and my smile immediately faded. My car was completely boxed in. Four black *Lexus* jeeps had double-parked, leaving my car in the middle. I tossed my lunch onto the passenger seat and headed back into the restaurant.

I walked in and the women in the place were still ogling the exotic man, as he stood at the counter placing his order. I walked straight up to the counter and interrupted: "Excuse me, but um, I'm completely boxed in because some of your patrons decided to double-park. Can you make an announcement for the Lexus' to move, please?"

The cashier looked at me scornfully.

I guess I had interrupted her flow with "Mister Exotic." She kissed her teeth, and was about to say something, but the man then spoke in the gentlest voice I ever heard.

"Oh snap, dat's my car. Mi so sorry. Cyan ya wait a minute? Let mi finish getting my food—then I a go move di car."

I stared up at him while my heart fluttered.

The only man that *ever* got that type of reaction out of me was Jordan Richardson! The exotic man stood 6'4" tall. I leaned my body into his.

"Now, see, waiting for you is going to make my food cold, and make me *late* for work!"

He then put his arm around my waist and pulled me in closer.

"If your food gets cold, then I'll just warm it up. You're not goin' to be late for work."

I then glanced at my watch. I had exactly forty-five minutes before I had to be at work. The mall was only ten minutes away.

"Look, I can warm up my food when I *get* to work! I'd like to do that before my shift starts, so can you *please* move your car?"

I turned to walk away—the guy then gently pulled me back towards him.

"Baby, why you so tense? Ease up. I'll just move the car just now." He turned back to the cashier and continued placing his order. He was drop-dead gorgeous, but that *didn't* give him the carte blanche to have me waiting.

I headed back towards my car.

I ate my lunch there, and realized that I had only ten minutes to get to work on time. I knew for sure that I was going to be late.

Just as I was about to go back into the restaurant, "Mister Exotic" and his entourage came walking out.

"See, just now I'm coming to move the car." I walked back to my car and started it up. I put on *Here Comes the Boom* by *Sean Paul* and *DMX*, because I needed something to speed off to.

He wasn't the *only* one that could put on a show!

Just as the first jeep pulled out, I quickly steered out of the parking space and did a wide U-turn onto the other side of Merrick Boulevard. I turned my stereo to maximum volume, and stole three red lights.

I made it to the mall parking lot in five minutes.

My great luck, I found a parking space right in front of the doors. I quickly dipped in and parked. Just as I was leaving my car, I noticed all four jeeps pull up to the curb. I shook my head and walked passed them. "Mister Exotic" hopped out—just as I walked into the mall.

"Damn, ma, wait up."

I continued walking as if I didn't hear him. The man followed me all the way to my job but, I *still* continued to ignore him.

I went straight to the backroom to clock in. When I came back out, "Sticks" was all over "Mister Exotic." I pretended not to see her or him, and continued towards the front of the store.

"Baby, how you just gonna walk pass me while this chicken head is all over me?"

I was pleased when he said that!

I played along: "See, I told you, honey. Most girls out here are scandalous sluts that hop on the *dick* with the quickness of a jack rabbit!"

"Sticks" was left speechless!

153

She walked away as the guy gave me a big hug and picked me up in his muscular arms. I had to remind him that I was at work, and that he needed to put me down.

"Lady, I'm so sorry. You must understand, I *never* seen such a b-e-a-u-t-i-f-u-l woman before!" Something about the way he said that made me warm inside! "Ah, where are my manners? My name is Shawn, and yours?"

The guy then extended his right hand towards mine, and I froze when I saw the tattoo on the back of his hand! The hairs on the back of my neck rose, as goose bumps attacked the surface of my skin. He noticed me staring.

"Oh, that's my nickname. Nothin' really. Them used to call me that from when I was back in Trinidad."

I couldn't believe it!

The man was too sexy to be a *ruthless* killer!

He'd sent chills through my body as soon as I met him. I thought that was the chemistry of attraction. It wasn't.

It was destiny.

The man that I had hypnotized was the one *I* was supposed to "take care of" for Rippa. I tried to remain calm.

"I'm Kai," I said softly while shaking his hand. I continued to stare at the guy's tattoo. "What do you prefer me calling you, 'Shawn' or 'Ding-Dong'?"

"You can call me *ANYTHING,* just as long as I can call you mine."

I blushed.

"Um, actually, I'm caught up in a bad situation right now, so you can call me a friend." I then looked down at my engagement ring with hate in my eyes—and a burning sensation in my stomach.

"Wow, it *can'tt* be! A woman as pretty as you unhappy? I'ma change that! Tell him that you're goin' to leave him and come back to Florida with me."

I giggled, and was about to come back with a witty reply, when Tony's voice boomed behind me.

"Yo, Kai! WHAT'S *REALLY* GOOD?"

I flinched.

The two men then sized each other up. Ding-Dong clearly towered over Tony, and tried to intimidate him by staring Tony down. Tony just stared back at him. After a few tense moments, Ding-Dong finally spoke.

"Ah, ya mus' be di toy-friend. Ya one lucky man. Ya 'ave a *b-e-a-u-t-i-f-u-l* woman 'erre, and ya cyan make her happy? Fuck up, and she a go be *my* wife before ya casket even close."

I could tell by the sudden appearance of an American accent that Tony's presence had irked him. I didn't even have a real conversation with Ding-Dong yet, and already he made a death threat towards Tony! Tony kept a blank expression on his face.

"YO, NIGGA, WHO THE *FUCK* IS YOU *TALKING* TO LIKE THAT?"

Ding-Dong smiled towards me.

"Baby, you 'ave a good day. Mi a go check ya later, ya hear?"

I didn't reply.

"YO, NIGGA, YOU AIN'T *CHECKING* NOTHING! THAT'S MY *FUCKING* WIFE YOU'RE TALKING TO!" Tony screamed. Ding-Dong smirked.

"Jus' cool. Remember wha' mi say. It a go happen. It really a go happen!" Then Ding-Dong strutted out of the store. Tony turned to me.

"Look at you, big playgirl! The *fuck* was that about?"

I had just found my mark. I was hired to *kill* Ding-Dong, but was quickly falling for him.

Tony and his *bullshit* had made my head spin.

"Please, Tony! I'm at work. We'll *talk* about this when I get home. Okay?" Tony shook his head and left the store without looking back.

Three hours later, Ding-Dong came back to the store. I *shivered* at the sight of him! The way Rippa talked about him—I thought Ding-Dong would've been a crude looking guy. Come to find out, he was the epitome of male beauty!

When Ding-Dong walked into the store, I was busy with a customer, but still managed to make eye contact. He then took a seat on one of the benches outside of the store. As I helped the customer, I'd admired Ding-Dong through the corner of my eye.

He'd changed his clothes and let his hair out. Ding-Dong's hair flowed down to the middle of his back in jet-black curls, being held back from his face with a *Rocawear* head band. Ding-Dong also was the same complexion as Tony, but his face seemed so much clearer.

155

When I finished with the customer, I'd sat right next to Ding-Dong on the bench. I whispered in his ear: "What are you doing here?" I immediately wished that I hadn't sat so close to Ding-Dong.

My palms started to sweat...

His *Platinum Egoist* cologne entranced me, and I lost a-l-l objectivity.

FUCK RIPPA!

I was not going to, in any way, shape, form or fashion, hurt Shawn a.k.a. Ding-Dong!

I *fucked* around and fell in love at first sight!

"I told you I'd be back. I'ma *MAN* of my word." As he spoke, I stared at Ding-Dong's perfectly white teeth, and noticed that he had a small earring in his left nostril.

"I'm glad to see that, but why?" I casually replied.

Ding-Dong shook his head and clamped both hands together in his lap.

"Mi nah really know. Earlier, when I left an' tell my boys dem wh'appen, dem jus' a laugh at mi! Dem say: 'Ding-Dong, ya mean fi say ya tell her husband ya a go *kill* him, an' ya barely know her?' Mi say, 'It nah matter. Mi *feel* like mi know her; understand? It's someting about her beauty dat have mi like damn, mi need her inna mi life.'"

I *couldn't* believe my ears!

"So *dat's* why mi a come back! Mi understand ya 'ave a likkle toy-friend, but mi wanna know ya still."

"Sticks" interrupted our vibe.

"Kai, don't be *acting* like you're not on the clock. Tell Romeo he gotta go! NOW!" "Sticks" then strutted off, nearly breaking her hips in an attempt to add a switch to her walk.

"Why you hatin', ma?" Ding-Dong replied.

"Sticks" turned around and got in his face: "Excuse me?"

"Why you hatin'? Ya was ready to gimme *ya* number, now, you wanna act all disrespectful? Wasn't you jus' inna di back of di store wit' some bwoy? A wha'? Ya nah workin' an' wanna *come* 'round an' tell people wha' to do?" Ding-Dong sucked his teeth. "Ya too *fuckin'* red eye! Learn fi cool."

Once again, Ding-Dong had put "Sticks" in her place.

I was pleased!

Rippa had hired me to *kill* this man, and there Ding-Dong was, defending me and trying to steal me away from Tony!

My life *couldn't* have gotten any crazier at that point!

"Ding-Dong, listen, we're about to close soon, so I'm going to need you to head out." He began to look sad.

"Dat's cool. 'Cept, I have one problem."

"What's that?"

"Mi nah drive out here—mi nah have a way of getting back home."

"I see. Can't you call one of your friends to come and get you?"

"I was kinda hopin' ya would drive mi back to my grandmotha house."

"Dang, Shawn! I *really* don't know you to have you *sitting* in my car like that. Besides, I have to head home to you know who after work."

Ding-Dong sucked his teeth again.

"Kai, ya nah heartless. Ya nah gonna leave mi here when mi dunno my way 'round."

"Alright...but you're going to have to wait like an hour or so."

"Mi would wait an eternity, ma-ma!"

He did just that.

Ding-Dong sat on the bench reading magazines, as I continued working.

* * * * *

I thought it would be a quick, little trip dropping off Ding-Dong.

I was wrong.

When I pulled in front of his grandmother's house in Cambria Heights, Ding-dong had invited me in.

"Come. Let me introduce you to Nana."

I gazed up at the house that looked like it belonged back in Florida. It was yellow with huge bay windows. The roof had red clay tiles, and the house was four-stories high, including the attic.

As soon as I saw Ding-Dong's grandmother my mouth dropped! His grandmother looked Chinese. I extended my hand graciously, "Nice to meet you," I said quietly.

She gave me a warm smile as she pushed my hand away.

"Now, any friend of Shawn is family. Come here, girl." She embraced me tightly.

157

Ding-Dong smirked.

"Now, Nana, that's enough. I don't want you to scare her away."

I thought to myself, *Scare? Nah, babes, I ain't going anywhere!*

That night, I enjoyed a quiet dinner with Ding-Dong and Nana.

How sweet!

romeo must die

Three weeks had pleasantly gone by, and I fell hard for Ding-Dong. He made it his business that I didn't want for anything. I ended up staying with him and Nana, having my every whim catered to.

I'd thought that I found Paradise!

I still ignored AJ while Tony and I were strictly on business terms. I managed to hook Tony up with Ding-Dong on a heroin connection.

That suited me just fine.

I had enough of New York and all of its bullshit!

I decided to leave for good. I figured that moving to Florida with Ding-Dong would do me good. Besides, I'd still have one hand in New York, in case I ever wanted to come back.

In a matter of months, I would have been inching towards the billionaire mark.

Well, at least, that was the plan.

Ding-Dong fell fast, and I was going to make the best out of the turn of events; even if it *killed* me.

Before my move to Florida could happen, I knew that I had to first pacify Rippa. I could never be with Rippa like I could be with Ding-Dong. Rippa would just *have* to understand!

Turns out, he refused to understand.

I managed to keep Ding-Dong in New York while I flew down to Florida. I left a message for Rippa saying that I was coming down, but he never called me back.

I decided to go anyway.

I returned to his breath-taking driveway around 5 AM one Sunday morning, and my nerves were shot. My fingers trembled as I pushed the intercom button. Uncertainty made my voice crack as I spoke into it. The same woman with the accent replied and the doors slid open.

Déjà vu.

I walked in slowly with weak legs, as my stomach turned wildly. I was beyond nervous and didn't know why.

No, I knew *exactly* why!

I tried to let the music that was playing in the background soothe me, as I continued into Rippa's house, and had stopped short.

I didn't make it pass the foyer.

Much to my surprise, and discomfort, Rippa sat there on one of the sofas while fifteen other men surrounded him. Apparently, they were waiting for me. I watched Rippa guzzle down half a bottle of rum before I got myself together to address him.

He cut me off as my lips parted.

"Why him nah dead yet, eh?"

I exhaled quietly.

"Dead?" I half-said, half-asked.

"Kai, don't come 'round an' *fuck* wit' me, ya hear?" One of the dudes from his entourage aimed an Uzi at me. "Mi say, why him nah dead yet?"

I couldn't talk fast enough for him. Rippa then jumped to his feet and headed straight towards me; still holding the bottle of rum.

My body froze...

Inches away from my face he stood, staring at me while I searched for my voice. I started to blackout, but the bottle of rum crashing to the floor stirred me back to my senses.

A wicked flame burst inside of me, and I found the strength to speak to Rippa.

"Dead? Why isn't he dead? You wouldn't be talking about Ding-Dong, would you?" My voice was still shaky, even though I tried to sound confident.

Rippa looked me dead in my eyes.

"Eh, eh, ya know *who* mi a talk 'bout! A wha' type of game ya play?"

I shook my head gently.

"Rippa, I'm not playing any types of games. You know, Ding-Dong doesn't have to die, in order for you to take over."

Rippa then turned away from me, as he threw his arms in the air.

"Wha' ya mean? Him nah haffi dead? Eh? Dat was di plan or ya forget?"

"Nah, I ain't forget. I just came up with a better plan."

Rippa turned around to the man that was still aiming the Uzi at me.

"See, Murdah, mi a tell ya from when ya tell mi say she an' 'im hook up; she a go fall in love an' fuck up everyting!"

Murdah never took his eyes off of me.

"So wha'? Mi a go *kill* 'er right now, boss!"

My stomach turned when he'd said that. Rippa laughed.

"Nah, man, let we hear wha' she haffi say first."

Feeling like the "Grim Reaper" was near, I hardened up.

"Look, *fuck* all of this bullshit, Rippa! I ain't scared of you or that *fucking Shabba Ranks* looking dude!"

The room became silent.

"Ding-Dong and Tony are business partners now. Ding-Dong is going to start supplying Tony and his father with heroin. You can have his piece of Florida when Ding-Dong is ready to move shop up North. Everybody gets what they want!"

Rippa was shocked! He quietly sat back on the sofa and lit a blunt. He took several pulls before responding.

"Nah, man. *Everybody* nah get wha' dem want! Ya see, ya a go back to Tony and tell him say I say, mi want fi supply di heroin. Mi and him a go run New York, Florida an' every *blood clot ting* in between! Ya hear? Tell Ding-Dong to go back a Trinidad. An' ya? Ya can disappear. Mi *nah* need you…but, mi want mi refund wit' fifty percent interest pon top of it!"

My phone started to ring. It was Ding-Dong. I quickly answered: "Hi honey."

"When are you coming back?" his voice seemed tense and hoarse.

I glanced out the windows and found strength in the rising sun.

"I'm almost finished working things out here. I should be back in New York later on this afternoon."

"Alright. Lata." *Click!*

I stared at Rippa.

"Look, at the end of the day, I make things happen, understand? Tony stays successful because of me. Ding-Dong is already more successful then you and Tony put together! That means more money for me. You, my friend, will just have to hold your position and be *thankful* that Ding-Dong isn't a killer like you! I'll bring your money with me on my next visit."

Rippa smirked.

"Alright, mami, we a go see 'bout dis an' see who a go *make* di most money. I thought ya were heartless, but ya not. Let mi find Ding-Dong come back a Florida an' 'im a go dead! Romeo mus' die, ya understand? ROMEO MUS' *FUCKING* DIE! Left outta mi house before mi a go make ya turn duppy!"

I turned away and *quickly* walked out of Rippa's house!

I *refused* to let it go!

I stood to make *too* much money off of Ding-Dong alone! FUCK THAT!

RIPPA WOULD JUST *HAVE* TO DIE!

* * * * *

When I arrived at back at *JFK Airport,* Ding-Dong and his goons were there to pick me up. As soon as he saw me, Ding-Dong's eyes lit up.

"Hey little mama, how was ya trip?"

I'd smiled cheerfully, hiding the fear that Rippa placed in my heart.

"It was great, baby. There are still some issues that need to be sorted out, but everything will work out for the best in the end."

He then smiled at me and helped me get into one of the *Lexus* jeeps. Ding-Dong sat down next to me and told his driver to go to the spot, as he reached for his ringing cell phone.

"Hey Chyna, mi be there in like fifteen to twenty minutes..."

My heart sank...

"...Who? Kai? Nah, she won't be around 'til lata on tonight..." Ding-Dong then rubbed my knee which had started shaking. "...Girl, stop worrying 'bout all of that. Mi be there...Soon come...Okay...Alright...One."

I pulled away from him.

"What the *fuck* is going on?" I whispered as soon as he clicked the phone shut.

"While ya were away, mi did some research of my own. Tony is one cool dude and mi like how ya'll have *everyting* situated out here. There's only one problem though."

"What?"

"Dis nigga right 'erre." Ding-Dong pulled out a picture of Rico. My left eye started to twitch! "Yeah, dis dude right here is *mad* trifling. Jus like dat *bitch,* Chyna."

162

"Oh word, how do you know this?"

"Well, it ain't take *too* long to find out dat Chyna was his girl, so mi went up to ya job, first *ting* dis morning, right."

"Uh-huh."

"And I saw her at the register. I asked for you. You know what she said? She was like, 'Why are you *fucking* with a loser like her?' I was like ah man. This *bitch* is crazy. So I got the number and hooked up a little get-together."

"Oh word?" I couldn't believe my ears.

"Yep." That was the last thing Ding-Dong had said as we rode up to Far Rockaway.

Before I knew it, we were in front of Rico's house.

My nerves started to get the best of me again!

I hadn't been on the Rock since Rico put me into a coma. To be in front of his house, on Rico's turf, made me very uneasy. Ding-Dong didn't notice. I watched as he called "Sticks" back.

"Come out front."

I couldn't hear her reply. Within seconds, "Sticks" was at the front door. I guess Rico wasn't home at the time.

"Just play along and everything will be cool." Ding-Dong acted as if everything was normal. Before "Sticks" walked out of the front door of Rico's house, he was already out of the *Lexus,* leaving me behind.

I WAS FURIOUS!

Within minutes, Ding-Dong hopped into the jeep that was in front of us with "Sticks".

My blood started to boil!

He drove off, and the rest of the jeeps followed behind him. I was full of questions but, I wasn't about to ask one of his cronies what was going on. At that point, I didn't know *what* to think.

Minutes later, we ended up on the Belt Parkway heading towards Coney Island. Just as my nerves settled a little bit, I noticed that the jeep Ding-Dong was driving made a left, while the jeep I was in and another one, made a right when we got off of the parkway.

I wanted to scream, but I didn't!

I continued playing along, knowing that eventually everything would become clear to me.

I closed my eyes and waited. It seemed like forever before the jeep's engine was turned off. The driver finally spoke: "Yo, Kai, wake up, sweetie. You gotta see this."

We had parked near the boardwalk, and I could see a couple in the distance. The driver handed me a pair of binoculars. It was Ding-Dong and "Sticks", chatting like they've been the greatest of lovers.

At that moment, I wished I had *killed* Ding-Dong like Rippa hired me to do! Mania evoked delusions, and I thought that I saw Rippa laughing at me.

I REFUSED TO BE MADE A FOOL!

The sound of my phone ringing snapped me out of my delirium. Rippa was calling.

"WHAT?" I hissed into the phone. Rippa was unfazed.

"Wh'appen, mami? Everyting criss?"

I cursed to myself.

"No, things are *fucked* up! What do you want?"

Rippa started to laugh.

"My, my, business mus' be tough inna di' city, eh? Mi nah trouble ya, mi jus' wanna apologize fi mi behavior earlier, dat's all. Mi must've smoked some badda weed."

I then reached to my side, searching for comfort in "Khara". She wasn't there. I forgot that I left "her" home.

I tried to calm down.

I started to say Rippa's name but I stopped short, remembering I was still with Ding-Dong's driver.

"Um, listen, if it's about the money, like I *said,* the next time that I'm down in Florida, I will return it. As a matter of fact, I'll give you double with the fifty percent, if you leave me the *hell* alone!" I startled the driver when I screamed.

Rippa remained silent at the other end of the phone. I got myself together, and was just about to snap my phone shut when, he finally spoke.

"Tsk, Kai, mi nah go *neva* leave ya alone; period! Is *you* who made *mi* who I am, so it's *only* right dat I honor ya by making ya mine foreva! Ding-Dong, 'im soon dead. Dat mi a *promise* ya! Tony, mi nah go deal wit' him. Kai, we *soon* be together! Next time ya come down here, mi a go bring ya back a yard 'an ya can have mi baby. I *love* ya, mami." Then Rippa hung up.

Ding-Dong was no longer important to me at that time. Rippa was!

Whatever game Rippa was playing with me, I didn't want *any* parts of! I was beginning to realize that I was in over my head by even talking to the man, let alone setting up to killing Ding-Dong.

Dazed and confused, I looked into the rear view mirror and caught the driver staring back at me. It was more like he was staring through me; like he heard every single word of my conversation. I held the stare, trying to protect my presumed innocence.

When the intensity became too much to deal with, I looked down at the binoculars. I turned them to the direction that Ding-Dong and "Sticks" were in and looked through them. I then rubbed my eyes to make sure they weren't deceiving me.

I couldn't *believe* that "Sticks" was sucking Ding-Dong's dick like it was her last meal, while he stood leaning up against a support beam underneath the boardwalk.

I hopped out the jeep and emptied the contents of my stomach onto the ground. The driver came out behind me. I guess he thought I was going to make a run for it and break up "Sticks'" groove. I looked at the driver sternly through bloodshot eyes.

Roughly wiping the vomit from my mouth with the sleeve of my shirt I turned to him: "WHAT THE *FUCK* DO YOU WANT?!" I guess that surprised the driver, because he then threw up his arms and shook his head before getting back into the jeep. Moments later, I followed.

I picked up the binoculars again and looked through them. I could see "Sticks" getting up as Ding-Dong rolled a condom off of his limp dick. At least the boy was *smart* enough to USE SOME PROTECTION! I then cringed, as they started heading towards where I was parked.

Ding-Dong had stopped short, and my phone started ringing. It was Ding-Dong.

"Yo," was all I could manage.

"What up, my nigga? Everything cool with you?"

I couldn't take it anymore...

I was physically weak and mentally exhausted.

I looked to the driver and he gestured with his hands for me to continue.

"Nah, everything *ain't* cool *motherfucker!*" I spat into the phone.

"That's good to hear. Listen, Blaze and Coolie went 'round da block so mi a go take ya whip, cool?"

"Whatever, nigga!" I was totally clueless until the driver told me to come on. As Shawn and "Sticks" approached the jeep, the driver and I dipped out the other side.

Side-stepping my vomit, he grabbed me by my waist and told me to crouch down, as we tip-toed to the jeep that was parked behind us. Ding-Dong took off and, once again, we followed behind.

new kid on the block

We drove in silence all the way back to Queens. I was disgusted with Ding-Dong and his cronies. Even after he'd dropped "Sticks" off on Jamaica Avenue and sat inside the jeep that I was in, Ding-Dong still hadn't said anything. The silence was broken when we pulled up in front of a quaint-looking home on Ridgefield Avenue.

Ding-Dong turned to me and smiled.

"It's our first, let's go inside." I followed him that far, so I continued to go along with no questions asked. On the outside it seemed like a perfect family home but, as *soon* as I entered the house and picked up that familiar scent, I *knew* that it wasn't.

It was a trap house.

"How many?" was all I asked.

Ding-Dong turned to me.

"Just a few. Tony said I could have some here-and-there as pocket money and shit. But pretty soon houses like this will deal strictly wit' the heroin. We get our first big shipment by the end of the week."

"Our?" I asked puzzled.

"Yeah, oh you thought I was bullshitting? I told you, I'ma *MAN* of my word! I said it's gonna be about us, so it's about us— running the *entire* eastern seaboard, baby."

I was still fuming off of the incident that had happened earlier with "Sticks", but I kept silent. As *soon* as we got to the back of the house, fiends started knocking! When I saw who the first customer was, I smiled like a kid in a candy store!

"Aye, yo, papi, lemme get this much worth of sugar."

"Lil' Magic" gave one of Ding-Dong's boys a one-hundred dollar bill, who in turn, handed her a small bag of cocaine.

Ding-Dong turned to me.

"She's my best fiend, yo."

Seeing "Lil' Magic" still addicted made me smile, but seeing her also reminded me of the last time I saw AJ.

I missed him…

Sadness started to steal me away from the moment.

I'd begun to wonder what would have happened if I'd just chilled and didn't go to Florida like AJ asked. I then made a mental note to call him to see how he was doing, as soon as I wasn't with Ding-Dong.

Needing an excuse to leave, I tried to start an argument: "Ding-Dong, what the *fuck* was that earlier?" He then nodded his head and walked over to where I was standing.

"It's about time, girl. For a minute there, I thought you were emotionless." He pulled me into a nearby room, closing the door behind us before he continued. "Look, Chyna could be you if she wasn't so naïve and a coke head. She has that *wild* ambition, just like you, but she don't know how to do this *shit* respectfully!

"Chyna knows me as 'Ding-Dong' a.k.a. her new boss. Gimme a month before *Rico* and his little clan are history! She let me come to the middle of Rico's hood, in front of his house to pick her up. She's a *bitch* that can't be trusted!"

My eyes widened in delight when I heard that.

Too bad Ding-Dong's plans were only a dream.

* * * * *

About a month went by before we got into any trouble. Tony had given Ding-Dong a legit apartment in Rochdale Village, and business was booming for everybody. Rico caught wind of this and wasn't too happy.

Ding-Dong and I were just about to pull out of the drive-thru of *Popeye's Chicken,* when we were surrounded by black *Benzes.*

I knew it was Rico and his boys.

Ding-Dong remained calm as Rico walked up to the jeep.

"Yo, my nigga, you that *motherfucker* they call 'Ding-Dong'?"

I quickly decided to give Ding-Dong a show of my own. I leaned over his lap and pressed the button for the window to roll down. Ding-Dong got nervous. "Wha' di *fuck* ah ya doing?" I put a finger to his lip and winked.

Rico's eyes bulged when he then saw me sitting in Ding-Dong's lap.

"Oh my bad, Kai. My bad, yo." Rico started walking away but stopped abruptly. "You really intend on continuing with this *bullshit,* huh? It's *fucked* up, Kai, but don't worry, I got ya *fucking*

168

card. Sorry about New Year's, yo." He then practically ran to his car and drove off.

Ding-Dong looked confused: "Wha' da *fuck* was dat 'bout?" I smirked.

"Loose ends, baby, that's all." My phone then started to ring. It was Tony. I missed him *so* much... "Yo," I sounded cold and distant. I couldn't believe that the hood alerted Tony so quickly. *Damn is he having niggas watch me!*

Tony's voice was full of concern, "Yo, you alright, baby." My heart ached!

"Yes, Mr. Cartagena, everything is okay." Tony still sounded loving.

"Why Rico roll up on ya like that? Ya'll need to watch him." Tony then took a deep breath. "Ma, things ain't *gotta* be this way you know. I don't know how you hooked up with that dude, Ding-Dong, don't get shit twisted though, me and pops do appreciate the connect, but damn, ma. I couldn't live with myself if anything happened to you."

Ding-Dong kept his eyes fixed on me, so I rushed Tony off of the phone.

"Yes, Mr. Cartagena, I understand. If anything changes I will keep you informed." I snapped my phone shut. "Ding-Dong, you gotta lay low for a minute." He looked perplexed.

"Da *fuck* for? So dat little *two-bit* hustler cyan say dat he *punked* me? FUCK DAT! As a matter of fact, I am laying low up here to take a break from the Caribbean action. Ma, do you *realize* how much *fucking* money I have? I don't *need* to be out here doing this shit! I do it for the thrill, so don't *ask* me to back the *fuck* down! Tell your man to back the *fuck* down!"

I was pleased that Ding-Dong and I thought on the same level.

We weren't the ones to back down easily!

I knew I made the right choice!

Ding-Dong would just have to understand that right then, Rico was his biggest threat.

"Um, calm down, fool. You don't realize what just happened do you?" Ding-Dong then shrugged his shoulders.

"What? Punk-ass dude whose main bitch is on my payroll, rolled up on us and got shook when he realized who I was with? I knew you had clout up here, lil' mama."

I shook my head.

169

"No, stupid. You roll around with three other, exactly identical, *Lexus* jeeps. Why did he approach this one on this side? How did he know that you were *even* back here?"

"Damn," Ding-Dong whispered to himself, as he lowered his head. "It had to be Chyna."

I *sucked* my teeth in disgust!

"Boy, don't tell me you went so over and beyond reason to fuck her head up. So much so, that you had her back here with you?" He remained silent. "Oh word? This is Chyna's work? Okay, lemme handle that bitch."

menage-a-trois

It took me a couple of weeks before I could get "Sticks" where I wanted her. It was the dead of winter, and we were about to leave work when, I'd overheard "Sticks" yelling at Rico for not being able to come pick her up.

"Listen ma-ma—"

"Fuck off, Kai!"

She cut me off before I could even finish. I humbled myself and walked right up to "Sticks"—I whispered softly in her ear: "Just cool it. Ding-Dong will take care of you; you know this. Ain't no need for us to be enemies."

"Sticks'" body language changed when I came near her. I'd sold her, giving me an instant plan to *kill* "two birds" with one stone. I immediately sent a text message to Ding-Dong. I needed him to have "Lil' Magic" arrive with Blaze carrying at least a pound of coke, before picking up me and "Sticks".

Ding-Dong agreed.

After work, Blaze pulled up with "Lil' Magic" in the front seat.

A smiled quickly danced across my face.

Blaze immediately jumped out of the jeep.

"Yo, ma, I gotta do a run so take the truck; I'ma roll with Coolie."

That came unexpectedly. Blaze then handed me a *Victoria's Secret* gift bag, as I hopped into the driver's seat. "Lil' Magic" gasped when she saw me open the door for "Sticks".

"Hi ma-ma. Let me introduce you to my homegirl, Chyna. Chyna meet Maritza." "Sticks" just gazed at "Lil' Magic" from the back seat speechless—I didn't know what to make of the situation. I told Ding-Dong I'd take care of "Sticks", and I had to do it right then and there before I'd lost his trust.

The two girls still didn't say anything to each other or me. I had to break the tension.

"Ding-Dong just wanted his favorite girls to have a good time tonight." They looked at me silently. I then reached into the "gift bag" and found my lure. "Look at the wonderful gifts he's given us." "Lil' Magic" and "Sticks" simultaneously gasped when they saw the kilo of coke.

My plan was simple.

I would get them both to overdose...

I started to drive out of the parking lot without knowing where the hell to go. Blaze must've called Ding-Dong because, by the time I hit Sunrise Highway, Ding-Dong was calling me. "What's good?" I answered.

"Before ya fuck shit up, take dem bitches to dat house mi showed ya over in Dodge City."

"Cool, but I'm with my homegirls right now. I'll holla at you later."

Ding-Dong started to laugh.

"Take as much time as ya need, baby girl. Make daddy proud."

I smirked to myself and turned to "Lil' Magic".

"Yo, it's gonna be like this all night, and I'm fitting to get fucked up. Why don't we just leave the phones in the car?"

To my surprise, "Lil' Magic" and "Sticks" both agreed.

When we got to the co-ops that were on Laurelton Parkway, I found a spot to park, and had instructed the ladies to get out. I'd slipped on my leather gloves.

I then pretended to toss my phone under the seat while checking for "Khara" in my handbag. "Lil' Magic" and "Sticks" both were *too* excited about getting high to even notice!

As I walked up to the door, I prayed that we wouldn't have any problems. I turned the knob on the door and it opened. I looked around and saw Blaze and Coolie in the distance and figured that I was safe.

"Come on, ya'll." I then took off my jacket as we walked inside, but left my gloves on. I was too caught up in planning the scheme as I went along that, I didn't notice the tension between "Lil' Magic" and "Sticks". I'd escorted them upstairs and decided on one of the bedrooms for my little party.

The girls followed behind me like faithful dogs!

"I really have to go to the bathroom," "Lil' Magic" squealed.

"Me too," said "Sticks". Just knowing they were about to get high, gave them the urge to use the bathroom.

That bugged me out!

Ding-Dong had obviously gotten to the house before me, and already had known what I was up to. Our minds were in sync.

When I opened the door to the one of the bedrooms, there was *another* kilo of cocaine in the middle of the bed. "Sticks" and "Lil' Magic" had finished using the bathroom and quickly walked into the bedroom after me. Both girls looked at the bag, then at me.

"Now, now, ladies, we *must* pace ourselves. We don't want to OD, now do we?"

I took a minute to look around the room and everything seemed cool. There were two bottles of *Alize* and a bottle of *Hennessy* on a table near the headboard.

The *Hennessy* was for me.

"Lil' Magic" couldn't *wait* any longer: "Can we start, Kai, please?" That was the first time that she'd ever addressed me respectfully.

I tossed the other kilo on the bed: "Do you!" I then reached for the *Hennessy* and poured myself a cupful. I sipped slowly, as I watched "Lil' Magic" put some coke on a nearby table, and line it up with a blade before inhaling it through her nostrils. She and "Sticks" started taking turns.

After the first three hits, the two girls got loose. First it was "Lil' Magic": "Damn, it's *hot* in here." She then proceeded to strip down to her underwear.

"Sticks" followed: "You are *so* right, gurrrl. Kai, you not hot? It's *hot* like whew!" "Sticks" then stripped buck-naked.

I stopped sipping the *Hennessy!*

"Ya'll alright?" I asked, feeling like the tables were turning on me.

"Sticks" looked at me and licked her lips seductively.

"Take off your clothes, ma-ma. Ain't you hot?"

"WHAT THE *FUCK* FOR?" I yelled.

"Sticks" then squinted her eyes as if I'd hurt her feelings. "Lil' Magic" had come to her rescue.

"Awww baby, fuck her. Remember the senior trip, Chyna?"

Senior trip? I didn't think it was possible. I felt "Sticks'" vibe earlier and thought that she might be bi-curious, but seeing her so comfortable buck-naked in front of me and "Lil' Magic"

173

sealed the deal. I had to ask to make sure: "What happened on the senior trip, lil' mama?"

"Sticks" bit her lip as she stared at "Lil' Magic". There was tense silence between them before "Lil' Magic" answered.

"You wanna show her so Kai can join us and we could *really* get this party started?"

"Sticks" nodded her head yes, before taking another hit of coke.

"Only if you promise to *eat* me out…like you did when we was in the cabin by ourselves!"

My eyes bulged. My stomach lurched, and I wanted to head out of there, fast! I quickly gulped down the remaining *Hennessy* in my cup, and started drinking from the bottle! I couldn't *believe* what was happening in front of my eyes!

"Lil' Magic" took off her underwear and proceeded to kiss "Sticks".

I was in awe.

I *never* saw two girls go at it!

I had to stay…

"Lil' Magic" sensed my discomfort and had looked up at me while she cupped one of "Sticks'" breasts in her hand.

"Yeah, get *fucked* up, ma-ma. Like it or not, I'ma turn *you* out, too."

I already knew that I was in control, even if I was under the influence of the cognac. I drank from the bottle as "Lil' Magic" kissed all over "Sticks'" body. She then pleaded with "Lil' Magic" to eat her out, and she did just that!

I lost count of how many times I heard "Sticks" climax.

I started to turn away from their romp when, I saw "Lil' Magic" walking towards me.

"Where the *fuck* are you going?" I said slowly.

"Lil' Magic" bit her lip again and reached for her bag that was on the floor by my feet. She never took her eyes off of me, as "Lil' Magic" then reached into her bag; so I stared back at her.

"Mami, you're next," "Lil' Magic" replied.

I was about to snap at her when, I realized "Lil' Magic" was holding a strap on… I've heard of them things but, until that night, had never seen one.

"You always carry that *thing* around?" I asked.

"Lil' Magic" licked the tip of the fake penis slowly.

"For sure, baby girl. You never know when you gonna need—"

"Sticks" then interrupted her.

"Yeah, ma-ma, I need it right now!"

I was shocked and amazed.

I sat there and watched "Lil' Magic" pump in-and-out of "Sticks". "Sticks" enjoyed every *moment* of it!

* * * * *

By that time, I had *so* much money saved up, that I *didn't* know how much money I actually had. Tony was still giving me my weekly allowance, and I had Ding-Dong just *throwing* bags of money at me! It had gotten to a point where money was the *least* of our concerns.

One of them, however, was being *FUCKED* by another girl right in front of me, while another was waiting for Ding-Dong back in Florida.

FUCK THAT!

I figured if I could have Rico at bay, I could do the same to Rippa.

* * * * *

Warm hands moving up my thighs, stopped me in thoughts: "What ya'll doing?" I half whispered. The *Hennessy* started to affect me. "Lil' Magic" didn't hesitate.

"I told you, you're next, ma-ma."

I had to think fast!

"Whoa, whoa, whoa! I ain't *fucked* up just yet." I was.

"Lil' Magic" was insulted.

"You mean to say you just watched me do my thing, and you ain't turned on?"

I tried to keep the vibe nice.

"Nah, freak-bitch. I *ain't* turned on. But wanna know how you could turn me on?"

"Lil' Magic" then started sucking on the tip of my index finger.

"Tell me ma-ma. You know that you can have the *both* of us, right?"

175

"Lil' Magic" and "Sticks" had kneeled before me, sucking on my fingers. I'd instructed "Lil' Magic" to get on the bed and spread her legs.

"Chyna, baby, eat this shit off of her *pussy* and I'll take one piece of clothing off." I poured a small mound between "Lil' Magic's" legs and "Sticks" hungrily lapped every crystal up. When she was done, "Sticks" looked up at me. I took off my shirt and the two girls licked their lips.

"Maritza, same thing." "Sticks" held both of her legs wide open as I poured cocaine in between them. "Lil' Magic" then went to work, and before I knew it, I was standing there in my bra and panties.

I couldn't believe these girls still hadn't over dosed.

Ding-Dong had known what he was doing when he'd given me two bags. I emptied the remaining coke unto the bed and separated in into two piles.

"The first one to finish gets to *eat* me the fuck out!" I returned to my chair and sat with my legs spread wide opened.

The girls quickly went to work on their piles!

It wasn't much longer after that. "Sticks" was the first to go. She slumped over quietly. "Lil' Magic" went to her aid.

"Sleepytime? No, no, Sleepytime, we gonna turn her out...okay, you sleep now, have her tomorrow." "Lil' Magic's" speech was slurred. I then yelled at her, fearing that "Lil' Magic" might stop.

"FINISH SNORTING THAT SHIT UP SO YOU CAN *FUCK* THIS SHIT UP!" She nodded so quickly, I thought that "Lil' Magic" was going to snap her neck. Seconds later, she was convulsing on the floor.

"Sticks" looked pale. I tried checking for a pulse but, I didn't want to get my finger prints on her. I took off one of gloves and slid my index finger under her nose.

I felt no air.

The same rang true for "Lil' Magic". I reached into my bag and pulled out the tarot cards. I put my clothes back on and picked up the gift bag, the bottle of Hennessy and my cup before heading out the door.

My work there was done.

I slid out of Dodge City virtually unnoticed. I called Ding-Dong as soon as I hit the boulevard.

"Hey baby."

"How did everything go?" he asked sleepily.

"Oh, sorry to wake you baby. I'll be home soon."

* * * * *

I woke up early the next morning to see if I had made the news again. Ding-Dong was no where in sight. I turned on the television and there it was—

"Breaking News: Today in Laurelton, Queens, cops discovered two females dead from an apparent cocaine overdose. Going on a tip, investigators believe that the two victims, Chyna Smith, age twenty-four, and Maritza Santiago, age twenty-seven, were associates of Rico Santana; a notorious drug dealer from Far Rockaway, Queens.

"Authorities are currently seeking Mr. Santana. Evidence left at the crime scene links him to the murder of Tyrett—"

I quickly turned the news off when the cameras panned to the tarot cards laying on the floor where I had left them. I thought for a minute, *I killed three birds with one stone.*

Just as I started to get wrapped up in my thoughts, Ding-Dong walked in.

"You better *pray* that Dodge City ain't harboring a *snitch* that seen my *fucking Lexus* parked up there last night, you understand?" He quickly began packing his stuff into suitcases.

That wasn't part of my grand plan.

"What the *fuck* are you doing?" I yelled to Ding-Dong. He continued packing his stuff.

"I got a *fucking* plane to catch, ma. My uncle is coming to get me in his private jet soon. I gotta be at *Mac Arthur Airport* at three o'clock this afternoon."

I was confused.

"Ding-Dong, you just *can't* up and leave. It'll make you look suspect." Ding-Dong then shook his head.

"If a *snitch* shows his *fucking* face, I will be a suspect! Blaze already had the cars scrapped. I hope you ain't *leave* no fingerprints behind, because 'One Time' will have you, too!"

"My prints aren't on a thing," I whispered, as I realized how much I put in jeopardy with one hasty decision. Ding-Dong looked at me.

177

"Look, I'm goin' to *chill* out in the Keys for awhile. Come with me. *Fuck* that job at the mall! We chill out for awhile; then come back to New York when the smoke clears."

Ding-Dong was *all* I needed.

Anywhere he went, I wanted to go.

"Then let's just go. If anything, Tony could come down to see me if he needs to talk to us, right?"

Ding-Dong nodded in agreement. I didn't even bother to pack. Most of my valuable stuff was in Rosedale.

I called Shelly and told her to go see Tony. He'd have her come back to the apartment and take over the lease.

Shelly could just keep whatever I left behind.

* * * * *

Around 1:30 PM that afternoon, Ding-Dong decided that it was time to go to the airport. We headed downstairs to meet with Blaze and the rest of Shawn's cronies.

Everything was quiet up until that point.

As soon as we stepped out into the sun, Rico rolled up on us bearing arms. He headed straight towards me.

"Yo, I'ma need you to report to work by the end of the day. Now that Chyna ain't around, you're officially back on duty!"

Ding-Dong was about to say something, but I spoke first.

"*Fuck* off, Rico. I got things to do." I walked away trying to play off the fact that I'd helped his girlfriend overdose, a little more than twelve hours earlier.

Rico remained calm, as he pulled out his one-shot and aimed it directly at Ding-Dong.

"Bitch, don't start *shit* you can't finish! I underestimated you, but best believe when this shit is all over, you'll be *all* over my dick again; just like in the beginning."

Niccolo's entourage had rolled by in black *Expeditions,* and Rico quickly fled the scene.

I *cringed* as I watched him drive away.

Ding-Dong looked as if he was about to question what had happened, but then decided against it.

out in the street dem call it...

Ding-Dong and I arrived in Tampa, Florida sometime that night. His uncle was very cordial and the plane ride was smooth. I had totally forgotten about Rippa, until I reached Florida. The thought of him and how adamant Rippa was on killing Ding-Dong had sent chills through my body, as soon as I got off the plane.

Ding-Dong's mansion was visibly twice as big as Rippa's. It looked like a magnified version of his grandmother's house back in Queens; having a marble walkway on the outside.

On the inside, it was equipped with state-of-the-art security.

I knew I'd be safe there.

I hoped I'd be safe there.

That feeling died when we started hitting the club scene later on that week.

I wasn't sure that I was ready to be out in the open knowing that, at any moment, Rippa could just jump out of the bushes and *kill* Ding-Dong!

Rippa always made good on his promises.

* * * * *

After a couple of months, I'd begun to have the time of my life down in Florida! Nothing bad really happened, and Rippa became a distant memory.

Tony continued sending me money.

Things were going so great, I sent for Shelly to come for a day so we can catch up on some things.

I picked Shelly up from the airport in my brand-new drop-top *Chrysler Roadster,* and took her to a small café not too far from one of the local beaches. Once we got over the initial hellos and bullshit, I got *straight* to business!

"What's been happening in New York since we left?"

Shelly shook her head from side-to-side, "I don't know where to begin."

"Begin with that bitch, 'Lil' Magic' and 'Sticks' bullshit," I said nonchalantly.

179

"Oh, the cops never could link it back to Rico. As a matter of fact, that nigga, Rico was being held on some bullshit charges that he beat when that whole shit went down. Word on the street is that the same person who killed Ty is responsible for what happened to 'Lil' Magic' and 'Chyna'. I ain't like that *bitch* for real, but she ain't had to die like that."

For a second, I admired Shelly's compassion. Then I remembered how I got to where I was.

I GOT THERE BY NOT GIVING A FUCK!

"I guess now her and Ty found their happily ever after in Hell." I started to laugh, but Shelly didn't find any of it funny. She stared off in the distant for awhile.

"So, how are *you* doing, Miss Kai? What are you up to now? What? Stealing husbands and boyfriends? Pushing drugs? Teaching 'How To Run The City 101' or 'Are You A Murderer For Hire' courses?"

A wicked smile danced across my face. I lowered my voice. "Oh my, Miss Shelly. A murderer? Me?"

Anger then rose within Shelly.

"You *fucking* murderer, don't play that *shit* off! I knew you killed Ty—"

"Oh dear!" I cut her off.

Shelly's voice was quickly gaining the attention of the other patrons in the café. I had to quiet her. "Shelly, you are my best friend, my ace-boom. You, out of *all* people should know me better than that. And besides, I'm a girl, remember? When's the last time you heard of a girl actually running the show? Get real."

That managed to calm her down.

I'd called *1-800-CRIMESTOPPERS* after I dropped her off back at the airport. I'd always known that Shelly would *fuck* me over if I let her. Too bad for her, I had another gun just like "Khara", and tarot decks that were missing two cards from them in the apartment.

I told the cops that Shelly was behind the murders.

* * * * *

At that time of our lives, Ding-Dong had taken me to so many different spots in Florida, that I forgot the names of most of them. One night, he'd decided to take me to a Jamaican club in Miami that was supposed to poppin'. When we got there, people

180

greeted us like we were royalty. Ding-Dong and I were quickly escorted to the VIP area.

That's when my fairytale ended.

Ding-Dong and I were grooving in a corner when, Rippa's voice tore through my ears: "Wh'appen, pretty?" He then turned to Ding-Dong. "Wha' a gwan, star? Long time mi nah hear from, Ding-Dong!" They hugged, and I immediately felt like I was at a disadvantage.

Ding-Dong pulled Rippa to the side, and they exchanged words quietly. Rippa slid up to me and whispered in my ear: "Ah, so, ya *ah* di Empress, fi real, eh? Nice. Mi a go check ya a likkle lata." He turned to Ding-Dong again. "Easy, Mister Ding-Dong; respect!" and left. I immediately looked at Ding-Dong.

"What was that about?"

Ding-Dong then took a sip of his *Heineken.*

"Nah worries, jus' some loser. If mi could jus' get *rid* of dat nigga, Rippa, my life would be so much easier."

I took a sip of my *Apple Martini* to try to steady my stomach. Something wasn't right that night. Too bad I had to wait until we got all the way home for me to find what the problem was.

Ding-Dong must've felt it too because we didn't go to his mansion in Tampa. Instead, we ended up at another one of his houses that was also in Tampa. I didn't ask any questions. I just quietly followed his lead. Once we got inside of his other house. Ding-Dong relaxed a little.

"Ma, shit doesn't *feel* right out 'ere. First ting in di morning, we bouncing right back to New York. Tings should be cool by now."

I agreed.

He picked me up and took me into the bedroom. Gently laying me on the bed, Ding-Dong made all the promises in the world to me. I smiled, knowing that I had exactly what I wanted and more. I was good to go.

Ding-Dong then got down on both of his knees while holding my hands in his. He stared into my eyes, and it seemed like Ding-Dong was about to ask me to marry him but, I'll never know…

Just as his lips parted, Rippa's voice startled us.

"Aye bwoy. Di Rippa a come fi ya." Rippa looked at me, and I started to plea with my eyes. "An' look, ya have di Empress here, too. Hi ma-ma, mi a go turn ya boyfriend inna a duppy, cool?"

I had no idea what a *fucking* "duppy" was, but hearing shots rang out as I got sprayed with pieces of Ding-Dong's flesh, gave me a good idea.

I wanted to cry.

I *desperately* wanted to cry but, I couldn't. Just as the gunfire stopped, I started laughing hysterically again.

Rippa had a perplexed look on his face.

"A wha' di bumba clot ah' ya problem, eh? Laughing like some damn idiot?"

I tried to stop laughing but I couldn't. I stood up and walked towards Rippa.

"Listen, I *ain't* no idiot. It's just that, how am *I* supposed to get paid for killing Ding-Dong when you killed him?"

Rippa didn't get it.

Neither did I.

Someone Rippa was with cried out: "Ya should jus' kill her, too."

Rippa replied, "For wha'? Dis *bitch* long dead, ya know. She jus' a walk an' carry she casket behind her. She nah trouble nah one. Leave her. Let's go."

They left the beach house and I followed behind them. I didn't even flinch when I saw Blaze and Coolie dead in front of the house. Rippa then let me get into his car, bloodied and all.

When we arrived at Rippa's house, I walked straight in like I owned the place and headed to the shower that was near the pool. I let the water run over my skin, as shock began to take over my body.

I heard Rippa enter the bathroom and sit on the toilet. His phone had rung.

"Yo, B…eh heh…dat long finish…di girl…nah, man, nah man… she wasn't even deya…eh heh….nah man…don't even worry about di money ting…it a my pleasure…okay…one…no problem, Rico." *Click.*

I couldn't b-e-l-i-e-v-e what I had heard! I threw back the shower curtain and walked naked past Rippa like he wasn't there. I managed to find some clothes in a room nearby, and left the house once I was dressed.

Rippa never came after me.

I walked into the night without knowing where I was going. I stopped at the first pay phone that I found. I picked up change from the road as I walked, and had just enough for one phone call. I called AJ.

Ring, ring, ring, ring, ring.

His voicemail picked up: *"Hey, you've reached AJ. Leave a message at the tone." Beep!*
I spoke quickly, hoping and praying that he would get the message in time.
"AJ, listen, it's Kai. I-wanna-chill. I-wanna-come-home-and-go-mimi! Please, AJ-I'm-on-my-way-to-the-airport. Please-come-get-me! I have *nothing* left, please!" The operator indicated that I needed ten cents for the next three minutes. *Click!*
I started walking up the road again when, I caught a flashback of the "Jane Doe" that I caught Tony with. I remembered how I made her walk up-and-down Guy R. Brewer Boulevard buck-naked.
I felt her shame.
Just as I did, a gray *Infiniti* pulled up to me.
"Miss, are you lost?" I nodded. "Well, hop in."
Delirium made me careless and I didn't recognize the voice at first. When I got comfortable and turned to the driver, I quietly gasped. He had tears rolling down his face. The guy then cleared his throat.
"I know that I'm the last person that you expected to see. Shit... You're the last person that I expected to see. But, here we are. I came up here to surprise my cousin. I wanted to meet his new fiancé. I didn't know it was you until I saw you guys at the club earlier. I didn't see when ya'll left, so I went to my uncle's spot. When he said that Ding-Dong hadn't come home and wasn't answering his phone...I don't know. I just felt the need to rush over to the hideout spot and then—"
The guy stopped as the tears overwhelmed him. I didn't want him to continue but he did. "I came up here to surprise Ding-Dong, and you. I got to the hideout too late... You looked like a zombie walking out of the house, Kai. Why did they have to kill him like that? Why, Kai? Why?"
I reached out to the guy and let him cry in my arms. I tried to give comfort.

"Your cousin was the *best* man I have ever known. Sure he was a drug dealer, but he had a heart—a big one! Understand that I *honestly* loved Ding-Dong, and had no connection to what happened tonight."

He looked at me through bloodshot eyes.

"YOU'RE LYING! YOU SET HIM UP BECAUSE OF ME, DIDN'T YOU?"

I rubbed his back.

"No baby. No I didn't. I didn't even *know* that you guys were related, up until this very moment. If you had taken the time to get to *know* me, the *r-e-a-l* me, before the fame of the drug game, then you would know that I am *incapable* of hurting the people that I love. If I had known that Ding-Dong was your cousin, I would've made sure that *nothing* happened to him! I would've given my *life* for him!"

"You mean that?"

"Jordan, baby, I mean that from the bottom of my heart. Ding-Dong was my everything, and I'd give *ANYTHING* to have him back with me right now! Get yourself together, okay? You gotta stay here and make the funereal arrangements and shit. I can't talk to the police. You understand that, right?"

Jordan nodded his head.

"Good. Can you please drop me off at the airport? I gotta get back to New York as quickly as possible."

"Are you going to be alright, Kai?"

I took a deep breath.

"No…I'm not going to be alright… After this, I am *never* going to be alright. I just lost the only thing that ever mattered in my life."

* * * * *

Jordan dropped me off at the airport and took off before saying goodbye. I watched the sun come up from the waiting area. Flashbacks of Ding-Dong flooded my mind, as I searched for tears to cleanse me.

I was so hurt but, I still couldn't cry.

I sat there in the waiting area and nobody bothered me until the sun started to go down.

Two uniformed officers approached me: "Ma'am is everything alright?"

I wanted to *curse* the officers out so badly, but was afraid they were going to kick me out of the airport. I still hoped AJ would come for me. I turned the officers.

"Oh yes, everything is quite alright. I've just been here waiting for my friend, Arturo Jesus Piscone. He's supposed to be picking me up."

Pleased that I wasn't a threat to national security, they left me alone.

I dozed off for a little while and awoke to see AJ standing over me.

"Hi mamacita; you ready?"

I didn't answer.

AJ then took me by the hand, and we got on the first flight back to New York.

caribbean connection

I stayed with AJ for about a week. He didn't ask me any questions about Florida, and I didn't offer any information either. After my first few nights with him, AJ did tell me how Maritza didn't have a proper funeral, because her family was ashamed of her. The city ended up burying her in *Potter's Field* cemetery.

All it took was that first week for me to devise a plan to tie up my loose ends. I'd set things straight with Tony, pay Rico back and start life anew with AJ.

In a few months, I would be twenty-five years old. I had been ripping and roaring without a care for the past seven years.

I was just about done!

Some one *else* could run the city!

I wasn't built for the horrors that the game held secret...

* * * * *

I knew my greatest chance at getting at Rico was just before he left town to go on his Christmas trip. I had a cousin that worked at the airport who ran Rico's name through the computer on a daily basis to see where he was heading.

I'd take care of him somewhere in between, and send someone else on Rico's flight, so it'll look like he never came back from wherever Rico was going. When my cousin called back saying that he had bought a one-way ticket to the Dominican Republic, my plan shifted.

I figured that I'd meet Rico there and get him to cross the border into Haiti with me. I had a lot of family back in Haiti that I never met. However, I did meet one of my cut-throat uncles who lived in Petionville. I called him and told my uncle I was coming to visit, and to make all the necessary arrangements.

The entire island was under political unrest and I probably wouldn't be coming back home, but I took the chance anyway.

The only person that knew that I was in town was AJ. I borrowed the money from him for my trip to Haiti, and promised to pay him back as soon as I returned. I told AJ that I needed to get out of the country for awhile. I gave him the number of the *Coconut Villa Hotel* in Port-au-Prince, Haiti.

AJ begged me not to leave, but I was intent on going.

Rico was scheduled to be in the Dominican Republic on a Sunday afternoon, I arrived at my hotel the Saturday before. After I checked in, I called my crazy cousin, Junior and let him know to come get me.

When Junior came and got me, I had to assure hotel security that we were family. One of the hotel workers had spoken English, and told me wild stories of kidnappings and ransoms.

That *wasn't* my concern at that time!

It wasn't until I hopped into my cousin's jeep and started driving around that I realized that, the shit that went on back home was *nothing* compared to what I saw in the streets!

The beautiful Haiti my father used to show me in books, no longer existed. It was no longer "La Perle des Antilles" (The Pearl of the Caribbean).

It was more like the *disgrace* of the Caribbean!

There was a lot of fighting going on, and the faces of people looked desolate and hopeless.

This was where Rico belonged.

We got stopped several times along the way, and I saw Junior actually shoot some men that tried to carjack us before we reached his uncle's house in Jacmel; a town nestled on the South-East coast of Haiti.

When we got there, Junior immediately went over the plan with me. It was simple. As an expert fisherman, he'd learned how to extract poison from blowfish. Junior handed me a bottle of premium, five-star *Barbancourt* white rum. I looked at him puzzled.

"What's this for?"

Junior answered me in his broken English: "When he's finish half the bottle—no more problem."

That's all I needed to know.

Junior promised me that he would take me over to the Dominican Republic in his jeep. I'd have to get Rico to get inside the jeep, and come back with me to Haiti for everything to work out.

Early the next morning, Junior and I rode out to the Dominican Republic. The Dominican Republic was nothing like Haiti. The natives were dancing around and having fun.

I quickly found *Confresi Beach* in Puerto Plata. Rico was staying at the *Sun Village Beach Resort* there. I sat at one of the tables and prayed that he would show up.

He did.

I was just finishing a plate of codfish and steamed plantains when, I heard someone call my name. I turned around before answering: "Rico, is that you?"

He was so surprised to see me. Rico came and scooped me up in his arms.

"Dang, baby girl! I tried to get away from all the madness back in New York, and I found my little piece of Heaven right here. How long you've been out here?"

"Almost two months," I lied. "I just needed to get away from all the bullshit back home, so I hid out here. I got family out here so they've been taking real good care of me."

"Oh word?" Rico said with a devilish grin on his face. "You gonna let me take *good* care of you, ma-ma?"

I blushed.

"Sure. Why not? I've been dodging you all this while. It's about time, huh?"

Rico agreed.

"Damn right! It's about time that you came to your senses girl."

I then grabbed Rico by his waist.

"Hey, you wanna go and chill at my aunt's house across the border? Ain't nobody there to bother us while we make up for lost time."

Rico fell under my spell.

"Sure babe."

We went back to my cousin's jeep which was parked nearby, and I pretended not to know Junior.

"Bonjour monsieur." My cousin turned to us and smiled. I turned to Rico. "Bare with me, my Creole is a little off." I turned back to Junior: "Ou kapab mennen monsieur sa avec mwen address sa?" I handed Junior a piece of paper with the address of the abandoned house. He looked at it and nodded.

"Wi, madmoiselle. Chita." Junior then opened the door of the jeep for us. Rico and I sat down in the rear and enjoyed the view, as we headed towards Jacmel.

It was a long ride back to Haiti. The abandoned house was just off a deserted road. As we were getting out of the car, Junior reminded me that everything I needed would be in the house, and to not drink from the poisonous rum bottle. He said it in Creole so Rico was left clueless.

We entered the house and Rico began asking me questions: "What was that man saying when we was leaving the cab?"

I replied softly, "Beats me. He spoke too fast for me to understand."

Rico left that alone but had another question: "So, Kai, since we all alone, can we finish what we started a few years ago?"

I *didn't* need this to go on any longer than it needed to.

"Sure why not." I gently placed my bag, which held the rum, on the floor, and began kissing Rico passionately. He gave into me and followed me into a bedroom.

Rico then threw me onto the hard bed and began to tear off my clothes. I let him have his way and I gave in completely to Rico. My cousin had the entire parameter of the house surrounded, so I knew that I wouldn't be disturbed.

Rico had begun feasting on me like he had the first time, and I was returning to Heaven. Losing track of time as I climaxed, I yearned to have Rico enter me. I had forgotten about the rum for that moment.

He'd seen the lust in my eyes and pulled away from me. I feared that Rico would repeat what he did the first time, and tell me to put my clothes back on.

Rico didn't.

Instead, he tore off his shirt revealing several tattoos. One of them caught my eyes immediately. He had "Baby Boy" written in script, followed by a rose across his stomach.

Tony came to mind.

I also noticed that Rico physically resembled AJ, but with less muscle tone. I disregarded it as coincidence and lost myself in the moment.

He then slid on a condom before entering me missionary style. After a few gentle strokes, Rico stopped: "Turn over, Kai."

"Why?" I asked breathlessly.

"I'ma cum too quick."

"And?" I said with a bit of an attitude. I pulled my legs from around Rico's waist and threw them over his shoulder.

Rico moaned.

"Damn, Kai…this shit is *sweet*… oh my god, this shit is so fucking—"

"Oh yeah? Yeah, nigga, I thought my shit was too small for you?" I snapped back, as I'd gyrated my hips against his. Sweat was pouring from every inch of Rico's body.

"Nah ma-ma…shit…I was wrong…I was—"

The end.

I guessed that six, maybe seven minutes had gone by before Rico was done. He collapsed on top of me.

"Damn ma, I need a drink."

That snapped me back to my senses.

"There's a bottle of rum in my bag."

Rico had walked out of the room naked and returned with the bottle. He had already started drinking from it.

"Damn, this is some strong shit!"

I'd begun putting my clothes back on.

"Yeah, I know. That's why I only drink it to help me go to sleep."

"Why you putting your clothes back on? I am *s-s-so* far from being done wit' you." Rico's speech was slurred. I didn't bother to turn around towards him. I continued getting dressed.

"Look, Rico, you can *fuck* me later on. Right now, I want to head to the main—"

Boom!

Rico had fallen onto the bed. I shook him.

"Rico? …Rico? …Rico?"

No answer.

A great weight was lifted over my shoulder.

I watched him for a half hour more and Rico didn't move. I yelled out the window for my cousin. I gathered my things and was about to leave.

Junior soon walked in: "Ban sa." I reached for the machete that was hanging from his waist. I turned to Rico who was slumped over the bed.

"You little fucker! Payback is a *motherfucking* bitch! A BITCH NAMED KAI! This is for Tony." I clutched the machete with both hands over my head and used all my strength, as I swung it down to cut Rico's dick off!

I ended up just cutting the tip off.

"*FUCK!* I guess this'll do." I reached into my bag and put the tip into an empty *Ziploc* sandwich bag. Then, I put that bag into another *Ziploc* bag that had dry ice.

"This will keep you fresh until Tony sees you."

I didn't care that my fingerprints were all over Rico. By the time anybody realizes that he's missing, Rico would be unidentifiable.

family affair

Everything worked like clockwork. I was back in New York worry-free, on a chilly Tuesday afternoon. AJ had picked me up from the airport.

"Did you enjoy your trip?"

"Did I?" I responded. "Hell yeah; I'm good. I'm ready to settle down. I went out there and got my head right. I'm done with all the bullshit."

AJ tried to hide his smile.

"I really hope that you mean that, Kai. I couldn't stand another heartbreak, you know? A man like me shouldn't have to deal with all that bullshit."

"And you don't, sweetie. I'm here now. You've got my undivided attention. All that's left to do now is find our happily ever after, and life will be cool."

AJ's face turned red.

"Do me a favor Kai, don't start making me promises and sweet-talking me. If you're going to gain my trust, you're just going to have to do your part to make this relationship work."

I agreed.

* * * * *

The winter was slowly rolling through and things couldn't have been any better. I enrolled back in school and started seeing my family on a regular basis.

I even got my job back at the mall.

All was well until I got a mysterious call from a Florida number. I was in the middle of class so I couldn't answer it. Beads of sweat started to form on my forehead.

The only person I knew in Florida was Rippa!

Rippa couldn't *possibly* have my new cell phone number because it was in AJ's name. I was just about to dismiss the thought when, my phone alerted me to a new voicemail.

Shortly after, my phone rang again. That time it was AJ. I'd sent him to voicemail. He called back. I'd sent AJ to voicemail again. Seconds later, he called back again. I'd sent AJ to voicemail while I silently excused myself from the class.

By the time I reached the hallway, my phone alerted me that I had seven new messages. I called my mailbox. It played the newest message first:

"*New message. Today at 10:53 AM: Babe, listen, it's me. I have an urgent family emergency. I know you're in class, but I'm going to be in front of your school before 11:15. Be outside. Next, new message—*" Click!

I hung up the phone and darted down the stairs to wait for AJ in the main lobby. As soon as I saw his white, *Nissan X-terra* pull up to the curb, I ran outside.

"Babe, what happened?" I asked while trying to catch my breath. AJ had tears forming down his face.

"They never found my baby brother," was all AJ said.

I didn't get it.

I then realized we were heading in the direction of Tony's house, so I didn't ask any more questions.

When we pulled up to Tony's block, Niccolo was already there. I could tell by all of the black cars and their tell-tell vanity plates.

AJ parked his jeep and went into Tony's house. I'd followed behind not knowing what to expect. Just as we entered Tony's home, I instantly remembered all the good times me and Tony shared together.

I looked up and there Tony stood, staring at me with his eyes full of regret. He shook hands with AJ before hugging me.

"Damn, ma, it's been a minute. I'm glad you're alright. Come here let me take a good look at you. Damn, girl." Tony looked to AJ as his voice cracked. "Take good care of her, bro."

AJ had simply nodded.

I saw Niccolo standing in the distance. I went over to hug him. Niccolo saw me coming and was about to walk away. He'd bowed his head.

"Kai, you're gonna need to take a seat, sweetheart. I'm so sorry; really, I am." He took me by the hand and sat me next to him on the sofa.

My hands started to shake.

Niccolo put his hands over mine to steady them. I looked at him.

"Mr. Cartagena, please. Tell me what's going on." Niccolo rubbed his eyes.

"Now that we're all here, we can discuss the matter at hand. As you all know, Antonio has had some problems on this side of town. All my life..." Niccolo stopped short in his address, as tears streamed down his face.

I'd squeezed Niccolo's hands before gently wiping away the tears from his cheeks. He kissed my fingertips.

"...All my life, I tried to keep the boys happy. Not for their mother, *fuck* that *bitch*—I curse on her grave, but for their own good. This hurts me so deeply because I feel that if I had been more honest, then the boys would have gotten along better."

I couldn't figure out *what* was going on! I searched Tony's eyes for answers while Niccolo continued.

"I hate to have to be the bearer of bad news... But after a month-and-a-half, they still have been unable to find your brother. Antonio, Arturo... I'm so sorry."

My blood boiled so quickly, that it began to ooze out my nostrils. I began to hyperventilate.

"Tony...what the *fuck*...is going on? You and AJ are brothers? Huh?"

Niccolo pleaded with me.

"Kai, please calm down before you end up in the hospital."

I *couldn't* calm down.

Tony and AJ had yet to explain to me what was going on.

"Tony, you *better* explain this *shit* to me, right now!" I'd reached for "Khara" and everybody jumped.

Dang!

I had forgotten that I left "her" at home again.

Tony then grabbed AJ, and they stood before me. AJ spoke softly, "I'm sorry, Kai. Being that I'm the oldest, I should have told you from day one. I tried to tell you to stay away from him, and I had no idea that you were with Tony; until that day you got into that argument with Maritza."

The room had begun to spin, as I'd taken in the information. AJ looked at Niccolo before continuing.

"Everybody thought that I was the son of Niccolo's half brother, Arthur. Arthur Piscone. I'm actually Niccolo's first son. Years later, Niccolo fell in love with Donna Blake, which is

Tony's mom; and they started a family. Arthur died over a dice game and Niccolo took me in."

AJ's voice began to get weak. Niccolo continued for him.

"Donna and I had planned to raise a big family. She was a very lovely lady in the beginning. After Tony was born, people began saying that the two boys looked like each other. My father *hated* the fact that I was with a colored woman, but still allowed me to work in his family business.

"DNA testing had just become available so I secretly had AJ tested. I found out he was mine, but never told anyone else. AJ didn't find out the results until he'd turned thirty.

"Anyway, to make a long story short, Donna fucked up everything by having a child for this man named, Chico Santana. He was strung out on heroin, but Donna insisted that she loved Chico. I put Donna up in a beautiful home in Garden City, Long Island, while she raised Tony and the baby she had for Chico. AJ went to live with my sister." Niccolo then let out a long sigh. "Kai, you understand that this stays here, never to be repeated again."

My nose had stopped bleeding.

I'd let out a nervous laugh.

"You don't have to worry about me—" It had just dawned on me. "Did you say that your ex-wife got involved with a man named, Chico Santana?"

The room remained silent.

"RICO SANTANA IS THE BABY BROTHER THAT'S MISSING?"

I was *s-c-r-e-a-m-i-n-g* at the top of my lungs!

I started hitting AJ with all of my strength, while he stood there letting me! Tony had to come and get me off of AJ.

My nose bled again.

"So, you knew, huh? Did Tony tell you how Rico put me into a coma, huh? He beat me *fucking* senseless! Tony tell you how Rico *threatened* to *kill* him every time he saw me by myself? And did you know that Rico hired somebody in Florida to *kill* Ding-Dong? My fiancé is *DEAD* because of him!"

Everyone in the room gasped.

"Yeah, his *fucking* name is Rippa! Yeah, Rippa tried to *kill* me, too. Now I wish that he *fucking* did. I *fucking* hate you!" I snapped. I turned to walk out of the house when, Niccolo pulled me back to sit down.

"I'm so sorry, Kai," was all he could say. The room remained quiet. "Listen, Rico was last seen in the Dominican Republic. From there, no one knows."

AJ turned to me.

"Ain't that right next to Haiti?"

I responded: "Yeah, and?" All eyes were on me. "Check my *fucking* itinerary! I was in Port-au-Prince the whole *fucking* time...never even left the hotel!"

They lied to me.

I lied to them.

Just then, the Florida number appeared again on my phone. Again, I sent it to voicemail. I then got up and went to the upstairs bathroom to wash my face. Tony followed behind me.

"I'm sorry, ma. You know my father, he's a made man. He lives by certain codes. One of them is silence. This was a big family secret." I remained quiet as Tony continued. "Ma, I got this in the mail not too long ago. You know anything about it?"

I quickly averted my eyes away from the *Ziploc* sandwich bag and remained silent.

I had nothing to say...

I felt embarrassed and ashamed...

At one point, I'd loved every single one of the brothers, even Rico.

I slept with all three of them.

When Tony and I came back downstairs, everyone in attendance was still discussing Rico's disappearance. I sat down next to Niccolo and vowed to follow my own "code of silence".

* * * * *

When I got back to AJ's house, I still remained quiet. He couldn't take it anymore.

"Damn, mamacita, are you going to say anything?"

I looked at AJ and went upstairs. I ran myself a bubble bath in an attempt to wash away the events of the day, but it wasn't any help.

Just before going to bed, my phone rang. It was Tony. I flipped it open and put it to my ear. Tony spoke: "Kai? I know you must've picked up the phone. Listen, just listen. I love you and I *never* meant to hurt you like this. I'm sorry. Just forgive me, okay? I still love—" *Click!*

I hung up the phone on Tony, and turned it off for the rest of the night.

baby mama

Two weeks went by before I'd begun to speak to AJ again. I blamed myself for being so blind. How could I miss the fact that both he and Tony had the same middle name?

Eventually, I'd forgiven AJ, but I held on to my secrets. AJ was so happy when I'd forgiven him.

During the two weeks that I didn't speak to AJ, he still managed to pamper and spoil me. As soon as we were on speaking terms again, AJ and I started making love every chance we got.

It wasn't long before I missed my first period...

It was two months after the confessions session at Tony's house and during finals.

I owned it up to stress.

Another month went by and still no visit from "Aunt Flow". People at my job started asking me what I was using to make my face glow.

I still didn't put two-and-two together!

I decided to go see a doctor to make sure that it was stress and nothing more. My plans got cancelled as soon as I pulled in front of my doctor's office. I was trying to parallel park when, I heard somebody calling my name.

The familiar voice sent *chills* through my body.

I pretended not to hear to him.

He walked straight up to my car: "Wh'appen, pretty?" I couldn't *believe* that Rippa was standing right in front my very eyes! He continued, "Every time I try callin' ya, ya neva answer. So, mi figure mi give ya a surprise. Surprise, mami."

I still couldn't move.

"Come, let we go *sit* down an' talk fi a likkle while."

Fear persuaded me to park my car and hop into Rippa's *Bentley*.

One minute, we were heading in the direction of Jamaica Avenue. The next, were driving through the back streets of St. Albans. My voice finally returned, "Rippa, where are we going?"

Rippa had a strange look in his eyes.

"To my house." I became scared.

"Nah, man, chill. Take me back to my car."

Rippa shook his head and continued speeding. We stopped in front of a house that was situated at the end of a dead end street. Rippa leaned over towards me.

"Just cool na', baby." He lifted up his shirt revealing a chrome nine-millimeter tucked into the waist of his jeans. Rippa then exited the car and started walking up the steps to the house.

I followed behind him.

I went quietly behind him until we reached the master bedroom. Rippa sat on the bed and proceeded to roll a blunt, as I stood in the doorway. He looked at me and sucked his teeth.

"Come now. Make yaself comfortable an' close di door behind ya." I did as Rippa said and sat down next to him, as I watched Rippa roll two blunts.

He took the first one, lit it and inhaled deeply. Rippa had let the smoke blow out through his nostrils before sucking it back up through his mouth. Rippa also took another heavy pull, and brought my face close to his.

Afterwards, Rippa pressed his lips against mine and exhaled the smoke into my mouth.

I began to cough.

He laughed.

"Alright, mami, take off ya clothes." Rippa threw his gun in a corner and took off all his clothes, before hopping into the bed.   I looked at Rippa like he was crazy!

"No, I ain't *taking* off my clothes!"

Rippa wouldn't take no for an answer.

"COME 'ERRE!" he yelled.

I didn't budge.

Rippa then jumped out of the bed and grabbed me from behind. He put me in a headlock, as Rippa dragged me up to the bed. It didn't take long for Rippa to literally rip my sweat suit off.

Before I knew it, I was in my underwear.

The second-hand smoke from his blunt had me dazed. I watched Rippa snatch off my panties, but I couldn't move. He held the blunt in between his lips, as Rippa parted my thighs and kneeled in between them.

For a minute I couldn't *believe* what he was about to do… But Rippa did it, disproving the myth that: "JAMAICAN MEN DON'T GIVE ORAL SEX." He took pulls of his blunt between *sucking* on my love sponge. Between the craftiness of Rippa's tongue and watching the thick smoke rise from between my legs, I was hypnotized.

I *jumped* when Rippa pulled down his boxer shorts and aimed his humongous cock at me! I cried out: "RIPPA, WHAT THE *FUCK* ARE YOU DOING?"

His breathing was heavy: "A wha'? Mi a go *breed* ya!" Again, Rippa tried entering me.

"Nah, man, chill! Where the condoms at?"

Rippa sucked his teeth, as he tried to pry my legs open with his knees. Rippa got frustrated.

"Alright, ah' so ya want it? Eh, you mus' understand dat ya *will* have mi child." As Rippa said that, he reached for his gun and it aimed at me.

"Rippa, don't do this," I tearlessly pleaded with him.

Rippa snubbed the blunt out before he pulled my legs open. Just as Rippa had gotten them open, he rammed his cock inside of me.

I kept *screaming* for Rippa to stop!

He put one hand over my mouth, while the other hand aimed the gun at my chest. I was in excruciating pain, as Rippa slammed into me for what seemed like forever.

It was only twenty minutes.

As soon as he pulled out of me, I tried to jump to my feet. My stomach hurt badly...

I managed to get onto my knees...

I was overcome with a feeling of dirtiness, as I watched Rippa's gooey sperm ooze out of me.

Rejected.

I reached for my clothes and Rippa left me alone. He was speaking to me, but I blocked him out and couldn't comprehend what Rippa was saying.

When he'd gotten ready to, Rippa had dropped me back off at my doctor's office. I walked in, with my clothes tattered and torn, and headed straight the receptionist.

"I've been raped," was all I remember saying to her.

* * * * *

I'd awakened later in the hospital. I overheard the doctor tell AJ that the bad news was that, I'd had some tissue damage, and that the pregnancy test came back positive. I heard the doctor explain to AJ that I had to have been pregnant before the rape.

I couldn't believe my ears.

I called out to AJ.

He came running to my side.

"Who did this to you?" was the first thing that AJ said.

"Rippa…"

Niccolo and Tony were also in the room. Tony shook his head. The doctor excused himself.

"Rippa held me at gunpoint and raped me."

I never felt so weak in my life.

AJ understood.

I heard Niccolo promise him that he would find Rippa and "take care of him".

A day later, the hospital released me. AJ came to pick me up, and we drove straight to New Jersey.

happily ever after...

The move to New Jersey wasn't so bad. However, nobody could find Rippa. Niccolo thought it would be best if AJ and I moved into the guest house on Niccolo's estate. He didn't want anything to happen to his first grandchild.

I was being catered to by Niccolo's maids twenty-four hours a day. I was unable to contact the outside world though.

Niccolo had forbid me to make any phone calls.

I underestimated Rippa's tenacity. Niccolo feared that any little thing could bring Rippa straight to New Jersey.

The spring turned to summer rather quickly. Before I knew it, I was seven months pregnant. I started having horrible dreams of Rippa ripping the baby from my stomach before killing me.

AJ tried to comfort me by planning my baby shower.

I didn't want one.

I felt that there was a good chance that I would never get to see my unborn child.

Niccolo saw the change in my behavior. He'd figured that I was going through hormonal changes. On some level I was but, as each day passed, the threat of Rippa's return grew greater. I wouldn't tell AJ or his father, because Niccolo swore that I was safe on his secluded estate.

I wasn't so sure of that.

By the middle of my eighth month, Niccolo had had enough of me moping around the place.

"Kai, you've been *so* sad throughout most of your pregnancy, you don't want to make my grandson a sad boy, do you?"

I wasn't too delighted about the addition of another boy into an overpopulated male family.

I just nodded at Niccolo.

He frowned.

"Bella, come…sit down. I think I have some good news for you." He called for AJ and we both sat down, as Niccolo began to speak.

"I've just gotten word from my Florida connect. Kai, the address you gave me for Rippa...well they've been watching the house. Some time between yesterday evening and this morning, the Feds came down on the house. The house is taped up. I think it's safe to say that we won't be hearing from Mr. Ripperton Everett a.k.a. Rippa for a long time."

For the first time in months, I smiled. I felt so foolish to let the fear of Rippa's return incapacitate me.

"Thank you, Nicky...thank you very much."

"Ah, Bella, seeing you smile is thanks enough. This is cause for a celebration." I then looked to AJ who seemed as if he had feared Rippa's return too. Niccolo continued.

"Look at you two love birds. I have arranged a little vacation for you in Puerto Rico. I own several villas down there. You'll be flown down there with a doctor on my private jet." Niccolo then poured himself a glass of wine. "Well, go start packing. The jet leaves at six o'clock this evening."

I couldn't believe that I was going back into civilization.

* * * * *

We arrived at *Newark International Airport* at 5:30 PM that evening. AJ had smiled proudly, as he helped me wobble around. I took a moment to reflect on how helpful AJ had been since the rape.

He'd managed to take a leave from his businesses, and had waited on me hand-and-foot. I was lost in my thoughts of AJ's love when, a voice broke me out of my trance.

"Wh'appen, pretty? ...Look like da belly 'bout to drop any day na'. Mi' a go call my daddy and tell him say him grandson a *soon* come."

I *jumped* out of my skin and turned to the voice! There were a lot of people at the airport, but I didn't see Rippa or anybody else talking to me. AJ noticed.

"Sweetie, are you alright? You look like you've just seen a ghost."

I started sweating heavily, while Gabriel started kicking around in my stomach. Gabriel was going to be my little angel. I rubbed my belly to calm him down.

"Oh, these *damn* kicks. It's like, every time this boy kicks, it's a brand new feeling. Whew...I can't *wait* until September."

What Niccolo had told me earlier that day, gave me a false sense of security.

I thought I had become delusional again.

Rippa was either dead or Federal property.

Either way, there's *no* way he could have been in New Jersey.

AJ and I got on the jet, and I didn't hear anymore voices. We took off in clear and calm weather. Even though hurricane season was approaching, the weather bureau said that there wasn't any hurricane activity going on between New Jersey and Puerto Rico.

I then looked at AJ, who had fallen asleep as soon as we hit the sky, then the seven bodyguards, my doctor and the stewardess, and felt safe.

I tried to rationalize why I thought I heard Rippa's voice. *How did Rippa know I was having a son?*

Impossible!

Just as I discounted hearing Rippa's voice as a delusion, I heard it again: "Just cool na', pretty. Rippa a come fi ya an' 'im, baby."

I looked around nervously.

The jet was eerily quiet.

AJ was still sleeping, but so was everybody else. I tried to yell but, my voice got lost in my throat.

Then everything went black...

no honor among thieves

Gasp...
Breathe.

Let me see if I can scream: "RIPPA!"
Nothing.
A flood of light breaks into the room. I hear someone moving around, but my eyes haven't adjusted to the light yet. As they do, my deepest fear manifests itself: "Rise an' shine, pretty."
I start to gag on my own spit.
"Eh? Wha' ya say? Oh…let mi take off dis *ting* 'erre."
I cry out in agony as the tape rips across my lips.
"Alright, much better? Na' wha' ya want?" Rippa starts rubbing my stomach. I try to kick him off of me, but forget that I'm restrained.
"FUCK YOU, RIPPA! UNTIE ME, YOU HEARTLESS SON-OF-A-BITCH!" *I know I need to calm down for Gabriel's sake. He's thrashing around inside of me. I need to get out.*
Rippa unties me and I leap out of the bed.
A shot rings out: *Bang!*
"Jus' cool na', ya try any of ya *fuckery*, and ya a go dead!"
I turn around slowly and see Rippa holding a *Guiness Stout* in one hand, and the chrome nine-millimeter in the other.
"Why, Rippa? Why are you *doing* this to me?"
He finishes off the bottle of stout.
"Why wha? See, ya too 'ard-'eaded. Mi a tell ya, ya a go breed before di end of di year, an' look how ya belly round so."
"Rippa," I hold on to my stomach to brace myself. "…this child is not yours. It's mine and AJ's."
Bad move.
I try to back up as Rippa quickly approaches me.
Too late.

Whack!

The bottle of stout makes contact with the left side of my face.

"A wha' dat, eh? Ya *mean* fi *tell* say dat *nah* my pickeney? Eh, eh? A PURE BULLSHIT! Mi can tell from how ya belly firm it a my baby!"

My stomach knots up as heat starts to ooze down between my legs. I look down, and see a stream of clotted blood flowing out of me. I turn to Rippa.

"See, a pure I-man baby dat. Even 'im cyaan tolerate *ya* lies! Mummy, send fi di doctor."

Tears are streaming down my face, as my fear of never seeing my baby becomes real.

"Rippa, I need to go to the hospital," I cry.

The doctor comes bursting in the room with a short, pretty, but older looking woman. I know him. That's Dr. Brown from Florida.

"She's hemorrhaging. We have to bring her to the hospital," the doctor announces.

Finally, somebody with some *fucking* sense!

"Why cyaan she 'ave di baby 'erre?"

"Ripperton, baby, she a go dead if she nah reach a hospital soon." Rippa's mother smiles gently at me before placing her hand on my stomach. "Son, you a go lose ya *child* if she nah reach a hospital soon!"

"Mr. Everett—"

"Come on, Kai. We *mus'* go to di hospital."

Rippa starts to light a blunt, but tosses it out.

* * * * *

The four of us get into Rippa's Bentley. His mother rides with me in the back seat and tries her best to comfort me. I see Rippa's mother's lips moving but I can't hear what she's saying. I have never been to Puerto Rico, but something tells me that I'm not in Puerto Rico. I'm in the Caribbean alright, but not Puerto Rico. We're driving through a lush forest area. I turn to Rippa's mother and whisper: "Excuse, but where are we?"

She fights back tears as she gently squeezes my hand. The car stops. I turn and look out of the window: "KINGSTON INTERNATIONAL HOSPITAL". I turn back to Rippa's mother. She says calmly: "We're in Kingston, Jamaica, honey."

I start screaming hysterically as tears start coming down my face. "Why, Rippa. Why?"

206

No one answers me.

The door opens. I want to make a run for it but, the nurses grab me and lay me down on a gurney. They quickly wheel me into the hospital. I can hear Dr. Brown giving out orders to the staff.

I look down between my legs at blood-soaked sheets.

"AJ...AJ!" I yell at the top of my lungs. Dr. Brown urges me to calm down. I get poked in the arm.

My rage begins to subside.

I slowly start to calm down, and begin to realize that I'm in great amount of pain. I want to yell, but my vocal chords have become disabled again.

I sob silently to myself.

I watch the nurses and Dr. Brown move around the room frantically.

He orders a cesarean.

A mask covers my face...

Gasp...
Breathe.

I'm much calmer now. The doctor speaks: "Kai, we're going to start in about five minutes."

My head feels light as I gaze down between my legs. They have my legs propped up in the stirrups.

That's all I can see.

A sheet covers my stomach, so I cannot see what the nurses are doing between my legs.

"Jus' na' di baby a come. Mi *soon* give ya a next one."

I don't move.

I just stare at Rippa, as he stares at the nurses.

Minutes go by.

I keep my eyes locked onto Rippa, as I feel a tugging sensation underneath my stomach. I wait for the pain to follow and then I hear him.

I hear my child.

The baby doesn't cry as they pull him from my womb. He coos softly, showing no damage from the hostile environment we just came from. Dr. Brown announces, "You have a baby girl! What shall you name her?"

A baby girl? My heart starts to race. *Did he just say "baby girl"?*

Rippa starts yelling: "A wha' kind of business dat Dr. Brown, eh? A wha' type of *fuckery* a *gwan* so? I's pure male seed mi a carry. Mi *nah* put a lil' *bitch* inna her!"

I watch the nurses clean off my baby girl.

"Her name is Anna-Bella!" My voice finally returns.

Rippa takes out his gun and aims it at me.

"A wha' ya do wit' my baby boy, eh?" For someone as rich as Rippa, you would think he'd get a tutor or something. He doesn't seem to understand that this is *not* his child!

It *can't* be his child.

Dr. Brown cradles Anna-Bella in his arms before handing her to me. Only minutes old and she already has her mother's charm. Dr. Brown looks at Rippa.

"She just gave birth. Please, let her and the baby rest."

Dr. Brown hands me Anna-Bella. I reach for my daughter and gasp as my heart leaps.

She's so pale.

Tears form in my eyes, as my fingers run through her thick, curly, light-brown hair. Anna-Bella gazes into my eyes and I smile. I recognize those honey-brown eyes instantly.

They're AJ's.

As I fall in love with my daughter, Rippa's mother breaks the silence that filled the room.

"Ripperton, ya sure that's ya chile?"

Rippa aimed the gun at his mother, sucking his teeth.

"Yes, mummy, mi sure dat's mine! Nobody can *tell* mi nah different. Soon as we leave outta 'erre, she ah go give mi my son. No *fucking* likkle gyal cyaan run di family business." Rippa turns around and aims the gun at me and Anna-Bella.

Dr. Brown orders him to put the gun away.

I close my eyes and grab Anna-Bella tightly.

Pop! Pop! Pop! Pop! Pop! Pop! Pop! Pop!

A hail of bullets rain down in the operating room.

I try not to panic.

Something pierces through my side.

I feel pressure, but no pain.

The sterile room begins to smell like hot, burnt flesh. Anna-Bella is ripped from my arms. I cry out: "Noooooo," as I reach for her.

My efforts are to no avail.

My arms are limp.

Anna-Bella's being taken away from me, and I can't move.

Shit!

"Come on, lil' mama, this lazy *bitch* doesn't deserve to be your mother. She too *fucking* cold to be a mother."

Pop! Pop! Pop!

More gun fire.

I don't recognize the voice.

Still no pain.

GIVE ME BACK MY CHILD!

Anna-Bella starts to cry, then the strange voice attempts to soothe her. "Awww, baby, don't cry. Let me clean you up, and we'll be on our way; okay, ma-ma?"

Anna is quieting down.

Give me back my baby!

That was no use.

My voice only exists in my mind.

I'm afraid to open my eyes.

Afraid of who that voice might belong to…

It isn't AJ.

AJ is not the violent type.

AJ wouldn't do this.

It isn't Rippa unless…he never did have an accent.

"RIPPA!" Oh damn! I still cannot speak.

"Now look at you. All fresh and clean. Dammit! Where do they keep the *fucking* baby clothes and shit? Awww, my bad lil' mama. I guess I'ma have to watch my mouth around you. It's cool though. Aight, here they go. Now let's get you dressed."

Anna is too quiet.

OH, GOD NO!

PLEASE DON'T LET MY BABY GIRL BE DEAD.

"Wow, lil' mama, you're mad quiet… In shock? Yeah, I'd be too. Shake it off lil' nigga…Wait! You ain't no nigga. Let me find out ya mama is a lowdown dirty hoe." He pauses. "Too bad

209

that good *pussy* had to go to waste. Oops! My mouth. Yeah, I know." Again he pauses. "Damn, lil' mama. I thought Rippa said you was his seed and shit. You don't look *nothing* like him… Nah, it can't be. It can't *fucking* be!"

The voice rushes over to me.

"You *motherfucking* bitch! You *better* not die!"

I feel something but, I don't know what it is.

DAMMIT, KAI…MOVE!

I can't.

"You *fucking* bitch! You had a *fucking* seed for me and didn't even fucking tell me. That's okay. I'm going to be a *good* daddy while you *rot* in Hell! YOU HEAR ME? Rot in Hell you stupid bitch!"

You're not AJ! I say in my mind. *Please don't be AJ.*

My eyes are heavy with fear.

I don't want to open them.

I hear rambling in the distance.

The voice speaks again: "I don't know who Kai thought she was fooling. It's alright though, 'cause I have my lil' princess. Ain't that right, lil' mama?" Anna-Bella starts wailing loudly.

Her cries give me the strength to open my heavy eyes. I open them slowly not knowing what to expect. I see a tall man with broad shoulders. Long curly hair flows from his pony tail.

AJ?

He picks up Anna-Bella and wraps her up in a blanket. He gently rocks her from side-to-side.

"Hush, lil' mama, don't say a word. Daddy's gonna buy you everything on earth, and if every damn thing *ain't* enough, daddy's gonna *kill* that *motherfucking* slut!" He turns around completely. I shut my eyes quickly but not before seeing him point a gun at me.

"What's the use? She's already dead. Come on, lil' mama."

Again, Anna starts crying.

I open my eyes and see the man's face.

I want to get up and get my baby, but I can't move.

Noooooo, don't take my baby! Please don't take my baby! I'm so sorry! I'm so sorry! I try so hard but, no sound escapes from my lips.

"Sshhh, sshhh, come on, settle down, princess. Don't worry, I'ma feed you before we get on the plane. I'm going to name you 'Donna' after my mama."

NO YOU RAT BASTARD! YA MAMA WAS A SLUT. GIVE BACK ME MY DAUGHTER! I don't bother trying to vocalize, but somehow, Anna-Bella hears me. Her eyes widened, and then she starts crying louder than before.

Damn!

For someone who is just a few minutes old, Anna-Bella's got a whole lot of sense. Yes, baby, look at mama.

The man looks at Anna-Bella and faces me.

I stare back at them in disbelief.

"Sshhh, she's gone baby girl. She's not waking up."

Oh, yes I amm motherfucker!

"Look, she's dead. Don't worry lil' mama, Daddy Rico is going to take good care of you."

GLOSSARY

54-11's - Sneakers priced $49.99 plus tax
730 - Code for crazy
Ace-boom - Best friend
A gwan - Going on/happening
'Ard - Hard
Aunt Flow - Menstruation
'Ave - Have
Ban sa - Give me that
Beef - A problem
Bi-curious - Inquisitive about bi-sexuality
Bid - Jail time served
Blood clot - A strong curse word. A Rastafarian term
Blunt, spliff - Marijuana wrapped in cigar paper
Bonjour monsieur - Hello mister
Bottom-feeding - Lowest ranking within a gang
'Bout it-'bout it - To be for real
Breed - Impregnate
Broke-ass - To be poor
Broke off - To pay off
Bubble - An unsightly keloid caused by a sharp object
Buck-naked - Nude
Bumba clot, Ras clot - A strongest curse word. Rastafarian term
Bwoy - Boy
Calli weed - Potent form of marijuana
Catch feelings, check for - To admire someone
Carte blanche - First choice privilege
Cha - Tsk
Clapped - Shot a gun at
Collared - Arrested
Cookies - Crack
Cooley, mooley - Nigger
Criss - Cool
Cyan - Can
Cyaan - Can't
Dat - That
Deadly-to-ras - Deadly as all hell
Dem - Them
Den - Them
Deya - There

Di - The
Discombobulated - Out-of-order
Do you - Focus on yourself
Duppy - Ghost
Dyke - Lesbian
E - Ecstasy
'Er - Her
'Erre - Here
Ewww - Nasty/disgusting
Fi, fah - For
Fittin' - About to do something
Flaked out - Sparkles that are mixed into the clear coat of car paint
Gyal - Girl
Goo-goo eyes - To flirt/Infatuation
Haffi - Have to
Hard rock - Courageous person
Heavy hitters - Major players in the game
Holla - Follow-up
Hood legend - Popular person in the ghetto
Hooptie - Used car
Hot-minute - Very soon
'Im - Him
Jus' cool na' - Relax
Kicks - Sneakers
Mama Beecho - Cock sucker. A Hispanic term
Merked - Killed
Mi - Me
M.I.A. Missing in action
On lock - Committed
One - Peace/good-bye
One Time - Police
Pebble beach - Any project roof
Peeped - Spotted
Pendejo sucio - Dirty motherfucker
Pickney - Child
Pigeon, bird, squally - Low class female
Puerco sucio - Dirty pig
Punk me -To intimidate
Put in work - Involve oneself in an illegal activity
Running game - Hustling someone
Shook - Afraid

Shotta - Thug
Sitting on - Having money stashed
Spit - Rapping
Someting - Something
Stuck on stupid - To be idiotic
The Ave - Jamaica Avenue in Queens
This-that-and-the-third - Everything
Ting - Thing
Titty bar - Strip club
Trap house - Place where drugs are produced/stored
Trick-out - To customize
Tro' me away - Throw me away/get rid of
Vex-I-Vex - To be upset
Vic - Victim
Wack-ass - Corny
Wan' - Want
Wha' - What
Wha' a gwan? - What's going on?
Wh'appen? - What happened
What's really good? - What's the deal?
Whip - Car
Wifed up - Marry
Wi, madmoiselle. Chita. - Yes, miss. Sit down.
Yankee - American
Ya, yaself - You/your/yourself
Ya heard? - Understand?

Page 36 – "Mira, ya no se donde estas mi amiga!" - Look, I don't know where my friend is.

Page 57 – "Mira, Sexy, No escucha La Bruja. Hasta pronto. Muchas Besos y abrazos. Te amo, mami, Te amo mucho. No olividas eso. Tu Nuevo novio." - Look, sexy. Don't listen to the witch. See you soon. Lots of kisses and hugs. I love you mommy. I love you a lot. Don't forget. Your new boyfriend.

Page 94 - Kai, monsieur ap pale avèk ou - Kai the man is speaking to you.

Page 191 - Ou kapab mennen monsieur sa avec mwen address sa? - Can you bring us to this address?

LADY SPEAKS THE TRUTH, VOLUME 1
Essay written by SHA

Growing up in Urban America isn't easy. Throw in the race, gender and age cards. You walk through life with iron-filled crates shackled to your ankles. How can you climb the ladder of success with so much holding you back?

This isn't about me outlining how to live your life or what's right and wrong—I don't know the answer to that. This is about me asking you to wake up! What's up, Urban America? Have we've become so complacent as to stop our complaining because we've been reassured that everything is new and approved, and comes backed with a money back guarantee if we're not satisfied?

I don't know about you but, I'm not satisfied! I'm not a part of the "walking dead" that rest assured in what they've been spoon-fed, that would've been the easy way out: I like it hard.

I don't think you understand me. As my third-grade teacher put it, I wasn't "born with a silver spoon in my mouth." I was born in Kings County Hospital in Brooklyn, New York. It happened sometime after the birth of "THE MONSTER" (HIV/AIDS) and just before the Crack epidemic hit hard.

Though my father owned a bodega and I attended parochial school, I was far from rich. It wasn't steak and lobster; 34th Street Miracle Christmas' and such. However, what we lacked in finances, we made up for through love and unity.

No money meant a closet filled with out-of-style clothes and ridicule from my peers; it was whatever! I was too focused on school to really give a damn. Then my body decided it wanted to start puberty at nine-years-old. Don't think that made me special, there were other girls in the fifth grade with bangin' bodies.

While they were using what they had to get what they want, I stayed in my books. Of course I wasn't popular with the boys, but everybody knew my name. Rhymes were my reason and Hip Hop saved me from the cruelty of the bullies. Well, at least, some of the time.

Being from BK, my ability to write poetry and to get lyrics from any song off the radio, made me tolerable. My strict Haitian father didn't allow me to hang out after school, go on go-away trips or participate in any of the bullshit that happened in my neighborhood. If it didn't happen on my stoop, I wasn't able to go.

Soon after, I was in Queens and desperately wanted to go back to Brooklyn. I thought I'd be much more popular back "home", but the reality was if I wasn't "doing it", I was wack. I accepted that. I had no choice but to be wack and watch every single move that everybody made.

Then I reached high school. I attended a school that made headlines for acid-throwing, gun-toting, monster-infected students! It was the closest one to my house, so I really didn't have a choice. It was then when I got the fever for the fast life. I wanted to be that chick with the fly dudes that pushed the baddest cars, dipped in jewelry of every caliber.

I started asking around for the fly boys from elementary school. Surely by then, I thought, they had to be on top of the game. Dudes were either in Spofford, just recently released from juvenile detention, dead or strung the fuck out on crack-cocaine. Real talk, a sixteen-year-old junkie is not a joke.

Then I started watching the older dudes. This was the era of *The Sleepwalkers*, *The Lost Boys* and others. My young self got a thrill walking through the neighborhood with the older boys checking for me, because of my over-developed body; that made the girls hate me even more. I was already catching hell because of my hair and swagger. Yet, that was dealt with accordingly. I'm not saying I won every battle, but you damn sure won't be able to call me cara cicatriz (Scar Face)!

It was all fun and games until someone got his head blown off in Brookville Park one hot summer night…That brought me to the reality of things. I sat back and started making connections. It didn't take too long to figure out who were the major drug dealers, the minor drug dealers, the wanna-be drug dealers, the stick-up kids, the car thieves and the wankstas (Suckers). Before long, I had them all figured out and knew most of their modus operandi; it was too easy.

For the rest of high school, I met a whole slew of characters. I met guys who were predicate felons at the age of twenty; guys who snapped their fingers and made anything you desired appear like magic. I'll admit, crime life is very enticing! But the end results are not.

I played my cards well, at that time, holding them close to my chest. I was very careful about who I was seen with and where. Undercover detectives were all over the place all the time. Every other day, somebody was getting locked up, and females were getting caught out there on technicalities.

That right there was what *really* made me think twice about all my moves. I lost count of how many females I've seen get charged with years and decades, just because they were at the wrong place at the wrong time. Damn those RICO and Rockefeller laws! They will get innocent people and first-time offenders caught up in the system every time.

Besides the jail time aspect of a hustler's life, I realized that Uncle Sam makes fun and games out of hustlin'. That's another reason I just observed the business of drugs. Tell me why a black man getting caught with crack rocks in BK will get at least ten years, but a white man getting caught on the island with cocaine will get a much lesser sentence? Doesn't crack come from cocaine? Wake up, Urban America!

Why is it that Caucasians dominate the welfare system, but yet African-Americans and Hispanics are portrayed as being the dominate races in the system? Isn't it strange how families stay stuck in the same situation generation after generation? Your momma had you at sixteen, her momma had her at fifteen and her momma had her at fourteen! Yet, all of you still live in the same project apartment? F.Y.I., the projects, no matter how "luxurious" some may seem, are designed to keep the masses psychologically disabled so we can perpetuate the cycle, over-and-over again.

Uncle Sam put up the projects. Uncle Sam allows drugs to come into the country. Trust that if America really wanted to be drug free, then we damn sure would be! Then what would the DEA do? Do you realize how many federal, state and city jobs would be lost if there wasn't any illegal drugs in America?

Thousands of people would be out of work and the economy would fall apart. The Great Depression wouldn't be able to compare to the economic state of America if drug money wasn't in circulation. Uncle Sam can keep his VESID vouchers and his rehabilitation programs: I know the score.

To my young people of Urban America: hustlin' is what it is. We all do it in one shape or another. For most of us, it's a part of life. Victims of our socio-economic status, we have to do what we have to do; just do it wisely. Know when to hit *HARDER*, know when to ease up. I thank God for that ability. Too many times I've come this close to being state property...I'm free. Wake up and you'll be too.

An excerpt from ***GHETTOHEAT***® by
HICKSON
A GHETTOHEAT® PRODUCTION

ASSED OUT

My money's tight - Shit ain't right
Don't know if I'm gonna make it tonight...
Stomach growlin'- Fridge empty - Landlord's howlin'
A nigga ain't gots the rent!
'Bout to be homeless - Livin' in a tent: Yo, I'm bent!
Light and gas cut - Fucked up in a rut
Shit gots to get better - Son, I need some cheddar!
Can't gets no job - Doors slammed in my face
"Sorry, I can't help you," says Mr. Cracker
Mind cluttered and sketchy - Thoughts all over the fuckin' place
Do I gots to rob and steal to pay these bills?
Get a lil' meal?
Damn!
What's the deal?
Clothes mad dingy
Lookin' crazy - shabby and poor
Gonna rob and steal tonight - Can't take this bullshit no more!!!
Nigga gots no clout
Feelin' trapped up in this heat
Son, I wants out!!!
Ready to scream - 'Bout to shout
"Somebody tell a muthafucka what this shit's about!!!"
Now a nigga evicted from home
Gots no place to go - Out on Eighth Ave. I roam
Sleepin' on the street
Pocket full of nuthin'
Still no grub to eat
Shiverin' in the cold - Prayin' for shelter
A meal - Shit, some heat!!!
"Can I live, son, can a muthafucka just breathe?"
Mmmph, mmmph, mmmph...The agony of defeat

An excerpt from ***SONZ OF DARKNESS*** by
DRU NOBLE
A GHETTOHEAT® PRODUCTION

"They won't wake up. What did you let that woman do to our children, Wilfred?" Marilyn nervously asked.

"GET IN THE CAR!" Wilfred shouted. The expression on her husband's face told Marilyn that he was somewhat scared. She hurried into the passenger's seat, halting her frustration for the moment. Wilfred didn't bother to glance at his wife, as he started the vehicle's ignition and drove off at rapid speed.

Marilyn stared silently at the right side of Wilfred's face for ten minutes. She wanted to strike her husband so badly, for putting not only her, but their two children through the eerie circumstances.

"I know you're upset, Marilyn, but to *my* people this is sacred; it's normal," Wilfred stated, while his eyes were locked on the little bit of road the headlights revealed. Marilyn instantly frowned at his remark.

"Andrew and Gary were screaming inside that hut, and now they're sound asleep. This is *not* normal, I don't care what you say, this is wrong, Wilfred. That bitch did something to our kids, it's like they're drugged! Why the *hell* did you bring us out here? WHAT DID SHE DO TO THEM?" Marilyn loudly screamed, budding tears then began to run down the young, ebony mother's face.

Wilfred then took a deep breath, trying his best to maintain his composure.

"Take us to the hospital!" Marilyn demanded.

"They don't need a doctor, they're perfectly healthy."

"How can you say that? Just look at them," Marilyn argued.

"Listen to me."

"I don't want to—"

"LISTEN TO ME!" Wilfred roared over his wife's voice. Marilyn paused, glaring fiercely toward her husband as he spoke. "The Vowdun has done something to them, she's given them gifts we don't yet know. Marilyn, the Vowdun has helped many people with her magic, she once healed my broken leg in a matter of seconds. The Vowdun has brought men and women fame, wealth, and cured those stricken with deadly diseases. It was even told that she made a man immortal, who now lives in the shadows."

"I'm a Christian, and what you're talking about is satanic. You tricked me into coming out here to get Andrew and Gary blessed—you're a liar!" Marilyn interjected.

"That is why we came to Haiti, and it has been done—the worse is now over."

As the couple argued, Gary Romulus eyes opened. He remained silent and unknown to his parents. The infant was in a trance, detached from his surroundings. Wilfred wasn't paying attention to the road ahead, his vision was locked on his wife as they feuded. Gary was however. The newborn saw what his mother and father didn't see, way ahead in the black night.

Two huge glowing crimson eyes stared back at the baby. They were serpentine, eyes Gary would never forget. They were the same eyes he and his brother, Andrew had seen in the hut; the Vowdun's eyes. Gary reached across and gently touched his older brother's shoulder, strangely Andrew awoke in the same catatonic state as his sibling.

"Everything is going to be okay, Marilyn. I tried to pay the Vowdun her price, but she refused," Wilfred said. Marilyn gasped.

"A price?" Marilyn replied annoyingly, refusing to hear her husband's explanation.

Andrew and Gary glared at the large red eyes, which were accompanied by an ever growing shadow that seemed to make the oncoming road darker. Lashing shadows awaited the vehicle.

"WHAT PRICE?" Marilyn then retorted, consumed with anger; she could easily detect the blankness of her husband's mind. Wilfred now was at a loss of words, even he had no knowledge of what the Vowdun expected from him, that was the very thought that frightened the man to the core.

The car was moving at seventy miles per hour. The saddened mother of two turned away from Wilfred's stare, at that moment, Marilyn couldn't even bare his presence. When her sight fell on the oncoming road, Marilyn franticly screamed out in terror. Wilfred instinctively turned forward to see what frightened his wife. His mouth fell ajar at the sight of the nightmarish form ahead of them. Filled with panic, Wilfred quickly tried to turn the steering wheel to avoid crashing.

It was too late.

The sudden impact of the collision caused the speeding car to explode into immense flames that roared to the night sky. The creature that had caused it suddenly disappeared, leaving behind its chaotic destruction and the reason for it.

Out of the flickering flames and screeching metal came young Andrew, who held his baby brother carefully in his fragile arms. An illuminating blue sphere then surrounded their forms, which kept Andrew and Gary unscathed from the fires and jagged metal of the wreckage; incredibly, the two brothers were physically unharmed.

Andrew walked away from the crash feeling melancholy. In the middle of his forehead was a newly formed third eye, which stared out bizarrely. Not until he and Gary were far enough away from the accident did Andrew sit down, and the blue orb vanished.

Gary then looked up at his older brother and cooed to get his attention. Andrew ignored him, he was staring at the flaming vehicle as their parents' flesh burned horridly, causing a horrible stench to pollute the air. Through glassy eyes, Andrew's vision didn't waver, the child was beyond mourning.

Finally, Andrew gazed down at his precious baby brother before he embraced Gary. Gary smiled assured, unfazed by the tragic event. With his tiny arms, Gary then tried to reach upwards, to touch the strange silver eye on his brother's forehead, playfully. Gary was as amused by the new organ as he would've been about a brand new toy.

"Mommy and daddy are gone now," Andrew then sobbed, as streams of tears rolled down his young face. He was trying his best to explain his sorrow. "I will never leave you, Gary—I promise," The young boy cried. Gary giggled, still trying to reach Andrew's third eye as best he could.

For the price of the Vowdun to bestow her gifts from her dark powers to the children, Wilfred Romulus had paid the ultimate price—he and his wife's lives. Their children were given gifts far beyond their father's imagination, and for this, they were also cursed with fates not of their choosing. The future held in store untold suffering.

Andrew and Gary were no longer innocent, no longer children of Wilfred and Marilyn Romulus—they were now *Sonz of Darkness*.

An excerpt from ***CONVICT'S CANDY*** by
DAMON "AMIN" MEADOWS & JASON POOLE
A GHETTOHEAT® PRODUCTION

"Sweets, you're in cell 1325; upper bunk," the Correctional Officer had indicated, as he instructed Candy on which cell to report to. When she heard 'upper bunk', Candy had wondered who would be occupying the cell with her. As Candy had grabbed her bedroll and headed towards the cell, located near the far end of the tier and away from the officer's desk and sight, butterflies had grown deep inside of Candy's stomach, as she'd become overwhelmed with nervousness; Candy tried hard to camouflage her fear.

This was Candy's first time in prison and she'd been frightened, forcefully trapped in terror against her will. Candy had become extremely horrified, especially when her eyes met directly with Trigger's, the young, hostile thug she'd accidentally bumped into as she'd been placed inside the holding cell. Trigger had rudely shoved Candy when she first arrived to the facility.

"THE FUCK YOU LOOKIN' AT, HOMO?" Trigger had spat; embarrassed that Candy had looked at him. Trigger immediately wondered if she was able to detect that something was different about him and his masculinity; Trigger had hoped that Candy hadn't gotten any ideas that he might've been attracted to her, since Candy had caught him staring hard at her.

She'd quickly turned her face in the opposite direction, Candy wanted desperately not to provoke Trigger, as the thought of getting beat down by him instantly had come to Candy's mind.

She couldn't exactly figure out the young thug, although Candy thought she might've had a clue as to why he'd displayed so much anger and hatred towards her. Yet, this hadn't been the time to come to any conclusions, as Candy was more concerned with whom she'd be sharing the cell with.

When Candy had reached cell 1325, she glanced twice at the number printed above on the door, and had made sure that she was at the right cell before she'd entered. Candy then peeped inside the window to see if anyone had been there. Seeing that it was empty, she'd stepped inside of the cell that would serve as her new home for the next five-and-a-half years.

Candy was overwhelmed with joy when she found the cell had been perfectly neat and clean; and for a moment, Candy had sensed that it had a woman's touch. The room smelled like sweet perfume, instead of the strong musk oil that was sold on commissary.

Right away, Candy had dropped her bedroll and raced towards the picture board that had hung on the wall and analyzed every photo; she'd become curious to know who occupied the cell and how they'd lived. Candy believed that a photo was like a thousand words; she'd felt that people told a lot about themselves by the way they'd posed in photographs, including how they displayed their own pictures.

Candy then smiled as her eyes perused over photos of gorgeous models, both male and female, and had become happy when she'd found the huge portrait of her new cellmate. Judging by his long, jet-black wavy hair, facial features and large green eyes, Candy had assumed that he was Hispanic.

Now that she'd known the identity of her cellmate, Candy then decided that it would be best to go find him and introduce herself; she'd hoped that he would fully accept her into the room.

As Candy had turned around and headed out the door, she'd abruptly been stopped by a hard, powerful right-handed fist to her chiseled jaw, followed by the tight grip of a person's left hand hooking around her throat; her vocal cords were being crushed so she couldn't scream.

Candy had haphazardly fallen back into a corner and hit the back of her head against the wall, before she'd become unconscious momentarily. Within the first five seconds of gaining back her conscious, Candy had pondered who'd bashed her so hard in her face.

The first person that had come to mind was Trigger. Secondly, Candy also had thought it might've been her new cellmate who obviously hadn't wanted Candy in his cell, she'd assumed by the blow that Candy had taken to her flawless face.

Struggling her way back from darkness, Candy's eyes had widened wide, at that point, being terribly frightened, as she was face-to-face with two unknown convicts who'd worn white pillow cases over their heads; mean eyes had peeked from the two holes that was cut out from the cloth. The two attackers had resembled members of the Ku Klux Klan bandits as they'd hid their faces; both had been armed with sharp, ten-inch knives.

Overcome with panic, there was no doubt in Candy's mind that she was about to be brutally raped, as there was no way out. Candy then quickly prayed to herself and had hoped that they wouldn't take her life as well. Yet, being raped no longer was an important factor to Candy, as they could've had their way with her. All Candy had been concerned with at that moment was continuing to live.

An excerpt from *AND GOD CREATED WOMAN* by
TAMIKA MILLER
A GHETTOHEAT® PRODUCTION

"Here's what I want you to do. I want you to cock that leg up right onto my shoulder. Can you do that for me sugar?"

I cock my leg up and place it on his shoulder so that my thigh is right up against his cheek.

"Now, here's what I need you to do next. I'm gonna hand you a bullet of coke. Open the bullet, and sprinkle some dust onto your thigh." I do as he says. The man turns so that he's facing my thigh. Takes a long, loud snort of the line, then follows it up by licking the residue.

"Now, unbuckle my pants, pull out my cock, and show daddy what you can do with that thing."

I reach under the guy's jellyroll, tug open his gaudy, gold belt buckle and unzip his *Wranglers.* I dig under the man's gut and search for his dick between the creases. I am met by a rank, musty odor.

When I finally find his sweaty, shriveled up dick, it's about the size of my pinky finger. I make tweezers out of my thumb and pointer finger and hold the guy's tiny, smelly dick between my fingertips like a straw.

"Don't be shy. Put that cock in your mouth."

I lean in closer and the funk hits me full force! I have to keep myself from gagging. When I touch the tip of his dick with my tongue, I taste remnants of old piss. I feel the acid in my stomach bubble up.

My gag reflex contracts, releases, contracts, then releases. I feel like I'm about to upchuck in the guy's lap. He places his hand on the back of my head and shoves it in his lap. The man's sweaty belly is pressed against my forehead.

"Suck it. Wrap those chocolate lips around my cock, sugar."

I take the tip of my tongue and flicker it against the side of his pencil-sized dick, barely touching it with my tongue. He grunts and groans. The man is trying his damndest, but the guy's so full of coke and whiskey that he can't get a hard on.

"Fuck, girl, can't you do no better 'n that? I heard you was a real pro-fesshunal." The guy continues to pump his limp dick against my lips, with no results.

This goes on for about twenty minutes. Then he finally blows his load and soaks my face with his funky spunk. It smells like trash-truck juice.

"Lord hammercy, girl, you are a gift on God's green earth." The man now tosses a handkerchief in my face. I rush to the locker room and wash the sticky, smelly spooge off of my face, but some smells leave an indelible mark in your brain. I can't wash my face enough times to rid myself of the stench.

When I get done cleaning up, I make tracks to the nearest exit. I don't even bother to look around for Smitty who usually waits around for me and walks me to my car.

I push open the emergency exit door and step out to the dimly lit parking lot.

Dusk is turning to dawn.

I dig in my purse searching for my car remote. My hand wades through the contents: tubes of lipstick, breath mints, wads of cash, sunglasses, spare change—and eventually, reaches the bottom lining where my car remote is. I yank it from the purse, lose my grip on the remote, and it falls to the ground. When I bend over to pick it up, I hear footsteps behind me. I turn to see who it is.

But it's too late.

A heavy object comes crashing down on the back of my head with blunt force.

I fall back onto the concrete. Drop my purse. The contents spill onto the pavement.

I am hit again. And again. And again

I scream.

A sharp pain shoots through my skull. A river of blood runs down my forehead—spills into my left eye. I hold my arms up, trying to block my head from another attack, and I am kicked in the face. The sole of a high-heeled shoe comes crashing down against my lips and nose. Then another shoe slams into my stomach.

I hear voices. Whispers.

I am beginning to lose consciousness. Everything becomes shadows. A blur.

I see the silhouette of a hand reaching towards my neck. My necklace is ripped from my throat.

"Bitch!" I hear Diamond's voice say. She jams her stiletto heel into my shoulder. "Get the bracelet," Diamond says.

China Doll snatches my bracelet from around my wrist, steps on it, applies all of her weight and cracks my wrist bone.

I scream out in agony.

My diamond ring is pulled off of my finger.

"Fuck you!" I hear China Doll yell. Then she spits in my face.

My pocketbook disappears.

I hear the door of the club burst open. Heavy footsteps run toward me. I hear Diamond and China Doll run off.

"Ma'am, are you okay?" I hear a man's voice say. I feel a strong hand holding my head up. The other hand cups my face. He wipes the blood from my eyes with his shirt.

I see the shadow of his face. It's the cutie pie that had been watching me from the bar. He pulls out his cell phone. Pushes three buttons: 911

Devastation. Brutilation. Elimination.

I fade to black…

An excerpt from *SKATE ON!* by
HICKSON
A GHETTOHEAT® PRODUCTION

Quickly exiting the 155th Street train station on Eighth Avenue, Shani, walking with her head held down low, decided to cross the street and walk parallel to the Polo Grounds; not chancing bumping into her parents. As she approached the corner, Shani contemplated crossing over to *Blimpie's* before walking down the block to the skating rink. She craved for a *Blimpie Burger* with cheese hero, but immediately changed her mind; fearing of ruining the outfit Keisha gave her.

Shani then headed towards *The Rooftop*, feeling overly anxious to meet with her two friends. As she walked down the dark and eerie block, Mo-Mo crept up behind Shani and proceeded to put her in a headlock; throwing Shani off guard.

"Get off of me!" Shani pleaded as she squirmed, trying to break free. Already holding Shani with a firm grip, Mo-Mo applied more pressure around her neck.

Trying to defend herself the best way she knew how, Shani reached behind for Mo-Mo's eyes and attempted to scratch her face. Mo-Mo pushed her forward and laughed.

"Yeah, bitch, whachu gon' do?" Mo-Mo teased. "SIKE!" Startled, Shani turned around with a surprised expression on her face.

"Mo-Mo, why are you always playing so much? You almost scared me half-to-death!" Shani said while panting heavily, trying hard to catch her breath.

Mo-Mo continued to laugh, "Yo, I had ya heart! You almost shitted on yaself! I could've put ya ass to sleep, Bee!"

"Mo-Mo, please stop swearing so much," Shani replied, as she smiled and reached out to hug Mo-Mo. Mo-Mo then teasingly tugged at the plunging neckline of Shani's leotard, pulling it down to reveal more of Shani's cleavage.

"Since when you started dressin' like a lil' hoe?"

Shani, quickly removing Mo-Mo's hand from her breast, became self-conscious of what she was wearing.

"I knew I shouldn't have put this on. Keisha made me wear this. Do I really look sleazy?"

Mo-Mo frowned. "Whah? Shani, stop buggin'. You look aiiight. I'm just not used to seein' you dressin' all sexy and shit."

Shani then looked towards Eighth Avenue to see if Keisha was nearby.

"Mo-Mo, where's Keisha? I thought you two were coming to *The Rooftop* together."

Mo-Mo then pointed across the street, as she loudly chewed and popped on her apple flavored Super Bubble gum.

"Yo, see that black Toyota Corolla double-parked by The Rucker? She in there talkin' to some Dominican nigga name Diego we met earlier. We made that fool take us to *Ling Fung Chinese Restaurant* on Broadway. Keisha jerked him for a plate of Lobster Cantonese—I got chicken wings and pork-fried rice."

Shani shook her head and chuckled, "You two are always scheming on some guy."

"And you know it! A bitch gotta eat, right?!" Mo-Mo asked, before blowing a huge bubble with her gum and playfully plucking Shani on her forehead.

Mo-Mo was a belligerent, lowly educated, hard-core ghetto-girl who was extremely violent and wild. Known for her southpaw boxing skill and powerful knockout punches, she'd often amused herself by fighting other peoples' battles on the block for sport. That's how Mo-Mo met Shani.

Last January, Sheneeda and Jaiwockateema tried to rob Shani of her Bonsoir "B" bag near Building 1. Mo-Mo observed what has happening and had rescued Shani, feverishly pounding both girls over their heads with her glass Kabangers.

She didn't even know Shani at the time, but fought for her as if they were childhood cronies. Since then, the two have become close friends—Mo-Mo admiring Shani's intelligence, innocence and sincerity.

In addition to her volatile temper, ill manners and street-bitch antics, Mo-Mo was rough around the edges—literally and figuratively. Eighteen-years-old and having dark, rich, coffee-colored skin, Mo-Mo's complexion was beautiful, even with suffering from the mild case of eczema on her hands—and with her face, full of blemishes and bumps from the excessive fighting, junk food and sodas she'd habitually drank.

Bearing a small scar on her left cheek from being sliced with a box cutter, Mo-Mo proudly endured her battle mark. "The Deceptinettes", a female gang who jumped Mo-Mo inside of Park

West High School's girls' locker room last year, physically attacked her. Mo-Mo took on the dangerous crew of girls all by herself, winning the brutal brawl, due to her knowing how to fight hard and dirty.

With deep brown eyes, full lips and high cheekbones, she highly resembled an African queen. Mo-Mo wasn't bad looking, she just didn't take care of herself; nor was she ever taught how. Because of this, Mo-Mo was often forsaken for her ignorance by most.

Awkwardly standing knock-kneed and pigeon-toed at five-foot-seven, big boned with an hourglass figure, Mo-Mo was a brick house! Thick and curvaceous with a body that wouldn't quit, she had ample sized forty-two D breasts, shifting wide hips, big legs with well-toned thighs. Having the largest ass in Harlem, Mo-Mo's behind was humongous—nicely rounded and firm. It automatically became a sideshow attraction whenever she appeared, as everyone, young and old stared in disbelief; amazed at the shape, fullness and size of her butt. A man once joked about spanking Mo-Mo's rear, claiming that when he'd knocked it…her ass knocked him back!

Her hair length was short, in which Mo-Mo wore individual box braids, braiding it herself; having real, human hair extensions. Often, her braids were sloppy and unkempt, having naps and a fuzzy hairline. Mo-Mo's coarse, natural hair grain never matched the soft and silky texture of her extensions, but she always soaked the ends in a pot of scalding, hot water to achieve a wet-and-wavy look.

Mo-Mo never polished her nails or kept them clean, having dirt underneath them regularly. Rarely shaving the hair from under her armpits or bikini line caused Mo-Mo to have a rank, body odor. Someone left a package at her apartment door one day, filled with a large can of Right Guard, Nair and a bottle of FDS Feminine Deodorant Spray with a typewritten note attached. It read: *"Aye, Funkbox, clean ya stank pussy and stop puttin' Buckwheat in a headlock—you nasty bitch!"* Mo-Mo assumed it was either a prank from Sheneeda and Jaiwockateema, or Oscardo—still sulking over Mo-Mo kicking his ass six years ago.

She'd now lived alone in the Polo Grounds, due to her mother's untimely death six months ago—dying of sclerosis of the liver from her excessive drinking of hard alcohol. Just days after

Mo-Mo's mother's death, she'd received a letter from Social Services, stating that they were aware of her mother's passing, her only legal guardian, and that she would receive a visit from a social worker; one who would be instructed to place Mo-Mo in an all-girls group home in East Harlem.

Mo-Mo had begged her other family members to allow her to live with them, but they refused, not wanting to deal with her nasty disposition, constant fighting and barbaric lifestyle. Nor did they wish to support Mo-Mo emotionally or financially, resulting her to rely on public assistance from Social Services. At that point, Mo-Mo hadn't any relatives whom she can depend upon—she was on her own and had to grow up fast.

Luckily Mo-Mo's eighteenth birthday had arrived a day before she was accosted in the lobby of her building by a male social worker, having the rude investigator from Social Services antagonize her with legal documents; indicating that she was to temporarily be in his custody and taken immediately to the group home.

Failing most of her classes, Mo-Mo barely attended school. She was in the tenth grade, but had belonged in the twelfth. Mo-Mo was still a special education student, now having a six-grader's reading and writing level. Her former teachers passed her in school, being totally unconcerned with Mo-Mo's learning disability. Their goal was to pass as many students as possible, in order to avoid being reprimanded by superiors for failing a large number of students. The school system had quotas to meet and didn't receive the needed funds from the government for the following term—if a large amount of students were held back.

Along with other personal issues, Mo-Mo was hot-in-the-ass, fast and promiscuous, having the temperament of a low-class whore. She was a big-time freak, a sex fiend with an insatiable appetite for men with huge dicks—becoming weak at the knees at the sight of a protruding bulge.

Mo-Mo's self esteem and subsidized income was low, but her sex drive was extremely high, having sex with men for cash while soothing her inner pain. She didn't sell her body for money due to desperation and destitute— Mo-Mo did it for the fun of it. She loved dick and decided to earn money while doing what Mo-Mo enjoyed the most—getting fucked! She was going to have frivolous sex regardless, *"SO WHY NOT GET PAID FOR IT?"* Mo-Mo often reasoned.

Academically, she was slow, but Mo-Mo was nobody's fool; being street-smart with thick skin. A true survivor, who persevered, by hook-or-crook, Mo-Mo was determined to sustain—by all means necessary.

"AYE, YO, KEISHA, HURRY THE FUCK UP!" Mo-Mo beckoned.

"Hold up! I'm comin'," Keisha replied with irritation in her voice; concluding her conversation with Diego, "My friends are callin' me—I gotta go."

"Can I see you again and get ya digits, mommy?" Diego begged, talking extremely fast with his raspy voice.

"Maybe! And no you can't get my number—gimme yours," Keisha snapped.

Diego immediately was attracted to Keisha's good looks, snootiness, nonchalant attitude and bold behavior. He smiled as he wrote his beeper number on the flyer he received for an upcoming party at *Broadway International*—while exiting the Chinese restaurant with Keisha and Mo-Mo an hour earlier.

While handing Keisha the flyer, Diego attempted to wish her goodnight, but Keisha interjected: "Can I get three hundred dollars?" she said, looking straight into Diego's eyes.

"Damn, mommy, what's up? I just met you an hour ago and you askin' me for money already?"

Keisha paused for emphasis.

"…Are you gon' give it to me or not?" Keisha coldly asked, still looking into Diego's eyes—not once she ever blinked.

"Whachu need three hundred for, mommy?"

"First and foremost, my name is Keisha, not mommy! And I don't n-e-e-e-e-e-d three hundred dollars—I want it!"

Diego sat silently, bewildered and turned on by Keisha's brashness.

"Diego, don't you want me to look cute the next time you see me?" Keisha asked innocently while batting her eyelashes; deceiving Diego with her fake, light-hearted disposition.

"So I'm gonna see you again huh, mommy?" Diego nervously asked, smiling as he pulled out a wad of cash from his pocket. His large bankroll, wrapped in jade-green rubber bands caused Keisha's eyes to widen.

"Uh-huh," she effortlessly replied while staring hard at Diego's money while turning up the volume on his Benzi box.

Diego was playing his *DJ Love-Bug Starski* mixed tape and Keisha bobbed her head, rocked her shoulders from side-to-side and rubbed her thumb swiftly against her middle and index finger while singing to *Money: Dollar Bill, Y'all* by Jimmy Spicer; "Dollar, dollar, dollar, dollar, dollar bill, y'all."

Diego looked at her with his right eyebrow raised, peeling off money from his bundle. He handed the bills to Keisha and hopelessly gazed into her eyes.

Keisha, who became annoyed with Diego for showing too much of an interest in her so soon, rolled her eyes and retorted harshly, "Gotta…go," as she attempted to reach for the car handle. Before grabbing it, Keisha pulled out a napkin from her brand-new, blue and white Gucci bag with the signature G's, wiped her fingerprints off the console and opened the car door with the napkin in her hand.

"Yo, Keisha, why you wipe down my car like that?"

Keisha ignored Diego's question and beckoned to Shani and Mo-Mo, signaling them by waving her right hand in the air, before quickly bringing it down to slap her right thigh.

"Yo, I'm ready, y'all—let's go!"

Keisha then walked around the front of Diego's car and proceeded to cross the street; now eager to enter *The Rooftop*. Shaking his head in disbelief, chuckling, Diego couldn't believe Keisha's sassiness.

"YO, WHEN YOU GON' CALL ME, MOMMY?" Diego yelled out to Keisha from his car window.

Keisha immediately stopped in the middle of the street, causing the flow of traffic to halt. She flung her long hair, looked over her shoulder and tauntingly replied, "As soon as you step-up ya whip, nigga. Do I look like the type of girl who be bouncin' around in a dusty-ass 'one-point-eight'?"

Diego froze as Keisha continued to speak.

"You don't even take ya whip to the car wash. And stop callin' me mommy!" Keisha concluded, flinging her hair again by sharply turning her head. She then stuck her butt out and switched while crossing the street.

Diego stared long and hard at Keisha's rump as she walked away, noticing how good her behind looked in her skin-tight jeans. He then drove towards Eighth Avenue, repeatedly hearing Keisha's last comments over in his head.

Keisha stood at the entrance of the skating rink and observed the huge crowd outside as—Shani and Mo-Mo greeted her.

"It's about time!" Mo-Mo snapped. Keisha ignored her and reached out to hug Shani.

"What's up, college gurrrl?" Keisha asked.

"Hey Keisha! I'm fine. I'm chilling like a villain." Shani replied awkwardly, not use to using slang in her daily dialect.

"Shani, it's 'chillin'' not 'chill-i-n-g'! Why you be always talkin' so damn proper anyway? I wonder sometimes, yo, if you really from the hood!" Mo-Mo snapped.

As Shani attempted to politely respond back to Mo-Mo, Keisha rudely interjected.

"So, Shani, how's DC?" Keisha asked, cleverly examining her outfit from head-to-toe without Shani realizing she had.

"I like DC so far. I'm very excited about attending Howard University. I just need to learn my way around campus," Shani answered. Feeling jealous and left out of the conversation, Mo-Mo interrupted the two.

"Can you bitches learn y'all muthafuckin' way inside this skatin' rink?" Mo-Mo snapped before entering *The Rooftop*.

"Mo-Mo be illin'! She betta watch her mouth 'cause I'm not the one!" Keisha retorted while rocking her neck and waving her right hand in the air.

Shani, experiencing cramps from her period and the stress from sneaking from DC to New York City for the grand opening of *The Rooftop*, shrugged her shoulders to relieve the tension she had felt, as she inhaled a breath of fresh air. Shani then slowly exhaled and quickly adjusted the plunging neckline of her scoop-neck leotard to conceal her cleavage—as she and Keisha followed inside.

An excerpt from *SOME SEXY, ORGASM 1* by
DRU NOBLE
A GHETTOHEAT® PRODUCTION

BIG BONED

"I need you, Melissa; oh I love your body! Let me taste you, mmmph, let me love you—just give me some sexy!" Jezebel begged while still squeezing the woman's luscious crescents. Melissa had no hope of resisting this sudden passionate impulse that flooded her.

She felt Jezebel's grip tighten on her, then a finger slowly traced between her curvaceous legs. The unexpected jolt of excitable pleasure caused Melissa to rise on her side, throwing Jezebel off of her. She palmed between her own thighs, trying to silence the rest of the roaring waves threatening to overcome her preciousness.

Jezebel couldn't take her eyes off of Melissa, as she breathed erratically, while Melissa couldn't help but to stare back with conflicting desperation. Melissa's hand reached out and grasped the back of the Native-American woman's neck, as she pulled Jezebel towards her forcefully.

Their lips touch, melded, then opened. Jezebel's tongue dove into Melissa's mouth, finding the versatile muscle was eager to wrestle her own. A groan vibrated down Melissa's throat. Her hand came up, and two fingers strung like guitar strings on Jezebel's upturned beady nipple—first playing with it, then catching Jezebel's hardened nipple between her index and middle fingers; closing it within tight confines.

Jezebel then straddled Melissa, the two women's hands meeting, immediately intertwining before their kissing ended.

"I wanted you since I first saw you; I've been wet ever since that moment. You're so fucking sexy, Melissa. I need you, can I have some sexy? Give it to me," Jezebel said in a low, hushed voice.

The twinkle in her beautiful brown eyes affected Melissa like an intoxicating elixir. Melissa watched on, as Jezebel took her captured hand and began to suck on two fingers with her hot, steamy mouth. Jezebel's checked hollowed, as she continued to close in on Melissa's dainty fingers.

Melissa, voluptuous and womanly, petals became slick, and damp—natural juices now running down towards her rounded rear end.

"I want you, too Jezebel, come get some sexy!" she pledged. Jezebel smiled as Melissa's fingers slid from her mouth, leading them down her body. With her lead, Melissa allowed her hand to enter into Jezebel's bikini. A glimpse of her fine, black pubic hair came into view, as Melissa then felt the lovely grace of Jezebel's vagina.

A soothing hiss breathed out of Jezebel. The moistness of her internal lake coated the fingers that ventures to its intimate space. Melissa then bent her hand so the bikini could come down, and she was grand the delightful vision of where her fingers ventured.

Jezebel's outer labia had opened, as Melissa's fingers split between her middle, like tickling a blooming rose. She tipped her hand up, and used her thumb to peel back the protective skin over Jezebel's engorged clitoris. The pink button revealed itself exclusively, and Melissa used her thumb to caress it; stirring up Jezebel's burning desire.

Melissa had never seen or touched another woman's pearl, but found that she'd loved it completely. Two of her fingers then slipped within Jezebel's hot, oily insides, and the Native-American woman had thrust her hips forward to take all Melissa had to offer.

"You're so hot inside; burning up my fingers, baby."

"Just don't stop; please don't stop what you're doing," Jezebel instructed. Her hips began to undulate, rocking herself to a sweet bliss. Jezebel rode Melissa's fingers like she would her fiancé's long, pleasure-inducing dick.

Melissa then curled her wet fingers back slightly, as she would if she were touching herself, searching inside for that magical area most women long to discover—the G-spot.

Melissa felt Jezebel's tunnel pulsate, and a shock ran through the humping woman, giving Melissa total satisfaction that she'd found Jezebel's spot; now also realizing that, by her being a woman, she had full advantage to knowing another woman's body, better than any man could.

ghettoheat®

THE GHETTOHEAT® MOVEMENT

THE GHETTOHEAT® MOVEMENT is a college scholarship fund geared towards young adults within the inner-city, pursuing education and careers in Journalism and Literary Arts.

At GHETTOHEAT®, our mission is to promote literacy worldwide. To learn more about THE GHETTOHEAT® MOVEMENT, or to see how you can get involved, send all inquires to: MOVEMENT@GHETTOHEAT.COM, or log on to GHETTOHEAT.COM.

To send comments to SHA, send all mail to:

GHETTOHEAT®, LLC
P.O. BOX 2746
NEW YORK, NY 10027

Attention: SHA

Or e-mail SHA at: SHA@GHETTOHEAT.COM.

Artists interested in having their works reviewed for possible consideration at GHETTOHEAT®, send all materials to:

ghettoheat®
P.O. BOX 2746
NEW YORK, NY 10027

Attention: HICKSON

GHETTOHEAT®: THE HOTNESS IN THE STREETS!!!™

ORDER FORM

Name_____

Registration #_____(If incarcerated)

Address_____

City_____ State_____ Zip code_____

Phone_____ E-mail_____

Friends/Family E-mail_____

Books are $15.00 each. Send me the following number of copies of:

____ CONVICT'S CANDY   ____ GHETTOHEAT®

____ HARDER   ____ SOME SEXY, ORGASM 1

____ SONZ OF DARKNESS   ____ SKATE ON!

____ AND GOD CREATED WOMAN

Please send $4.00 to cover shipping and handling. Add a dollar for each additional book ordered. ***Free shipping for convicts.***

Total Enclosed = _____

Please make check or money order payable to GHETTOHEAT®. Send all payments to:

GHETTOHEAT®
P.O. BOX 2746
New York, NY 10027

GHETTOHEAT®: THE HOTNESS IN THE STREETS!!!™